ROAD OF BONES

By Michael Harbison

Martin Sisters Publishing

Published by

Ivy House Books, a division of Martin Sisters Publishing, LLC

www. martinsisterspublishing. com

Copyright © 2012 Michael Harbison

ISBN: 1-978-937273-46-7
Fiction/Thriller
Printed in the United States of America
Martin Sisters Publishing, LLC

DEDICATION

For my parents, Joe and Barbara, who gave me everything.

An imprint of Martin Sisters Publishing, LLC

Chapter One

Detectives hit your doorstep on a Sunday morning, know your name and need your time, the news is never good. Standing on my porch, Al Marner of the College Heights P.D. flashed a credential and made an introduction, then dabbed sweat with a folded tissue, depositing a trail of paper crumbs on the bulge of his prominent forehead.

"Jackson Boyd?" he inquired.

Three or four steps behind Marner a second man eyed the block as if he expected my kids to launch an ambush in the next few minutes. Had to be another detective. Cheap suit, tired look, underpaid half-frown creasing his mouth into a scar. Their department-issue Ford ticked in the sunshine at the curb, and the reflection on the windshield shot bullets of light my way, matching the intensity of Marner's eyes.

"Yes, I'm Jack Boyd."

Marner pointed to his friend.

"This is Detective Nat Vasquez of the San Bernardino County Sheriff's Department. We'd like you to come for a talk."

College Heights sits at the eastern fringe of Los Angeles County, an oasis of trees, quiet streets, and no surprise, colleges—

a suburban bliss that once graced most of Southern California—and Detective Vasquez, looking a decade younger than Marner, was clearly out of his jurisdiction. San Bernardino County started at city limits, which explained Marner's presence since College Heights was his beat. Unfortunately, Vasquez's presence needed no explanation.

"Am I under arrest?"

Marner let the question freeze. Waiting for the thaw, my eyes scanned the street and my brain cranked, wondering if neighbors stood behind drapes, watching the show. I glanced at the Sawyers' place. Mrs. Green's. Even Dave Manker's, though I knew it was empty. No one paced grass, nodding in my direction. They knew I worked around cops, and under normal circumstances, police at my house in the morning would not cause alarm. That said, the past week had been anything but normal.

"You're not under arrest, Mr. Boyd. We just need to talk."

When at the receiving end of police attention, unless you're an idiot, the rule is shut your mouth and get a lawyer. I had spent countless Saturday nights watching COPS with Abby, yelling at the TV as some mope spilled his guts after breaking his girlfriend's face, all while the nodding cop listened like a patient priest at confession. I knew the rule, but standing in the morning light, I took a deep breath and did the idiot thing.

"Let me take care of my dog and lock up the house."

Minutes later, alarm set and dog in garage, I walked to the Ford—past the mums Abby had planted the weekend before along the cracked walkway bordering our too-brown grass—took a glance around the neighborhood, unsure when I would be back, grateful Abby and the kids were gone and safe and not in front of our home asking questions.

Moving to the car, the detectives walked a couple paces ahead, saying nothing. No cuffs. No stiff, guiding arms. If I was their prisoner at that point, my captivity seemed voluntary. At the Ford, Marner slid behind the wheel and Vasquez rode shotgun. I wedged into the back, canting sideways to keep my knees from banging the front seat. Outside the glass, my neighbors' windows glowed gold in the early light, but no one stared my way. Nonetheless, as Marner pulled from the curb, I figured they all knew.

The last house I looked at stood next to mine and belonged to Carlos Moreno.

Dark.

Silent.

Dead.

Then Detective Marner punched the gas and my world receded. When my eyes moved forward, Detective Vasquez twisted at a hard angle and stared. A few beats later, he spoke for the first time. He looked my age, but his voice held gravel, as if he gargled with sand each morning, and he sounded much older.

"We appreciate your cooperation, Mr. Boyd."

I gave a slight nod.

Vasquez shifted a bit more.

"I'm surprised... You haven't asked what this is about."

Tires slapped the road.

Beats passed.

We had been moving south a few minutes—catching a green light across Baseline, another at Foothill—about halfway to the station. College Heights was a small town, a Midwestern life raft upon L.A.'s suburban sea. That said, it was not Mayberry, and Detective Vasquez was probably not Barney Fife. We would be at the station in a few minutes, and once we were there, questions would fly. I fixed my eyes on Detective Vasquez and decided to give my first answer.

"I know what this is about, Detective."

*

The College Heights Detective Bureau consists of four detectives, a lieutenant, and an evidence technician. Two of the detectives I knew well enough to call by first name—Matt Spray and Dale Griffin; my son played tee ball with their kids—and I had visited the building a dozen times to consult, and on at least ten other occasions for a Citizen Police Academy. Wasn't exactly unknown territory, but my previous visits had originated from the front door, and this time, Marner and Vasquez led me in through the booking entrance. For obvious reasons, the scenery change ate at me, and as we neared the door, Marner's hand gripped my upper arm, guarding against any sudden change of heart.

There was none.

We passed a booking desk staffed by a thin blonde chewing a fat wad of gum, then stopped at an empty bench sporting six pairs of open handcuffs. Vasquez told me to sit. He didn't cuff me. Then he walked down the hall to an open office and talked to someone inside, glancing my way now and then to make sure I stayed put.

Business was Sunday light. Other than the blonde, the booking area was empty. Here, suspects arrived, were printed and processed, then led down to a basement jail. As a Tier 1 detention facility, the College Heights jail had room for a dozen losers, and no one stayed longer than forty-eight hours. Once arraignment had taken place, custody of the accused usually migrated to the Los Angeles County Sheriff's Department and the subject transferred to one of the larger downtown jails—Men's Central, Twin Towers, gladiator arenas with no happy endings. Considering Vasquez's involvement, I would probably head east to San Bernardino County's West Valley Detention Center. Different destination. Same bad news.

The blonde exhaled, blew a bubble that popped like a gunshot, then glanced my way as she cleaned gunk off her face. She put the gum back in her mouth, and her gaze shifted down the hall toward Vasquez. I turned and looked that way.

Dale Griffin stood next to Detective Vasquez, wearing a flat look that told me I'd be getting no special treatment. Outside, being a friend or neighbor held weight, but in here, I was a paying customer, nothing more.

Griffin handed Vasquez a manila envelope and then stepped back into the office. Vasquez stalked toward me and pointed down another hall.

"This way, Mr. Boyd."

The interrogation room was nicer than I expected. More like a sparse office than a place where people confessed to the dark impulses of the human heart. Burnt orange paint coated three walls, and a window of mirrored glass dominated the fourth. In the center of the room, two chairs sat tucked beneath a single clean table, the surface unmarred by graffiti or stains, pristine enough to pass for an altar except for the eye bolt rising from its center and the handcuff sitting there cocked and waiting.

Vasquez told me to sit.

Then a tech wheeled in a cart holding a TV and DVD/VCR combo.

Vasquez thanked the man and closed the door.

"Need to make something clear, Mr. Boyd." Vasquez moved to the wall opposite the glass and leaned back, crossing his arms. "This is a preliminary interview. Your presence is voluntary…You're under no obligation to answer questions, and for now, you can leave at any time."

For now.

I knew the drill. Detective Vasquez's case was in early innings. I was here because he wanted to lock me into a statement, do the prep work for later. He figured if he came on too heavy right away, I'd bolt for the door or lawyer up, thus the *no obligation* bullshit. Smart move on his part but wrong on both counts. I wasn't going anywhere.

"I get that, Detective…I want to talk."

"Start by telling me when you were last at MicroLine Security?"

"Last night."

"What time?"

"Shortly before midnight… For approximately thirty minutes."

Vasquez glanced toward the mirrored glass. Beats of indecision tapped his face, and then he stood and took the manila envelope to the AV cart. Sixty seconds later, after some wrong-pushed buttons, he popped a disc into the DVD tray and turned on the TV. With all the certainty of a true believer, I knew what I was about to see.

Surveillance footage has always looked somewhat unreal to me, possessing an achromatic, sanitized quality that turns even the bloodiest horror show into something clean and well scrubbed. The world's violence brought to you not in color, or even the duality of black and white, but in a flat, neutral gray.

Watching the TV, I saw myself step to the double glass doors at MicroLine headquarters in Ontario. I watched as the security guard rose from his post and moved toward me. Recognition dawned on the man's face, and the evident tension growing in his body suddenly dissipated. He unlocked the door and let me in. Unfortunately for him, we weren't alone long. As I stepped inside the building, a third man—wearing a clown mask—walked into the lobby and put a gun to the guard's head. The subsequent footage lasted thirty seconds, showed me locking the double door and then joining the guard and the clown. After that, the screen went black.

Detective Vasquez turned off the TV and faced me.

"That you, Mr. Boyd? Locking the door?"

"Yes."

"Last night?"

"Yes."

"I need to advise you of your rights."

Detective Vasquez grunted a Miranda warning as I stared at the TV, unable to see my reflection in the black screen. No color, no neutral gray, just a barely glimpsed me floating in darkness. When Vasquez finished, he sat in the chair across from me.

"Knowing your rights, you still want to talk?"

"Yes."

"Without a lawyer?"

"Yes, Detective. Record everything I say."

From the look on his face, Vasquez had expected a different answer. He paused for a beat and then pointed over his left shoulder. Near the ceiling, a camera looked down on the table. A faint red light flashed.

"You're live, Mr. Boyd."

"Before we start, I have a question."

"Okay."

"The security guard... Did he live?"

Detective Vasquez glanced at the mirrored glass and waited as he decided how much information to give without getting something in return. Within a few seconds, he came to a decision and pulled a frown.

"Last night at twelve-thirty, San Bernardino County Sheriff's deputies responded to a 911 call at MicroLine Security and found the lobby door shattered. Upon entering, they conducted a search and discovered"—he glanced at his notes—"Roger Saldana, a company security guard, unconscious in a sixth floor office. Mr. Saldana had been shot in the side and his right hand had been amputated at the wrist. Someone chopped it off with a fire axe."

Acid churned my guts.

Detective Vasquez pursed his lips.

"What can you tell me about that, Mr. Boyd?"

"You didn't answer my question. Is Roger alive?"

"He's in surgery as we speak."

My stomach did a fresh dance.

I looked at the floor and commenced talking.

MICHAEL HARBISON

Chapter Two

Ten days earlier, the day Special Agent Fisk of the FBI ruined my life, winter had looked primed for an early arrival. The alarm went off that morning at six-thirty, and smelling rain, I was last to rise. Stayed in bed an extra five minutes, tried to snooze and avoid the day as Hondo's muzzle sagged the mattress and blew dog breath up my nose. At last, the Labrador's Alpo-tainted breeze drove me from the sheets.

After a quick pee in the downstairs bathroom, I headed to the kitchen and vowed for the hundredth time to fix the john in the master bath. Like most fifteen-year-olds, my daughter loved mirrors, and morning competition for toilet time was fierce. Thank God my son was only six. By the time he noticed girls, Sara would be in college and the upstairs bathroom would be free.

"Morning," I said, walking into the kitchen.

Carter dug into his cereal bowl. A plate of toast sat next to him. Near his bowl, a pile of Legos rose like a mini skyscraper, and as the kid ingested Fruit Loops with one hand, he added levels to the structure with the other. Eying his work, I grabbed a coffee cup and headed for the pot. My son's engineering skills impressed— multileveled projects requiring patience and planning, built amid the chaos of the kitchen or anywhere else he had some free time. Not bad for a kid diagnosed with autism the week before preschool, a diagnosis recently upgraded to Asperger's syndrome—a higher-level disorder on the autism spectrum, known to induce deep focus and concentration—but still worrying enough to cause sleepless nights. Some days he was like every other kid on the block, other days, his feelings came wrapped in body armor. Special needs or not, the boy's concentration ability exceeded my own, and I figured architecture was in his future, or maybe bomb disposal.

"How long you been working on that?"

"Since Scooby Doo."

"How high are you going?"

"Until it falls down."

Standing at the stove, my wife Abby scrambled eggs over a blue fire, robe cinched tight, eyes on the clock, calculating a prompt start to everyone's day. She spotted me, curled a lip, and then killed the flame.

"You were supposed to run the dog this morning," she announced. "You know he hates the garage when he's missed his run. He howls all day."

"It's gonna rain." I glanced at my flowering paunch. "Must have pressed the snooze."

"He hates you."

"No way. Hondo's my only friend. We're practically brothers." I panted like a dog and Carter shot me a grin. My morning got a little warmer. "Besides, it's Marty's day, believe it or not."

Picking at her eggs, Abby barely moved. Maybe a flinch at the mention of Marty Goodman's name. "Another visit already. That was a quick month."

"Time goes faster and faster," I said. "Especially with these monsters around."

I ruffled Carter's blonde hair and sat.

The boy concentrated hard as he added more blocks to the project.

"Who's Marty?" he asked.

Asperger's sometimes made it difficult for him to identify with things not directly related to him—something about an empathy deficit—so the question popped up on a monthly basis.

"Marty Goodman lived next door to me when I was a kid. He was like a second dad."

"Why does he have his own day?"

"He lives in a special hospital, so each month he has his own day when I visit."

Carter nodded as if that made perfect sense. "I want two dads," he said.

"Eat your breakfast," I grumbled.

Sara came down from the bathroom then and pulled up a chair. Glancing at her, I grabbed some toast.

"And how are you this morning? You know it wouldn't kill you to share the toilet now and then. My bladder's not what it used to be."

She poured Kashi into a bowl and gazed at her phone as she texted. For a while, breakfast unfolded in relative silence. I drank warm coffee and munched cold toast, while at the stove Abby ate eggs from the pan and monitored the clock like a soldier eyeing a determined enemy. My wife, every bit the harried professional. Officially, her workday as principal of Chavez Elementary in Pomona started at eight. Unofficially, she considered it a sin not to be first in the parking lot. After a few minutes, she dropped the half-eaten eggs into the sink and shot everyone a communal frown.

"Hurry up kids. We're gonna be late."

I got the hint, swallowed coffee, and said, "I'll take them to school today."

Abby's frown became a lopsided smile. "Sure you have time for both? You're supposed to go shopping."

"Shopping? For what?"

"Weekend barbecue? Your neighbors? Ringing a bell yet?"

Oh, that. In Southern California, summer ran from May until late October. Throughout the season, the families on our street got together once a month to give thanks for the sun—a public food fest we called a block party back in the day. This year, we had drawn hosting duty for October's shindig, but a weather change was settling in, and I was secretly hoping for a washout. No shopping trip, no barbecue, no nada.

"No problem...I'm shopping on Friday."

"The day before the party?"

"I'm telling you, it's gonna rain."

"It's not going to rain."

"You see the clouds out there? I'm telling you, something's coming. Anyway, Carter's off school Friday...some kind of teacher holiday, so I'll have time for shopping."

Abby looked skeptical but let it die.

I continued. "And work should be light today...so I can take them both to school."

Carter attended first grade at Dylan Thomas Elementary—a public school on the south end of town—and Abby dropped him each morning on her way to Pomona. Sara attended Portola Middle School, not far from where grassy foothills turned to pine trees and College Heights became the San Gabriel Mountains. The extra drive to take Carter would cost me twenty-five minutes—time enough for Hondo to crap on the rug or eat the sofa as retribution for his missed run, which meant the pooch would go along for the ride. I would then have to return home and put Hondo in the garage before heading to work. Quite a hassle. But my wife would be happy, which meant I wouldn't have to sleep with the dog later that night.

Abby patted my shoulder. "Easy day, huh? Must be nice...all that free time."

Munching toast, I ignored the jab. In another situation, there might have been a sting, but that morning, I sat halfway through a six-figure severance package from MicroLine Security, owned my own business, and things looked bitchin'. I'd go in to the office around nine and be home in time to make fish sticks for dinner. Then, after Carter's tee ball game, I would spend an hour or two with Marty Goodman.

A near perfect day.

At least that had been the plan.

*

When Special Agent Fisk stepped into my place of business, Digital Recovery & Investigations, I was with a client, so he took a seat in the lobby and waited. My assistant, Evan Fisher, approached my office—nothing impressive, just a cubical walled by frosted glass—handed me a business card, mouthed the letters F-B-I, and then left. Placing the card on my desk, I looked back at Jane Selig and gave an apologetic nod.

"Sorry about that. Please, continue."

Mrs. Selig took a deep breath and resumed her story. "A week after Don's accident, I found this in a safe deposit box."

She placed a container on my desk and then rubbed her palms against her jeans as if stripping a virus. Her damp blue eyes, streaked by either lack of sleep or crying, yawned like craters, and her voice carried a scratchy rasp. Glancing down, I peered into the container—some type of Tupperware made for salads—and spotted two metal-encased computer hard drives.

"Craig—my son—says they're from a laptop."

Out in the lobby, beyond Jane Selig's tired eyes, the FBI man paced carpet, looking out at the clouds. My office resided in Pomona, wedged between a nail salon and a Mexican chicken joint, not far from the Superior Court building, and from the way the courthouse flag snapped in the breeze, it looked like the weather outside had deteriorated. The weekend barbecue looked doubtful, and despite the gravity of Jane Selig's story, I suppressed a smile.

"Yeah, Mrs. Selig, those are hard drives."

"Craig checked them. He said they're empty, or that everything was deleted. That's what you do, right? Get back deleted files?"

She wiped more germs from her hands and jammed her fingernails into her jeans. Her husband had died a few weeks earlier in a car accident, and his insurance company was contesting the payout, claiming the crash had been intentional. She was so upset that if her nails tore through fabric and hit skin, she'd probably draw blood without flinching, maybe dig until she scraped bone. Staring at me, she licked her lips and nodded toward the drives.

"I need to know what's on them... That's what you do, right?"

"Yes, ma'am."

"Even if the information has been deleted."

"Yes."

"You find people's secrets."

"That's one way of looking at it."

"How's that possible?"

Clearing my throat, I nearly launched into a dissertation on hard drive architecture and forensic recovery techniques—slack space, swap files, fixed storage versus portable, how pressing the delete key erases no information from a device, just reallocates that drive space for overwriting—but looking at Jane Selig, I knew she wouldn't care. She was pretty and fit, in her late forties with a lot of life left to live, but so crushed by grief that if death himself showed up at her doorstep, she'd probably invite him in for coffee and open up a vein. We all handle grief differently, but Jane Selig's method resembled a slow-motion dismemberment, like lopping off limbs with a pair of nail scissors. For that reason, I gave the most uncomplicated response I could muster.

"We use software to recover the deleted files."

Her nails stopped digging. "That's what I want," she said. "Recover the files. I don't care what it costs."

Her business had come my way through a mutual acquaintance, Danny Devlin. Mr. Selig had functioned as Devlin's financial advisor—Devlin owned the auto body shop where my brother worked, and from what I knew, needed little advising—and according to Danny, Mrs. Selig could pay well beyond my normal eight-hundred dollar fee for a non-litigious recovery. From what I'd been told, her hillside villa overlooked the bedroom community of Walnut, and the view stretched from the San Gabriel Mountains to Orange County. On clear days, downtown Los Angeles was visible, but on smoggy days, brown haze probably obscured the next block. Southern California in a microcosm. With a house like that, money was probably the least of her concerns, but I felt I had a professional obligation to warn her.

"Deleted material can be recovered." I glanced at the FBI agent waiting in the lobby and lowered my voice. "But you may not want that."

She flashed me a look.

"Why not?"

"The insurance company can force me to testify in court about the contents. Depending on what I find, that might cause problems...you know, questions." I cleared my throat before proceeding. "Was your husband depressed? Did he keep a secret diary? Did he have thoughts of...well, hurting himself?" I paused to let the possibilities sink in. "Maybe it is best you move forward, Mrs. Selig."

Her eyes hardened. "My husband didn't commit suicide, Mr. Boyd. Do you want my business, or should I take it somewhere else?"

I gave a nod. "Yes, ma'am, we want your business. I just want to prepare you. Even the best marriage has secrets. Things spouses keep private for whatever reason. Not just affairs or hidden bank accounts, but small stuff you'd rather not know. Did your husband hate your cooking? Was he unhappy with how you dressed? Did he think you were unkind?" Not to mention the taste most men had for pornography, and not the sanitized Playboy version, either. In my experience, hidden hard drives usually meant hidden life, and discovering the secrets of a loved one after they had died was one certain way to negate everything they had once meant to you. "Sometimes things should stay in the past...especially if we're no longer around to clarify our intentions."

Jane Selig's eyes darted to my wedding ring. "If your wife died, wouldn't you want the truth?"

I thought that over and shrugged. "I'd want what's best for my children."

"Well, my son is grown, and I want the truth, Mr. Boyd. How long will it take?"

Like any business, in digital forensics, we strive to give the client what they want, so I lifted my hands in the universal gesture of surrender and said, "You can come by next Wednesday, any time after noon."

"Thank you."

After taking her check and escorting her past the FBI man, I opened the front door and watched her step into the rain as a gust of wind tore into the lobby. Then I closed the door, read the business card Fisher had given me, and glanced at the man in the rumpled blue suit, who was about to ruin my life.

"Special Agent Fisk. How can I help you?"

Chapter Three

What people euphemistically called a real estate correction gripped most Southern California neighborhoods by the throat, and my street was no different. No matter how innocuous the language, calling the event a correction was like referring to lung cancer as excess cell growth of the respiratory system. The words sounded prettier; the results were not. Home values had declined fast in our town and then dove hard for the basement. Soon, overextended neighbors disappeared in the night, leaving three empty houses with browning lawns on my street. One of the abandoned properties sat next door to mine, and that was the problem.

Special Agent Fisk took a chair, opened his attaché, and withdrew a manila folder.

"You're getting a new neighbor," he said. "The vacant house next to yours sold to a group named ConcreMex. They're a Mexican cement company establishing a presence in the U.S."

Fisk stared at the manila folder. Despite the morning hour, half-moons of fatigue cupped his eyes and cigarette odor rose from his skin as if he had spent all night in an ashtray. He was portly, balding, and unimpressive, the kind of guy Bin Laden's grandma could beat the shit out of, not the bold image the feds liked to portray these days. My assistant Evan Fisher looked on with interest until Fisk glanced back at him and frowned.

I nodded toward the front office. "Why don't you man the desk, Fisher?"

"It's quiet out there."

"Then you should be able to handle it. Close my door, please."

Fisher grumbled and closed the door. I looked at Fisk.

"Can a foreign company own American real estate?"

"Perfectly legal, I'm afraid."

That was news to me. It sounded wrong and unfair, which in the realm of international relations, probably meant that it was true.

"On paper, ConcreMex is owned by a group of multinational investors. In reality, a man named Javier Aldama y Obregon has control. Do you recognize the name?"

"Should I?"

"Only if you spend time in Mexico."

I shook my head. "Most of the news from down there isn't good...and we have three kids. The closest we get is dinner at *El Torito*."

"Probably smart."

"He's trouble, right? I mean...why else would the FBI care?"

"I'm afraid so."

Out in the office, the phone rang. Fisher answered and then yelled, "Are you available?" Fisher was my sole employee at DRI and on most days a godsend. He could mount any memory device—hard drive, iPod, cell phone—and come up with data. With the ones and zeros of code, no one was better. When it came to dealing with people or handling basic office tasks, he was mostly a zero.

"Take a message."

Fisher grunted. "Ten-four."

Across the desk, Fisk waited.

"Sorry about that."

The FBI agent shrugged. "No problem. You have a business to run, and I'm cutting in to your time. Computer forensics?"

"A two man shop for now. We do contract work for private investigators and businesses. Clients hire us to search home computers. Nothing exciting—divorce proceedings, cheating spouses, people caught surfing porn at work on company time."

"You once worked for MicroLine Security—upper management, if I'm correct—contracts with the federal government, the military, Fortune five hundred corporations. That must have been exciting. A long drop from those heights to searching home computers for porn. Why'd you leave?"

A few beats passed, and I shrugged. "You're not here to discuss my work history, are you, Agent Fisk?"

Fisk rolled his lower lip. "Actually, that's Special Agent...and no, I'm not."

"So this guy Obregon. What's the problem, exactly?"

"He goes by Aldama. In Mexico, the first surname is the father's; the second belongs to the mother. It's a male-dominated society. Nobody goes by their mother's name..." He trailed off and waved a hand. "Never mind. Not important."

Special Agent Fisk opened the manila folder, withdrew three glossy black and white photographs, and placed them on the table.

I looked down, took them in, and instantly wished I had not.

"Javier Aldama leads *Asesinos de La Sierra,*" he said.

Even limited with *El Torito* Spanish, I made a rough translation: *The Mountain Assassins.*

"*Asesinos* is a rising drug cartel challenging the Sinaloa and Gulf cartels for control of Tijuana since the Felix brothers got into trouble."

It was news to me. I managed a confused shrug.

"These men were Mexican federal police." Fisk pushed the photos closer. "Aldama had them killed."

Glancing at the photographs, I winced. The scene was something out of a slasher movie, the kind Sara watched on

Cinemax late at night when she thought everyone was asleep. Cut off heads, gallons of blood, and one detail the goriest horror flick would never have dared: the mouth of each detached head cradled a severed penis between its teeth.

"Aldama wants control of TJ," Special Agent Fisk explained. "These men got in his way."

"Jesus Christ." My guts did a seismic shift. "The guy who did *that* is moving next door?"

Special Agent Fisk shook his head. "Javier Aldama won't enter this country except to face trial for murder, narcotics trafficking, and a dozen other sins I could name without opening a bible. Despite what you hear on the news, our border enforcement is top notch. Official points of entry are highly secure, and a man like Aldama would never cross the desert with illegals." Fisk leaned back and wiped a bead of sweat from his brow. "Doing so would insult his dignity."

"Thank God for dignity."

"Don't thank him yet." Special Agent Fisk scooped the photos off the table and filed them away. "Like I said...you're getting a neighbor."

He produced a fresh photo. A black and white shot of a dark-haired guy standing next to a Chevy Suburban. Sunglasses concealed the man's eyes and an expensive suit cloaked his frame, but he looked a decade younger than I did—around thirty—and in much better shape.

"Who is he?"

"Carlos Moreno. We doubt the name is genuine. Sources say he's a former member of Mexico's Airmobile Special Forces Group, and he works for *Asesinos* as a hit man. In Mexico, they call them *sicarios*, and they're only sent north after very specific targets."

Special Agent Fisk dropped the photo, set his hands on the table, and waited as things soaked in. Once the facts settled, an obvious question floated to the surface.

"Who's his target?"

"We don't know."

"Can't you stop him from entering the country?"

"We have no evidence that Carlos Moreno has committed any crime in the U.S. or Mexico, and he has dual citizenship, so we can't keep him out."

"What about Aldama? He's a drug dealer. Seize the fucking house. Surely a drug cartel can't own a house."

"ConcreMex owns the property. We have no proof that Aldama, or anyone else associated with *Asesinos,* owns the company…none that would stand up in court anyway. We need the cooperation of the Mexican government to prove that, and cooperation is sporadic at best. Technically, when Moreno moves in, he will be the company's tenant."

"When is he moving in?"

"Soon."

My anger flared. "Lock him up then. That's your job, right? Put him in jail."

Special Agent Fisk shook his head. "Not going to work that way."

"Why not?"

"Moreno's target is unknown. We need eyes on him to see where he leads. The purchased house establishes a link between him and Javier Aldama. Once we determine his target—and it is almost certainly a Mexican national—we can pressure the Mexican government to go after Aldama. Once they move, we'll pick up Moreno."

"That's a vague-sounding plan."

"There's more." Special Agent Fisk looked at the papers. "We can't tell you everything…for obvious reasons."

"So you're letting this guy move next door to my family?"

"For now."

"You have to be kidding."

"It's no joke."

Crunching numbers, I looked for some way out but came up with zeroes. "This can't happen. You're not doing your job. I'll call my congressman, or the damn police. I have friends in a half-dozen departments. They'll…"

As a threat, the statement sounded weak and desperate—exactly the way I felt—and I regretted the words the second they cleared my tongue.

"We are doing our job," Special Agent Fisk said, "and sharing this information with anyone would be a mistake. First, even if local law enforcement wanted to help—which I doubt—they'd place a call to the FBI and discover this conversation never took place. How would that look for you and your business? Second, it could draw attention to your family…and drug cartels play by harsh rules, Mr. Boyd. You saw the pictures. Imagine your wife or one of your children like that."

My blood pressure redlined. I waited for it to subside before looking back at Fisk.

"You're telling me this why, exactly? I don't want to know any of this. What am I going to say to my wife? How am I going to sleep at night?"

"You tell your wife nothing." Special Agent Fisk spoke low and slow as if talking a jumper down from a bridge. "You're upset, Mr. Boyd. That's understandable. I want you to bury that anger deep and use it. The United States government needs your assistance, and in this fight, anger keeps you committed."

A few beats passed. My question seemed to come from nowhere.

"How can I assist the United States government?"

Fisk smiled as if a fat trout had swum up and gulped his hook.

"For starters…do what everyone does in the suburbs. Be a good neighbor."

*

Halfway to Carter's school, I placed a call at a red light and waited beside an idling U-Haul that towed a car with Iowa plates.

In the truck, a wide-eyed couple and a kid scoped out the city like natives getting used to indoor plumbing. Southern California was overcrowded, expensive, and indifferent to new arrivals, but they kept coming, ignoring the smog, fires, and hot desert winds, hoping for a shot at something better. It was a delusion shared by most Angelenos—the expectation of a better tomorrow despite today's bullshit.

The light turned green. The U-Haul pulled away in a cloud of smoke. Then Les Suarez picked up my call.

"District attorney's office."

"Lester, what's shaking?"

"Who's this?"

"My feelings are hurt."

"Boyd?"

The question was curt and pointed, not exactly filled with love.

"The one and only."

"It's been months. What's up? I was heading to a late lunch. Which, by the way, you should pay for, considering you stiffed me last time."

"Just a friendly call, Les. No need for hostility."

"Yeah, right…and my knob grew three inches last week. You know the county budget sucks. We got no cash for new software. You better make your play somewhere else."

"Come on. No sales pitch. Yours truly no longer works for MLS."

"You left MicroLine?"

"Started my own shop."

"That's probably good. I've been hearing hurtful things about MLS. They say Reed's buying ShredFast. Going to alienate people hawking evidence elimination with one hand and forensics recovery with the other. Cops get pissed easily, and they hold grudges."

"Hadn't heard about ShredFast. Probably bullshit."

"Yeah…even Reed's not that dumb. You really out?"

"I'm out."

"Then why are you calling me?"

"I have a question."

"If you're out, why should I answer?"

"Because the cyberstalker case made your career…and you owe me."

A long beat followed.

Nine years earlier, Les Suarez had been an LAPD detective in North Hollywood when an attractive Russian immigrant walked in to the station and accused a prominent Hollywood agent of attempted rape. The guy had come to her apartment in the middle of the night, used a hide-a-key to get inside, then roused her from a dead sleep and asked politely if she wanted him to use a condom. She started screaming, and the guy apologized, then left a business card and told her to call if she changed her mind. After a visit from Detective Suarez, the agent confessed to finding the woman's address on a swingers website. The profile claimed she liked rough, anonymous sex, described where she hid her apartment key, and invited men to get creative waking her up. Detective Suarez suspected an ex-boyfriend of placing the ad, but interviews with the guy proved fruitless until I found computer evidence that ultimately put him in the clink for five years. After law school at Pepperdine, Suarez was no longer a cop, but part of the district attorney's High Technology Crime Division.

"Memory coming back to you, Detective?"

"It's Investigator these days, Boyd, and you're in no position to blackmail me. How's your scumbag brother?"

The question was a not-so-subtle reminder that Suarez had long known about my brother's felonious past, kept quiet about it while MicroLine built a relationship with law enforcement, and wasn't about to let me forget. A fair point. Nothing turned a cop against your product faster than a brother doing a four-year stretch at Pelican Bay.

"So we owe each other. Mutually assured destruction, I guess."

"What do you want?"

"You guys deal with feds, right?"

"More than we'd like. Why?"

"You ever hear of an FBI agent named Dennis Fisk?"

Another long beat of silence. Near the school, the San Gabriel Mountains came into view and the rain grew stronger. Waiting for Suarez's response, I parked along the curb opposite the playground and killed the engine.

"We're living in a post 9/11 world, Boyd. You go asking about the identity of federal agents and people get jumpy."

"Yeah, I know. You heard of Fisk, or not?"

"Why do you need to know?"

"Just do."

"C'mon, Boyd."

"You like your job, Lester?"

"That cyberstalker thing was years ago."

"It made your career, and you would have missed the evidence without me. No doubt, you're a master of the digital universe now, but back then, you didn't know shit, and I saved your ass. News gets out, that could be embarrassing."

Suarez exhaled into the phone. "No. I don't know Fisk."

"But you've heard of him?"

"Didn't say that."

"But you're going to ask around?"

"Are you in trouble, Boyd?"

"Every day of my life...but not with the feds."

Another few beats.

"Okay, I'll ask around, but this cuts the cord. I don't owe you shit. After this, you owe me lunch."

"How about Philippe's? They got a Turkey dip these days, healthier than beef. I'll drive into town next week."

"I still carry a gun," Suarez noted. "I'd probably be tempted to shoot you."

"I'll wear Kevlar."

29

"Then I'll aim for your head."

"You love me, Lester, I know it. You'll call when you have something?"

"Yeah, sure."

Suarez cut the call.

Two blocks up from the school, the U-Haul pulled to the curb and parked in front of an apartment building. The family piled out, Dad lifting his hands for a stretch, bouncing up and down like a receiver who caught the game winning catch. The woman and kid came over and gave him a big hug.

Perfect family, ready for a better tomorrow.

I crossed the street to get my son.

Carter had tee-ball that night, and Abby had some kind of budget meeting at school, so I was on-deck alone for dinner. That was fine. I needed space to think about Moreno, had to come up with a plan and needed to do it fast. As Marty Goodman once said, you don't plan an escape route during the fire. You get it wired before you ever smell smoke; that way you're two steps ahead of the flames.

Truth was, I felt three steps behind already and figured things would soon get very hot.

Chapter Four

In my experience, blood seemed to dry in a Rorschach pattern that assumed the nature of whatever one was thinking about at the time. Standing in Principal Lofton's office, staring at the blood on Carter's formerly white tee shirt, the way it had dried into the shape of a human head with two eyes and a hard line that looked like a mouth, I saw the face of Carlos Moreno.

"What happened? You hurt yourself?"

Carter sat on a subcompact chair reading a book about construction trucks and saying nothing.

"He's fine, Mr. Boyd. There was an altercation. Carter wasn't involved. He was in the bathroom when two boys started fighting. One was beaten quite severely."

Abby had told me about fights at her school, Chavez Elementary, and they got ugly. Back in my Romper Room days, kids satisfied violent impulses with loud talk and chest thumping, but not anymore. Two weeks earlier, one of Abby's first graders had shown up at Chavez with a steak knife in her backpack, all because someone had been *bothering* her. Dylan Thomas Elementary was probably the same. Different zip code, same human nature.

"I'm sorry to hear that, Mrs. Lofton. Carter must have been upset."

There was long pause before the woman resumed speaking. "Well, that's the problem. He wasn't. He was close enough to get bloodstains on his clothes, but he returned to class and took his seat without telling anyone. When his teacher noticed blood, Carter told her a boy was hurt in the bathroom. By that time, the student was unconscious."

"Is the kid okay?"

"He lost two teeth. He'll be fine, but I'm concerned about Carter's behavior."

Despite her circuitous route, Principal Lofton's destination became obvious. Political correctness being what it was, I knew getting there would take time and decided to shorten her trip. I asked Carter to wait outside and looked across the woman's desk as she laced her fingers and placed her hands in her lap.

"Asperger's Syndrome can affect the capacity for an empathetic response, Mrs. Lofton. You're aware of that. I'm sorry Carter took so long to report the fight, but his delay wasn't intentional. He wasn't covering things up."

Mrs. Lofton engaged in a long, premeditated silence. As I waited, her unhappy face pinched under a nest of gunmetal hair, and the combination of the two carried the ominous nature of a loaded weapon. It wasn't difficult imagining a line of kids outside her office, pissing their pants as they waited for an ass chewing. Made me wonder what Carter had endured before I showed up, and thinking about that pissed me off.

"You can't make excuses for him, Mr. Boyd. Good parenting easily becomes overprotection, and that isn't good for a boy like Carter."

"What kind of boy is that? He's a good kid, Mrs. Lofton."

"However, the school has strict policies. Anyone failing to report an act of violence is as culpable as the perpetrator, and suspension is mandatory."

"Culpable?" My tone shifted up a gear. I tried to put it in check before things got ugly. "He's six years old. I'm not sure what you're getting at, but you can't suspend my son for lacking a response he's incapable of producing. That wouldn't be fair."

Another long pause, then Mrs. Lofton let out a long sigh. "I understand you're upset, Mr. Boyd, but this isn't personal. Carter's a wonderful boy, and everyone loves having him here."

Her tone suggested the opposite might be true. I got it. There were special needs students at Chavez, and Abby said the help they required took time from other students. IEPs. Special tutors. It was a resource drain, and the expense for a single child, who may or may not benefit from all the extra help, fostered resentment among parents and staff. That said, we were talking about my son, and other parents could get stuffed.

"What's your point, Mrs. Lofton?"

"If Carter gets special treatment, other children notice and discipline suffers. Your wife is a principal, Mr. Boyd. I'm sure you understand."

I glanced at the clock. Sara's dismissal bell had already rung. With the rain coming down, she wouldn't be happy about waiting around, and unhappy teens were never good for one's home life.

"How long is the suspension?"

"He spent the day in the office. He knows he did wrong. That's enough punishment for now, but I think the time has come to suggest an alternative to the current situation."

What alternative? To which situation? To the fact that my son had a disease or syndrome, or whatever euphemism one cared to use? That he was sometimes unlike other kids? That his feelings came wrapped in a hard shell surrounded by barbed wire? Or to the fact that a paid killer would soon be living next door us? Did Mrs. Lofton have a magic bullet for that situation?

"What suggestion?" I asked.

Mrs. Lofton coughed like a salesmen about to offer a special discount. "There's a private school called The Phoenix Academy which opened recently in Upland. It's expensive, but curriculum is tailored for students with Asperger's Syndrome, and Carter might find the environment more…comfortable."

Abby had brought me a brochure for the place two weeks earlier. We'd talked about Carter going there and then let the idea die. Expensive was an understatement. Sixty grand a year. No way could we swing that. But I counted a few beats, as if thinking over Mrs. Lofton's proposal, not wanting to sound defensive when I told her to go to hell.

"Are you telling me Carter is no longer welcome at Dylan Thomas?"

"Mr. Boyd, we're both aware Carter has a right to attend public school. I'm merely suggesting a semester or two at a specialty institution might help. If Phoenix doesn't suit, he can always come back to Dylan Thomas."

For months, I had convinced myself Carter was improving— misdiagnosed with autism, then misdiagnosed again with Asperger's. Maybe the doctors were wrong. Maybe he would grow past his quirks and blossom into a normal child. On the other hand, he could end up like my brother, Ransom, doing a stint in state prison. As I pictured that, a bolt of shame ran through me, as if I had sided with Mrs. Lofton and the rest who saw Carter not as a boy with boundless potential, but as an inconvenient problem to manage.

Screw that. My son was normal. Different maybe, but normal.

I cleared my voice and glanced at the clock. "Thanks for the information, Mrs. Lofton. I'll discuss it with Abby."

Then I left.

Leading my son to the car, I noticed parents watching us in the halls and wondered at their thoughts. Had they heard rumors about my crazy kid? Did they resent the attention Carter required? Did they think he was nuts, retarded, whatever? If anyone had been stupid enough to say so, male or female, I would have knocked out their teeth.

Screw Principal Lofton and her overprotective bullshit.

How could anything be too much when it came to protecting your kid?

*

That night, hours after the rain had stopped, the Dodgers were down by three runs with two out in the middle of the fifth when the Giants' center fielder had to pee. Unable to wait, the player unzipped and sprayed clover as a fly ball sailed over his head with the bases loaded. Instantly, half a dozen cell phone cameras shifted for a close-up. I glanced at Abby and forced a grin. Looking at her own phone, she watched something on the screen and seemed pissed. I considered asking her about it, but then my phone rang, so I left the bleachers and took the call.

"This is Boyd."

"Where are you? Sounds like a riot."

Investigator Suarez.

"Watching my kid's tee-ball game. What's up?"

"They winning?"

The centerfielder zipped tight and hunted for the ball as the batter rounded third base and streaked home.

"They are now. What did you find out?"

"Say it first: the slate is wiped clean."

"Whatever."

"I want to hear you say it."

"Okay...the slate is wiped clean. What did you get?"

Air blew into the phone, as if Suarez had popped a hemorrhoid donut, and the hiss went on for a long time. When at last he spoke, a new kid was at bat, and beyond the bases, the centerfielder frowned down at the clover as if he had stepped into his own puddle of piss.

"Word is Special Agent Dennis Fisk works out of the Bureau's Riverside field office. He was on the banks squad and then moved to OC."

"OC? Orange County?"

"Organized crime, you idiot."

"Would that include drug cartels?"

Suarez took a while to answer, so I watched the game as the batter took a base and a fresh hitter approached the box. Carter was on deck, swinging the bat, wearing a huge grin. If they survived another inning, the Dodgers would notch their first win of the season and earn a trip to Chuck E. Cheese. Looking to the stands, my son's eyes were huge and damp, like big pepperonis splattered with grease.

"Yeah, OC includes cartels," Suarez said at last. "Look, that's all I have on Fisk…Now, what do you have for me?"

"Lunch at Philippe's."

"Not good enough. What's this about?   FBI agents, drug cartels? You'd better not be involved in anything stupid, Boyd."

"I'm not."

"That doesn't sound convincing. Are you doing freelance work for the feeb? Computer stuff?"

The kid at bat whiffed the ball a few times—How do you whiff from a tee?— then hit deep into right field and made it to second base. Carter flashed a grin and stepped to the plate.

"Something like that. Can't really say."

"Just be smart, Boyd. The feds use people like you."

"What kind of people?"

"Disposable people. The kind who aren't federal employees protected by unions. Whatever you're helping with, if it goes south, the bureaucratic fingers will point your way, I promise. The feds are assholes. They don't care."

"You've hurt my feelings, man. I can look after myself."

"So what is it? Tell me."

"Don't know yet."

"Can't be the Italians. The Italians are done in L.A. OC is different these days. Must be the Mexicans or the Central Americans. The feeb going after MS-13? Share the love, brother."

Carter took two practice swings. A stiff ocean breeze swayed the tee, and the ball jerked as if electricity ran through it. Feeling a chill, I pictured Moreno standing on my driveway, grabbing Abby and the kids, putting a gun to their heads one by one. The breeze grew stronger.

"Fisk contacted me, and I needed to know if he was legit. Now I do. I appreciate your effort. The slate is clean."

Suarez sighed again. "Yeah, fine. It was worth it to put us square. Now, who solved the cyberstalker case?"

"L.A.'s greatest detective, Les Suarez. All by himself."

"L.A.'s future district attorney, Les Suarez. Don't forget it."

"Whatever you say, Lester."

"People get curious when you start inquiring about feds. Just so you know, I'm using the most disgusting public phone you've ever seen, downtown on Broadway, so there's no record of this call."

"Downtown?"

"The mayor's having some kind of shindig at The Orpheum tonight, hanging with the junkies and hobos. Thought I'd better press the flesh. To be honest, I'd rather watch your kid's ball game."

"Spoken like a true public servant."

"Yeah, I'm a prince. Call me next week about that lunch; there's something I need to run by you. And screw the turkey dip. If you're going to Philippe's, you gotta have the beef."

"Sure, we'll get the beef."

"Take care of yourself, Boyd, and be smart. The feds like to hurt people, and the drug cartels will kill you dead. That makes you the meat in the sandwich, my friend, and no matter what, people always eat the meat."

Suarez hung up.

I put away my phone and concentrated on the game.

Carter stepped into the batter's box and nailed the ball at the second baseman, who bobbled it, then threw to first base for an out, closing the inning. Next at bat, the Giants scored four runs and won the game. Chuck E. Cheese would have to wait.

That night in bed, I stared at the ceiling and pictured dead Mexican cops. After checking the doors and windows, setting and resetting the alarm, I had turned in around ten, pretending to be asleep when Abby slipped beneath the covers an hour later. She had been pissed about something all night. After Carter's game, our conversations stuck to the functional and mundane—we watched TV, got Carter through his bath, and maintained the routine until the kids were asleep. Then I feigned exhaustion and went to bed— a strategic move to buy time, think about Fisk and Moreno and how much to tell my wife.

"You're not asleep," she said, rolling onto her side.

Not responding right away, I listened to her breathing and tried to gauge the tone of her voice. Not exactly pissed, but clearly irritated.

"You're not asleep, either."

"What's the matter?"

"Nothing."

"You ignored me all night."

"I wasn't ignoring you. You seemed a little wound up at the game, so I was giving you space."

"I don't want space. I want to talk."

"Now?" I mumbled. "It's late. We'll talk in the morning."

"You didn't tell me about your day."

"You didn't tell me about yours, either."

"I don't want to talk about my day."

"There's nothing to tell about mine. Normal day."

"Really? What's normal for you these days? I don't even know what you do anymore."

"Nothing but free time, according to you."

"Come on…"

Flat on my back, I stared at the ceiling and thought of Moreno, then recalled Fisk's last request before leaving my office at DRI.

"We'd like to use your property for surveillance. I want cameras facing Moreno's house, and the trees in your backyard offer an unobstructed view," he'd said. "We'll maintain your family's privacy. Installation will occur when no one is home. A trimming crew will show up; your trees will get a light cut. My team can have cameras in place within thirty minutes."

Chewing it over, I took a while to respond. Our house butted against the foothills on the border of a wilderness park, and the terrain was rolling and open, dotted with oaks and groves of eucalyptus, networked by fire roads and trails. Twice a month, I joined a community watch organized by my neighbor Dave Manker and patrolled the trails, looking for homeless people lighting campfires and kids drinking beer or smoking. At nearly two thousand acres, the park was huge, and should have offered Fisk numerous surveillance options that didn't require endangering my family.

"What about the Patriot Act? Can't you just do it without my permission? You guys have all the power now. Why bother asking?"

"I'd prefer you cooperated, Mr. Boyd. You're going to need friends, and I'd like to be one."

Fisk was right about that. With a killer next door, we needed friends, preferably the kind who carried guns and had access to reinforcements. Still, the idea of cameras pointing toward my house put a sickening twist in my guts.

"Will my house be visible?"

"Just Moreno's."

"I don't want my family showing up on YouTube."

"That won't happen. You have my word."

"Fine…use my trees, watch every move that bastard makes. But if things go sideways, and you people don't come like an army, this hits every newspaper in the country."

Fisk had cracked a half smile then and left. When I got home that afternoon, the trees in my backyard looked the same, and staring up I saw nothing but leaves.

Abby cleared her throat and interrupted my worries.

"Earth to Jack. You say I'm the one being distant?"

"Yeah, sorry," I said. "I should have told you earlier. We have a problem."

"Only one? What an improvement."

"It's Carter."

I detailed the fight at school, our son's lack of reaction, and my conversation with Principal Lofton about the Phoenix Academy. Before I finished, Abby's face wore an expectant look, as if she had sniffed an opportunity. But she was about to enter a very expensive room, one we couldn't afford, so I cut her off right away.

"Tuition for private school is impossible right now, Ab. There's no way."

"We made a mistake sending him to public school."

"No, we didn't."

I looked across the sheets. Moonlight fell through the window and painted her blue. Between her eyes, deep creases grew into canyons of frustration bordering on anger, and I proceeded delicately, not wanting to fall in.

"Carter's six. We need to give it more time. He needs to be in a regular school. That's his best shot at being normal."

"He is normal. Don't say that."

"Okay, you're right. But if he's normal, he doesn't need a special school, does he? And anyway, even if we wanted to send him there, we can't afford it."

Between the mortgage and car payments, two hungry kids and everything else, our monthly nut could choke an army of squirrels, and Abby paid the bills, so she knew money was tight. Not ready to concede, she fired off a quick counterattack.

"We can afford it."

"You plan on robbing a bank?"

"The equity credit line. Even with this housing market, we're above water."

"Now isn't the time for a loan, Ab. We have no idea what the housing market's going to do. My business is okay, but we're building a client base. You know that. The credit line is our backup if things go south."

"Things already went south, Jack. You lost your job at MicroLine."

"I didn't lose anything. It was a buyout, and you know it."

"Whatever."

Time to get this out of the way. Long story short, I left MicroLine because Leila Krebs, a human resource temp, accused me of sexual harassment. The charge had been bullshit. MicroLine, however, had been looking to downsize upper management at the time, so rather than fight the charge, I took an offered buyout and started my own shop. There had been a non-compete clause in my contract, but Leland Reed, MicroLine's CEO, and a personal friend, promised not to invoke as long as DRI steered clear of their clients. The deal had been a good resolution to a bad situation. MicroLine avoided a lawsuit, Leila Krebs got some extra cash, and I started a new career as a digital forensics bottom-feeder. None of it had sat well with Abby, though, and my willingness to take the deal without fighting Leila's charges had left her with some heavy doubts. That was understandable. When Abby was a kid, infidelity had infected her family the way alcoholism and violence had afflicted mine—first a cheating mother, then her dad—producing one domestic earthquake after another.

"Is that why you're so pissed off tonight? You're thinking about Leila?"

"Not thinking."

"What then?"

"She sent me an email. Tonight, at Carter's game."

"An email? About what?"

"The message was blank. Like she was taunting me."

"She has nothing to taunt you with, Ab. Why didn't you tell me?"

"Have you seen her?"

Facing my wife, I reached for a hand. "I haven't seen Leila Krebs in three months. There's nothing going on. There never was."

"Then why is she contacting me?"

"I have no idea.

"Well find out, and tell the bitch to stop."

"Sure… Okay."

Abby took another breath and held it.

When Leila had made the accusations, I'd panicked and claimed we had never been alone together, hoping the whole thing would go away. That part was untrue. I had bought her lunch a few times, consumed too much wine, and told racy jokes. When Abby found out, she hadn't been happy, and by lying, I had only made things worse. There in bed, thinking of what was coming our way, I felt the same tug. Fisk. Aldama, Moreno. Keeping the truth from Abby made me feel dirty, but nothing good would come of her knowing. At best, we'd start packing in the middle of the night and skip town by morning. At worst, she'd call the police and demand round-the-clock protection. Not good options from which to choose. As I'd tried to explain to Jane Selig earlier that afternoon, sometimes the truth wasn't better.

Abby exhaled.

I squeezed her hand.

"We don't need to decide Carter's entire future tonight. He's in the first grade. We'll keep moving forward. He stays where he is for now and we see how it goes. If he doesn't improve, we discuss therapy, or maybe the Phoenix Academy."

Abby stared for a long time and then pinched my chest.

"Promise?"

"Promise.

She kissed me. When the kiss ended, she turned onto her side and pressed back until we formed a single bending curve on the mattress. I listened to her breathe, and as our rhythm grew slower, the day's stress drained away. I forgot about Fisk, Moreno, and Leila Krebs, and within minutes was drifting into the dark.

Then Abby rolled around, faced me in the blue moonlight with a questioning look, and ruined everything. "I forgot to ask... How was Marty? You must have gone during lunch."

Just like that, I jerked awake.

Shit.

Special Agent Fisk had dropped his bombshell, and in the ensuing blast, I had drawn a blank on Marty's special day. Lying there, counting breaths, I tasted shame for several moments—a bitter taste like raw almonds—and then forced it down.

No big deal.

I had never missed a monthly visit before, not once in over two decades, and one thing was certain: even if Marty was upset, he sure as hell wouldn't complain.

Marty Goodman hadn't spoken a word in over twenty-two years.

MICHAEL HARBISON

Chapter Five

Puffs of air bloated Marty's chest with the mute force of a punctured bellows, and as he breathed, a putrid stench—one part decaying teeth and two parts wasted life—rose from his mouth. A thin white crust—like a salt rim encircling a dry lake—stained his lips, giving them a faint, bluish tint. Grabbing a plastic cup and straw from the bedside table, I drew some water into the straw and then beaded it along the shoreline of his mouth.

"How you doing today, Marty?"

The old man flinched at my voice, then felt liquid and opened his mouth, lapping up the water. His tongue darted in an out, as if it functioned independent of the brain, the only living thing inside Martin Goodman's skull.

"You look tired," I said.

Marty's left eyebrow twitched, the hairs knotted and thick like coiled electrical wire. He looked no different from a month earlier—old, stubborn, barely holding on—at a point of stasis beyond which nothing waited but death.

Placing the cup on the table, I sat back in the chair and looked out the window. Evergreen Nursing Center was in a San Bernardino residential neighborhood, near the mountains at the eastern shore of the Inland Empire. Marty's window overlooked a garden of hibiscus and gardenia, and when smog wasn't thick, pine-dotted foothills were visible, and sometimes a hawk floated by on the wind. None of that mattered to Marty, of course, but if the old man ever woke up, at least he'd have something nice to look at.

I leaned back in the chair as a young kid with a silver nose stud walked into the room carrying an empty urine bladder.

"Time for a diaper change, Mr. Goodman. Running late... Your tank must be full." The kid noticed me and stopped. "Sorry. He's usually alone."

"No problem."

The kid went to the bedside and unhooked a full urine bag. He replaced it with an empty and then eyed me from across the room.

"Family?"

"No."

The kid shrugged.

"Mr. Goodman doesn't get many visitors. That's gotta suck...to be like that...and nobody even knows you're a vegetable."

"Marty's not a vegetable." I pointed at the bed. "And be careful what you say. He's listening."

"You think he hears us?"

"Yeah, I do."

"They say we should talk to them. Sometimes that feels a little too freaky."

The kid finished with the bladder and moved to the bed, pulling up the sheet and blanket and exposing Marty's toes. The nails were long, yellow, and cracked, and it seemed wrong they should grow while the rest of the man withered. Then the kid produced a nail trimmer and started clipping.

"So how do you know him if he's not family?"

"You're new around here, right? I haven't seen you before."

"Three weeks. I know you have your badge, but they say we're supposed to ask about visitors."

Evergreen's staff churned faster than a cage of meth-addicted rabbits—low wages and creeping death made for a tough work environment—and faces changed on a weekly basis. Over the years, Marty had shuffled from one place to the next, mostly when his benefits changed. Evergreen was the nicest by far, but the patient-to-staff ratio was high, and that morning, no one had manned the front desk. So I walked in, issued myself a visitor's badge, and roamed the halls, taking in room after room of gray hair dying in slow motion. Despite Evergreen's relative virtues, my monthly visits usually ended with me driving home, staring into the sunset, weighing the merits of late-octogenarian suicide.

"He was my next-door neighbor," I said. "A long time ago…before all this. When he was normal."

The kid nodded and his nose stud wagged.

"I spend all day with these guys, but they never talk. I drain their bladders. Change their diapers. Try to keep them comfortable. Sometimes I invent stories to go with the faces. You know, give them a past. This one was a bar singer or that one a movie star. Passes the time, you know."

"I get it."

The kid pointed at the bed.

"Not Mr. Goodman, though. Everyone knows his story."

All of a sudden, I wanted to leave, but I took a few deep breaths and forced myself to stay rooted in the chair.

"His wife bashed his head in. He beat her up or something, so she grabbed a baseball bat and almost killed him. He called the police, then slipped into a coma. She did like nineteen years in prison or something."

I removed a piece of lint from Marty's cheek and suppressed another urge to leave.

"Didn't happen that way," I said

"Oh?" The kid's nose stud flared. "You know about it?"

"Marty's not a vegetable. He's in what they call a minimally conscious state. He makes sounds and responds to stimuli. He can

47

move a little and probably hears us, so you need to watch what you say."

"I've never seen him move."

"He moves. And Marty never beat Janis. He didn't call the cops that night, either. Also, to be completely accurate, she did twenty years, not nineteen. They let her out because she got cancer. Compassionate release or something like that. The cancer went into remission. She teaches some kind of acting class these days. Janis always thought she should have been a movie star. She was a beautiful woman once."

The kid leaned back against the wall and glanced at Marty.

"The other guy said nineteen years."

"What other guy?"

"Looked like you, only meaner. Visited a few weeks ago."

"Sounds like my brother."

"I see the resemblance," the kid said. "He looks older."

"Four years younger," I told him. "That's what alcohol and prison do to you."

The kid nodded and glanced at Marty again.

"So what really happened to him? I mean, all I heard are rumors."

I shrugged and kept quiet.

"Come on?"

"It was a long time ago."

"You don't forget something like that when it happens next door. You were his neighbor, right? You must remember."

Of course I remembered. Had Marty Goodman not had his brains bashed in, I probably would have gone down a different path in life—maybe coaching or professional baseball; I was that good once. Probably would have attended a different university, never met Abby, never had my kids. Never worked at MicroLine. Janis and Marty had been my first taste of criminal violence, and had they never happened, the pressing need I felt to balance the scales between people who do wrong and those who use their gifts for good might never have sparked. Before Marty's exile into oblivion, we had spent hours discussing my future and, to a lesser extent, that of my brother. Who knows—if Marty had stuck around, maybe Ran would have avoided prison. The permutations were enough to drive a guy nuts, but the fact was, Marty had ridden a bed for more than two decades, and at some point, all untapped potential becomes part of history.

The kid stayed rooted to the wall. He wouldn't move until I told the whole story, so I kept it brief.

"I heard fighting one night…went over and pounded on the front door. There was no answer, so I let myself in. Janis was unconscious at the bottom of the stairs; Marty was at the top in a pool of blood. I called the cops and paramedics. The rest is pretty much as you said. Marty turned into this. The cops arrested Janis for attempted murder. I testified at her trial, and she never forgave me. What happened before that is anyone's guess."

The kid whistled long and low, like a tumbling bomb about to burst.

"You saved his life."

I shook my head.

"Hardly what I'd call living, kid. He might have been better off if I never made the call."

"You visit him, at least. That counts for something."

"Sure, I visit once a month. Marty's like my priest. I tell him things…he listens… No arguments between us. It was always that way."

I thought of Special Agent Fisk and of the man about to move in next door. I had wanted to tell Marty about Carlos Moreno, just to get it off my chest, but the kid was there, so I stayed quiet.

"He's having a good month," the kid said.

"How's that possible?" I asked.

"Two visitors and some good news."

"Oh yeah? What's the news?"

The kid went to the nightstand, opened the drawer, and pulled out a newspaper clipping.

"Your brother left this. Mr. Goodman's wife croaked six months ago."

Glancing down, I read the short article from the *High Desert News*, a daily from Victorville, California. Janis had served part of her prison term near there. The article stated that Janis Sanchez-Goodman, age 69, had died from a recurrence of cancer. That was it. No mention of a house in Fontana, a troubled marriage, or a prison term for the attempted murder of her husband, a man I had once considered a second father. Behind the article, a paperclip held a curled photograph of a boy clutching a baseball bat. I recognized it as one of the baseball cards Marty made for us neighborhood kids.

"I read it to him," the kid said. "Thought it would make him happy. You know…that she was dead."

I looked at Marty.

"Did it?"

The kid shook his head. "Not even a smile."

I stood and walked to the door, then turned and looked at the old man. "Marty wouldn't be happy about Janis dying," I told the kid. "He loved her. Probably still does."

The kid pointed at Marty's wasted figure on the bed. "Even after that?"

I nodded. "Even after that."

*

Thirty minutes later, I tapped on my brother's apartment door and watched a grinning Latino kid on a tricycle carve circles in the driveway. The wheels smacked the cracked asphalt, and the kid's helmeted head jerked as if taking one invisible punch after another. Eleven a.m. on a Thursday. Why wasn't the boy in school? A thin Vietnamese woman carrying a baby stepped from the next-door apartment and barked at the kid in Spanish. The circling stopped. The kid ditched the tricycle and darted inside. As he passed, a hint of Down's syndrome flashed around his eyes. Glancing inside the woman's apartment, I spotted four other kids on the floor, all special needs, two of them wearing helmets, and thought of Carter.

The woman glared my way.

"He not home," she snapped.

"Yeah, I figured that out."

Ran's apartment was in south Pomona, ten miles from College Heights, but with chickens roaming yards and cornrows crowding satellite dishes, the place seemed to occupy a different zone of latitude. A coat of dust covered the complex, except around my brother's doorstep, which looked well scrubbed and orderly.

"He late," the woman announced.

The baby on her hip began to squirm. The woman's small waist offered no purchase, and the child slipped toward the asphalt, tugging the woman's jeans down to reveal red underwear. She didn't seem to notice or care.

"You know when he'll be back?"

"Three weeks late."

"He's been gone three weeks?"

The woman shook her head, switched from English to Spanish, and then ended with a flurry of Vietnamese. Almost dropping the baby, she thumped her chest and said, "Rent!"

Counting three fingers, I saw the light.

"He's late paying rent?"

She gave a thumbs-up and winked.

"How much does he owe?"

"One thousand."

Doing a quick calculation of mortgage, car payments, and grocery money, I walked to my car and wrote a check, then wondered what to tell Abby about the missing funds. With his stint in prison and questionable friends, Ran wasn't her favorite person. The irony was, he loved Abby deeply, always had, and maybe in a way that under different circumstances would have made me jealous.

"You know when he'll be back?"

The woman shrugged.

"Maybe for lunch. Who knows?"

"You got a phone number for him?"

"Who you?"

"The guy about to give you a thousand dollars." I lifted the check so she could see the numbers. "I'm his brother."

"Brother should know number," she griped.

"Yeah, well…he moves around a lot."

The woman snatched the check and hurried into her apartment. Moments later, she came back and handed over a receipt, the lower margin scrawled with my brother's digits.

Accepting the receipt, I said, "Don't tell him I paid you."

"Why not? He your brother."

"He doesn't like me interfering."

The woman shook her head and went inside.

Returning to the car, I called the number and left my brother a message, extending an invite to Saturday's barbecue. The call was pointless, though—Ran would never come. It was an exercise in hope, as my driving there had been, thinking we could discuss Marty Goodman, Janis, and all the other things.

I turned the key and drove to MicroLine.

Chapter Six

At the eastern edge of the Ontario Airport, MicroLine's six-story complex looked better than I remembered—spotless glass, bright paint, a bold corporate logo shining with the arrogance of a company mining a gold rush. Twelve years earlier, when MicroLine opened shop, Leland Reed and I had staffed a two-room office on Holt Avenue and ridden the digital tidal wave as law enforcement struggled not to drown. Penal code violations looked the same—blackmail, embezzlement, murder—but the Internet boom meant evidence came in long strings of code, which to your average cop looked a lot like hieroglyphics. Reed, an artist in computer languages, had devised a method for collecting that evidence and preserving it for court, giving the white hats a fighting chance in a black hat world.

Entering the lobby, I headed toward a desk guarding the elevators. The security man, Roger Saldana, looked up, saw a familiar face, and smiled. I had walked past the guy hundreds of times, but I hardly knew him. Had I been aware of his fate in the coming days, I would have made more of an effort.

"Mr. Boyd. What's up?"

"How go things?"

"You know, busy. Coming back to work?"

"Just a visit."

Saldana dug into a drawer, produced an access card that doubled as a visitor's badge, and handed it over. MicroLine housed a regional digital forensics lab used by corporations and law enforcement agencies throughout the Inland Empire. With evidence and e-discovery around, security was tight. The badge controlled access to various areas of the building—some restricted, others not—and provided real-time tracking information to the security control room. Visitors wandered off path for long, someone from security would come looking.

Saldana wrote my name in his log and noted the entry time. "Probably a good thing," he said. "They're cutting back again. Mr. Reed's making this place lean and mean. Rumor is he wants to sell. But what do I know? I'm just a guy with a gun."

He tapped the holstered automatic riding his hip.

"Reed won't sell." I adjusted the badge on my shirt pocket. "That's why he never took the company public. He couldn't bear someone else running his baby."

"I don't know... Vector Dynamics made an offer last month. The Board turned it down, but I hear Reed's angling for a better price... Bad thing for me, Vector uses contractors for security. I could be out of a job."

"Don't sweat rumors."

"If you say so," he said, unconvinced.

"Tell you what. Let you know if I hear anything. How's that sound?"

Saldana bobbed his head and forced a smile. "Sure."

I sniffed the air, ready to change the subject. "Place smells a little stale."

"Too much bullshit around. Harvey Rezko's security chief now. Leaves his stench on everything."

"I had a dog like him once."

The guard laughed.

Heading to the elevator, I swiped the access card through a reader alongside the door and waited as the camera next to the elevator swiveled and took my close-up. If anybody else—a vendor or a visiting client—stepped under the lens, an escort would come down. Not Jack Boyd. Being tight with Leland Reed came with privileges. Easy access was one of them.

On the third floor, three paces out of the elevator, a ponytailed Indian guy wearing a Tony Hawk sweatshirt and carrying a squirt gun stopped me in the hall. Behind him, a cubicle farm spread to the windows, and beyond the glass, an airliner taxied onto a runway at Ontario International, leaving a heat shimmer in its wake.

Manjit Singh pointed the gun at my chest and grinned.

"Reach for it, Boyd."

"Manny. You survived downsizing, huh? So much for natural selection."

Singh directed the gun toward his mouth, fired off a stream of water, and slurped. "You're looking at the VP of Projects and Expansion. Not just a bitchin' title, either. Came with a hefty pay raise."

My old job. I took a few beats to reply. "What expansion?"

"Reed pulled the trigger on the SHU."

"You're guys are building the SHU?"

"Going operational in a couple of weeks. Reed's holding formal announcement until next month. Gonna be huge." Singh pointed to the jet on the runway. "Money's rolling in on 747s."

The SHU—or Secure Housing Unit—had been my final pitch before leaving the company. With one of the newest digital forensics labs in the region, MicroLine already had a large market share, especially in the Inland Empire, but it wasn't the only game in town, and competition grew tougher by the year. Guidance Software in Pasadena dominated the show, but Vector Dynamics was a close second. Building the SHU, a high-security evidence acquisition and storage facility that met federal national-security standards, would entrench MicroLine as a top-tier digital forensics company. Seconds after I finished my PowerPoint pitch, Reed dismissed the idea. National security upgrades would be cost prohibitive. Gravy flowed already, more than MicroLine could lap up. Why alter the recipe? Obviously, his opinion had changed.

Singh flashed a deep frown. "C'mon, man. Everyone knows the SHU was your baby. Reed became convinced it was the hot ticket."

"When?"

Singh slurped another drink from the gun. "Three months back. Maybe two. Leila worked on him."

Right after my buyout.

"What the hell does Leila know about forensics? She's a human resource temp."

"Reed brought her upstairs, gave her more responsibility. She was on track for permanent status. Then, three weeks ago, out of nowhere, she pulls the plug."

"Leila's gone?"

"Just up and quit." Singh's mouth froze and his eyes grew wide. "That doesn't mean you should come back, though. This place sucks now. Nobody screws around. I can't imagine what it'll be like once the feds drop by with evidence. Honestly, if I wasn't in my hole all day, I'd quit."

"Relax, Manny, I don't want my old job back."

"Good." Singh gave a relieved nod. "Hey...SHU is a prison term by the way. Where they keep the badasses. Reed wasn't happy when he found out. We had an ad campaign set up, had to dump the whole thing. He thought you picked the name because of your brother, like some kind of homage."

"I did."

"We call it the bunker now."

"Who came up with that?"

"Yours truly."

"I like it."

Over Singh's shoulder, beyond the cubicle farm, the jet screamed down the runway and pitched skyward, making an escape into the clouds. I thought of what Singh had said about money rolling in, what the guard had mentioned about the sale of the company, and spotted a pattern.

"Maybe things are changing for a reason," I said. "The downsizing, the bunker."

"Meaning what?"

"Maybe Reed wants to sell the company. He's making it more attractive...trying to up the price."

Singh made a fart noise. "Vector Dynamics? Total bullshit. Reed's never taking his mouth off this tit. If there were the slightest chance, I'd abandon ship. Anyway, what do you care? You have your own company to worry about."

He was right about that. Much as I sometimes missed being at MicroLine, nothing compared to running my own show. Smaller scale, less exotic cases, but at least I called the shots. No conference calls. No board meetings. Just a quick word with Fisher and decisions got made.

"I like being the boss."

"And business is good, right?"

"Sure."

Singh cocked an eyebrow. "Must be if you're already working with the feeb."

I took a moment to respond. "What do you mean?"

"You're working with the FBI, right? Business must be good."

"What makes you say that?"

Singh rolled his shoulders. "Nothing."

"Out with it, Manny."

"Before Leila split, some fed came around looking into your background. He spent a lot of time in HR. Everyone kind of figured it meant you're working for them."

I took a few seconds to respond. "What did he say?"

"Don't know. Leila talked to him."

"Does Reed know?"

"Yeah...and he's not happy."

Anger built for several beats. I pictured Fisk roaming the halls, asking questions. A background check made sense. The FBI wouldn't hit someone's doorstep without doing background. That said, if Fisk gave the impression I was working with the feds, Reed might assume I was poaching MicroLine's clients.

"This agent...what did he look like? Pudgy guy? Bad suit?"

"Nah, this guy was tall. Sharp dresser."

Didn't sound like Fisk. The feds had sent a different agent. Either way, I needed to talk to Reed, inform him this had nothing to do with business. Now wasn't the time to screw up my severance deal.

We continued down the hall, moving toward an elevator door. A cardkey slot and a number pad rode the wall beside the jamb. Some type of bio-scanner rested above the keypad. The door was beefy, like the entrance to a safe or a decompression chamber. Singh tucked his squirt gun into his shorts and dug out a cardkey.

"Good talking with you, Manny. Need to see the boss and get this straightened out."

"Reed's in San Diego, working some corporate meltdown. That Hartmann-Rydell merger—big mortgage house CEO coming back from Mexico had kiddy porn on his computer. Customs found it and the guy pulled the pin, killed himself mid-merger. The deal went belly-up. An army of lawyers is gearing up for World War III, so Reed's imaging company files."

"Since when does Leland image files?"

Singh rolled his shoulders. "They're paying for the privilege. Claims it'll take a week. My guess is that's bullshit. He's probably surfing at Solana. There's a sweet swell coming up from Mexico. You might want to call him, though. He was pissed you're working with the feds."

"I'm not working with the FBI."

"You'd better tell him that."

"I will," I said. "See you, Manny."

Singh nodded toward the elevator. "You want to see the bunker? Quick ride down to the basement. Hard drives chirping away like an army of crickets. Practically your baby. Might as well take a look."

My lips moved to say yes, but then a metal vise clamped my shoulder.

"You're not cleared for that."

The voice landed hard, like a jab and uppercut followed by a blow from a sledgehammer. I turned and met the glare of Harvey Rezko, MicroLine's security chief. Six foot three and linebacker wide, Rezko looked Marine Corps fit. A year before leaving MicroLine, I hired the guy, and his resumé had gleamed diamond bright—time in the Marines, Vietnam, twenty years with the United States Secret Service. We got along for six months, and then during his first performance review I suggested to Reed that Harvey lacked managerial finesse. Somehow, word got back to Rezko, and our friendship died. Standing in the heat of his gaze, I did my best to smile but felt like a kid about to have his car keys snatched away.

"What's up, Harv?"

"What are you doing here, Boyd?"

"Came to see Leland."

"Mr. Reed isn't here. You're no longer an employee, and you're not a client."

Rezko plucked the visitor badge from my chest.

"That's right."

"You have no reason to be here, then." He pointed to the reinforced elevator leading to the bunker. "You sure as hell got no reason to go down there."

Singh butted in. "I control bunker access, Rez." The Indian walked to a keypad, swiped a card, and placed his left eye next to the scanner. After the scan completed, the elevator door opened. "C'mon, Boyd," he said.

Spreading my hands, I stepped back "I have things to do, Manny."

Singh frowned and ducked into the elevator. The doors closed.

Rezko glared. "I'll escort you out," he said.

"I know the way, Harv."

"You might get lost and end up harassing the ladies."

We turned and walked back down the hall. Once inside the elevator, Rezko punched the lobby button. I watched the numbers drop and felt the security chief's gaze. Sloped beneath a fitted dress shirt, Harvey's back and shoulders seemed to support the roof. When he spoke, his voice rasped like Clint Eastwood fighting a bad case of strep throat.

"Business not so good, Boyd? I hear you're stealing our clients."

I cleared my throat, put a little edge to my voice. "You're cranky this morning, Harv. Been taking your Metamucil? Regularity plays an important role in a positive disposition."

"You shouldn't come around here."

"Far as I know, Reed is the boss. He tells me to stay away, I'll stay away."

Rezko's eyes narrowed into a challenge. "I heard you asking your little brown friend about Leila Krebs. You need to leave that girl alone."

"Whatever you think happened between Leila and me, you're wrong, Harv."

"Yeah...I doubt that."

The bell dinged as we reached the lobby. Rezko's lips twitched. The security man tugged his shirt and prepared to exit. I pressed the door-closed button and locked us in.

"Now that I think about it, since Reed isn't around, I have a question for you, Harv."

Rezko glared.

"Move your finger, Boyd."

"You're an ex-fed. Ever hear of an FBI agent named Dennis Fisk?"

Staring at my button finger, Rezko's eyes narrowed.

"Why are you asking?"

"Trying to confirm his identity, see what kind of guy he is. I want to know if I can trust him."

"Take your finger off the button."

He meant it this time, so I did.

The door opened.

The lobby seemed quiet with Roger Saldana away from his desk.

"You can leave now," Rezko said, pointing toward the door.

I stepped into the lobby. Then, a few paces from the exit, I turned and faced the elevator. Standing there, arms crossed, Rezko stared out like a bulldog watching a sick kitten.

"What about Fisk?" I asked.

Rezko shook his head.

"Never ask about a federal agent's identity, Boyd."

A few beats ticked by. I shrugged off the admonition and said, "Oh yeah? Why not?"

The doors began to close and Rezko fired one last shot.

"People get killed."

Chapter Seven

Grabbing a quick breath, I stopped and looked at Detective Vasquez. He leaned against the wall, riding the same position, wearing the same mixed expression—a hot cross between professional skepticism and outright disbelief that sucked all the moisture from the room. I tried to swallow and my throat screamed.

"Could I get some water?"

Vasquez nodded toward the mirrored glass.

A door opened and footsteps moved down the hall.

Above my head, the room lights burned like an overheated sun. Contrary to first impressions, the place wasn't that nice—muted paint, sticky residue on my chair, thick layer of grime filling chipped linoleum like scabs clogging a wound. It seemed like a motel room you arrived at in the middle of the night, only to find that by morning, subtle variations in the carpet had turned into an army of scurrying bugs.

Wiping sweat, I nodded at the camera. "Before I continue, I want Fisk here. He needs to back me up."

"Changing your mind about legal representation, Mr. Boyd?"

"No…but I want Fisk."

Detective Vasquez grabbed a breath and glanced at the mirrored glass. I pictured Marner, or maybe Dale Griffin, beaming telepathic signals from the other side, telling Vasquez what to do.

"We've contacted the FBI. They're tracking down Special Agent Fisk. Obviously, it's your right to stop talking."

My desire to see Fisk had nothing to do with my rights. I needed to be sure his men had eyes on Moreno and that Abby and the kids were safe. Once I knew that, nothing else would matter.

"Any chance I could use my cell phone?"

"There's no coverage in here."

"Outside then? I'm waiting on a voicemail."

"Give me the number. I'll have someone retrieve your messages."

I wrote our voicemail number and password on a piece of paper. Then someone came to the door with my water. Vasquez gave them the number and handed me the water. After guzzling half the bottle, I glanced back at the detective.

"Should I go on?"

Vasquez held up a hand. "Let me get the timeline straight. You went to MicroLine recently? Before last night?"

"Yeah, last week."

"And prior to that?"

"I hadn't been for a few months. Not since I left my job."

"Since you were terminated, you mean?"

"I wasn't terminated, Detective. It was a buyout."

"Okay…but if you left on amicable terms, why hadn't you gone back? I mean, you work somewhere twelve years, it becomes part of you. Coworkers become friends. Why not go back for a visit?"

"You know the answer to that, Detective, but I see where you're headed. I was embarrassed after what happened with Leila, but I wasn't angry about losing my job. Last night had nothing to do with settling a score against MicroLine. It was all about Moreno."

Vasquez gave a nod. "All right."

"Should I continue?"

"One more thing—the no compete clause in your contract. Mr. Reed promised not to invoke it as long as you steered clear of MicroLine's clients. Is that correct?"

"That's right."

"And was that a written promise or something between friends?"

"It was between friends."

Vasquez nodded as if a shaft of sunlight had just illuminated the dark path at his feet.

"So if MicroLine sold to a new owner, that new owner would be under no obligation to honor the agreement. I mean, if they wanted, they could shut down your business, right, Mr. Boyd?"

The detective's question made sense. It cut through all the bullshit and drove head on at the beating heart of every crime.

Motivation.

I resumed talking.

Chapter Eight

When I arrived home with Sara, a moving van blocked my driveway, five brown guys hauled boxes through the dead grass next door, and Carlos Moreno stood on the sidewalk, talking to my wife and son. Heart thumping, fingers wrapped around the wheel, I fought the urge to gun the engine, drive at Moreno, and watch him sink under the radiator. Instead, I parked along the curb and helped Sara limp out to meet our new neighbor. She had twisted her ankle playing volleyball at school that morning—she sent everyone a text announcing the injury—so it took us a while to join the crowd. When at last we stepped onto the sidewalk, Abby yanked me close and patted my head as if I were the dog.

"This is Jack, my husband."

Moreno flashed perfect teeth in the sunlight. His skin, the color of creamed coffee, hugged tight muscles that probably cost hours in the gym, and dark brown eyes, puffed from genetics or fatigue, dominated a lean face that tapered to a square jaw made of stone.

"Charlie Moreno." He thrust out a hand. "Nice to meet you. The truck is no inconvenience, I hope."

Flawless English. No accent. Just a slight deviation in syntax. Moreno held my gaze as we shook. To be honest, maybe it was a guy thing, but the killer's grip felt a little weak.

"Jack Boyd. Welcome to the neighborhood. The truck's fine."

Moreno smiled. "Thank you."

Abby lifted her hands. "I didn't know the place had sold." Her eyes landed on me. "Did you?"

I shook my head and lied. "News to me."

Abby grinned. "We're happy. Very happy. Vacant houses are never good for a neighborhood. They're an eyesore. You'll have the place fixed up in no time, I'm sure."

Moreno surveyed his sunburnt grass and shuffled his feet. Looking at him, I forgot Special Agent Fisk and his cameras, the dead Mexican cops, the past thirty-six hours of fluctuating dread, and saw a stranger handed a honey-do list by my wife.

"Give the man a few hours to unpack before you ask him to mow the lawn, hon."

Abby shot me a look. "That's not what I meant. I'm just glad someone's moving in."

"You're right, of course," Moreno acknowledged, "the yard needs work. I don't start at the office for a few days. The place will shape up, I promise. You'll probably hear more noise than usual. Please, bear with me."

On the lawn, Carter chased Hondo in circles and pulled his tail, making him bark.

"I doubt noise will be a problem," I said.

Moreno's brown eyes shifted left. "And who is this?"

Sara, balanced on one foot, leaned against Abby's BMW and smirked.

I said, "This charmer's my daughter, Sara. Normally, she'd shake hands and introduce herself, but she's a teenager and has forgotten her manners for a few years."

Abby smacked my arm. She went to Sara and bent down, pressing the ankle wrap. "How is it, sweetie?"

"Better when somebody helps me upstairs."

"Don't be rude, dear. We have a new neighbor."

"I'm not being rude. I want to sleep."

Carlos Moreno moved forward. "What happened to your leg?"

Sara curled a lip. "Twisted it playing beach volleyball in P.E. This Bambi got lucky with a heater so I boomed her. Crashed hard and my ankle rolled."

"Let's have that again…this time in English," I said.

Moreno helpfully explained. "A lousy player got lucky with a spike. Sara made a spike of her own but landed wrong." He looked at Sara and smiled, then pointed at her foot. "Can I look?"

The curled lip morphed into a grin, and my daughter nodded.

"You seem to know a lot about volleyball, Mr. Moreno," I said while the killer groped Sara's leg.

"Please…call me Charlie. I know a little from ESPN." His fingers explored her ankle and calf. Pressed, slid, rubbed. Halfway through the exam, he smiled up at me. "Years ago, I was in love with one of the world's best players—Holly McPeak. Unfortunately, she never knew I existed." He released my daughter's leg with a pat and then stood up. "I don't think it's broken. A bad sprain, perhaps. Ice it for three days, and then use heat. Thirty minutes on, thirty off. Make sure to check for abnormal discoloration. Good circulation is mandatory for healing."

"You a doctor, Charlie?"

Moreno smiled. "I sell concrete. My ankles gave me terrible problems when I was in the army. Of course, you may want to get an x-ray."

"Of course."

Moreno looked at Sara again. "Do you have a swimming pool?"

Sara fired a disdainful look my way and shook her head.

69

"Well, once my pool and spa are heated, you'd be welcome to use them for physical therapy. With your parents' permission, of course."

"We'll try the ice," I said, "and take it from there."

Moreno nodded as a loud crash echoed from the moving van. A string of profane-sounding Spanish followed. So far, the truck's contents seemed to consist of cardboard boxes and low-quality Goodwill furniture. No TV. No appliances. Maybe the cartel was running short on cash. There was another bang, and then Moreno's cell phone chimed and the neighborly conversation died. He looked at the phone's display and frowned.

"I have to take this call, and I believe my supervision is required with the movers." He nodded at Abby and Sara and addressed me directly. "It's been a pleasure meeting your family, Jack. You've made me feel welcome."

The statement was formal-sounding bullshit, but I recalled Special Agent Fisk's request to make nice and offered my hand.

"Sure thing."

Moreno shook it and left, answering his cell phone as he walked to the moving van.

"Charming man," Abby said. "Impeccable manners."

"I'll give him that."

Ahead of us, Sara was limping toward the front door, leaving us alone. Abby bent down, lifted her briefcase, and gave me a look. "You sound doubtful. He seemed nice."

I shrugged as the wind blew. Above us, sycamore trees waved back and forth and I stared up, looked for cameras, and wondered who stared back.

"Time will tell."

Abby began walking toward the porch. Glancing at Sara, balanced on one foot and waiting by the front door, I decided to plant the first seeds of suspicion.

"Did you see how he touched her leg?"

"Give it a break, Jack. He was trying to help."

"Being in the army doesn't make you a doctor, and there's no way in hell she's going over there to swim. He's moving in, but that doesn't mean we have to be pals."

"Yeah…well, you can't ignore him."

I glanced next door. Moreno was still engaged in an animated phone conversation.

"I don't intend to ignore him," I said.

"That's good, because I invited him for Saturday's barbecue. He's bringing tamales or some type of steak."

"You invited him without asking me?"

"We invite everyone on the street. What were we going to do, exclude him because he's new? That wouldn't be nice."

Abby's attention shifted to Sara then. I watched them go inside the house. Wrapped in her mom's arms, my daughter looked like a little girl. Wounded, vulnerable, seeking comfort. She smiled when Abby swiped a lock of hair from her eyes and pinched her nose. I hung back, let them have their moment, and glanced back at the moving van.

Moreno's phone call had ended. He stood to the side of the loading ramp, talking with one of the movers. The words fired out in rapid, incomprehensible Spanish. The body language, however, was universal.

The man smirked and gave Moreno some lip.

Moreno wagged a finger and motioned the man to lean close.

The man did and Moreno spoke.

Even from a distance, the mover's face seemed to pale.

*

After my third pee of the night, I peeled back the sheet and tried to climb into bed without shaking the mattress. The room was still, computer hum and the low chirp of crickets giving off a hiss of white noise, the only sounds breaking the silence. Glancing next door, I spotted the second floor of Moreno's home, convinced myself the killer had no intention of breaking into my house and murdering my family, then readjusted the pillow and lay down.

Abby's eyes were open. Probably a bad sign.

"Have you been drinking beer?"

"What?"

"That's like the tenth time you've peed."

"Drank a lot of water tonight."

"I heard you in Carter's room. Is he up?"

"Sleeping."

"What were you doing in there?"

She hadn't asked about my visit to MicroLine yet. I had no answer to give about Leila's email, so I'd considered myself lucky and not brought it up. Perhaps luck had run out. Abby was one of those women who liked deep conversations in the middle of the night, something about isolation giving birth to intimacy, which sounded like Oprah-induced bullshit to me, so I stared at the ceiling and stayed quiet.

"What were you doing?" she repeated.

"Checking his window. The latch is loose."

"He's on the second floor, Jack. The alarm is on. He's fine. We're all fine."

"I know."

"What time is it?"

"Past two. Go back to sleep."

A sudden burst of light painted the ceiling. Leaning left, I spotted a naked bulb illuminating a bedroom on the second floor of Moreno's house. Rolling to my side, I saw nothing more. From my window, trees blocked the view, and only the bulb was visible through the branches. To see inside the house, I needed to return to Carter's room. Unable to think of another reason, I stuck with the night's theme.

"Shit. My bladder's defective...or else I'm getting old."

Abby sighed and wagged a finger. "Forty's coming soon, sweetie. We'd better check your prostate."

"Funny, Ab."

Stepping into the hall, I crept back to Carter's bedroom. Harry the Hamster trotted on his wheel beside the closet, and Hondo lay on the floor at the foot of the bed. My son breathed low and steady, blonde hair mashed against his pillow. The dog, used to the intrusion by now, didn't look up as I moved toward the low, double-hung window that gave a perfect view of the upper floor of Moreno's house.

Across the fence line, the killer stood in a bedroom overlooking his pool, bathed in light from an overhead bulb, pumping iron. I crouched low next to the glass and watched him move.

Long and sinewy, the man had a distance swimmer's body—full of lean muscles coiled with power, and the way they twisted and curled as he worked out reminded me of a python killing its prey. The athletic physique probably came in handy decapitating Mexican cops.

What weapon did he use?

A knife?

A sword?

Shit, probably a machete.

After Fisk's visit, I had researched drug cartels on the Internet. Unlike the mafia, they loved publicity and had adapted quickly to the digital age, hosting websites, offering downloadable theme songs, even posting assassination videos on YouTube.

Gulf.

Sinaloa.

Morelos.

Highly oiled machines that functioned like mini-states complete with territory, diplomacy, and armies ready for combat. Moreno was one of their soldiers, and stripped to the waist under the harsh light, he looked the part. Muscles like body armor. Scars on his back and chest, gleaming like battle wounds.

Hondo clicked over and joined me at the window.

The two of us stared next door as puffs of dog breath fogged the glass.

I patted the dog's head.

"That's our neighborhood killer, my friend. Be alert."

Moreno stopped lifting weights then and switched to martial arts. His muscles grew fluid, seemed to levitate from one move to the next like mercury flowing over a bed of polished stones. He threw punches, kicks, and elbows, concentrating on a single point in the air, focusing all his energy and force toward its destruction.

BAM.

BAM.

KICK.

Watching him move, I felt the last shreds of security fly away, just as they had years before, staring through a different window the night Marty and Janis Goodman argued. That night, with brutal speed, the bat crushed Marty's skull, and the last reliable piece of my world had shattered. My mother's death and father's alcoholic decline had set me adrift, but Marty and Janis left me treading water in a hurricane, tasting salt water, wondering how drowning would feel. That insecurity had taken years to repair. Now I stared out my son's window and felt the water move close again.

BAM.

BAM.

KICK.

"You're not touching my family," I said through the glass.

BAM.

BAM.

KICK.

Then the workout stopped.

Moreno's light went off.

Hondo settled into a lump beneath the window, and Harry abandoned his wheel and went to sleep. After twenty minutes staring into darkness, I checked the window latch again, kissed my son, and crept back to bed.

Chapter Nine

Costco on Friday morning. Carter wearing a retractable leash clipped to my belt loop. He had an extended holiday at school, and thanks to an improved weather forecast, we were stocking up for the next day's barbecue. When it came to big box stores and kids, early shopping was best—broad empty aisles and full shelves— that way the restraint device wasn't a problem for other customers. The kid should have resented the hell out of the tether—he was a big boy now, as he never tired of pointing out—but I made a game of it, telling him to bark like a dog if he had a problem. I had just bent down to grab a case of Sweet Baby Ray's Barbeque Sauce when my son began to growl. Glancing left, I spotted Special Agent Dennis Fisk, dressed in jeans and a faded Corona tee shirt, standing next to my son.

"Does your kid bite?"

Dumping sauce into the cart, I shrugged. "Only when he's angry."

Fisk gave Carter a mean smile. "What is he now?"

My son receded into the space between two pallets.

"Scared. Like his old man."

Special Agent Fisk continued up the aisle. He moved past my cart and examined the contents—steak, chicken, a million ears of corn, enough paper goods to deplete a forest in Washington—then nodded as if he approved.

"Meet me at the dog food," he said. "We need to talk."

*

Standing next to a thigh-high pallet of Alpo, I asked Carter to count out a hundred cans while Fisk looked on with bemused detachment. Carter said his teacher had only taught him to count to thirty. I asked him to try and then glanced up and down the aisle, making sure we were alone.

"Moreno moved in yesterday," I told Fisk.

"We know. I told you…we're watching."

"He spends a lot of time in the backyard talking on a cell phone."

The agent shrugged. "Probably a burner…a throwaway. No way to tap in unless we have the number."

Fisk's presence reassured me that I wasn't alone, and as I stood there my blood pressure dropped a few points. The night before, after watching Moreno's workout, I had triple checked the doors and windows, then set and reset the alarm, and still had trouble falling asleep. How hard would it be for a man like Moreno to break through glass or disable a security system? If he wanted to get in my house, was a deadbolt going to stop him?

"To be honest, I hoped this whole thing might be a joke."

The special agent wagged a finger. "The federal government doesn't joke, Mr. Boyd."

"Some of my friends…they're wise asses. I thought maybe they put you up to it. I never spotted cameras in my trees. Never saw your people. I had doubts."

Special Agent Fisk watched Carter. "And now?"

"Now I'm scared shitless."

He looked back at me. "Probably a wise tactical mood, but try to relax."

I exhaled a long rush and then glanced at Carter. "How many cans you got, son?"

"Fifteen."

"What comes next?"

"Sixteen."

"Good boy. Keep counting."

"Smart kid," Fisk noted. "Let's hope his old man is the same. Don't freak out on me, Boyd. This thing has barely started. You need to keep your head until it's finished. We're out there, even if you don't see us; we're watching. Hang tight for a few weeks. We'll figure out why Moreno is here, and you can have your life back."

All of a sudden, gripping my shopping cart felt like manning the wheel of a runaway truck. My heart thumped hard, jackhammer bursts, and hot and cold patches broke out on my skin. What was it? Adrenaline? Anger? Fear? Maybe a combo of all three, capped by an overdose of exhilaration. After all, how many people meet the FBI at the local Costco in the morning? Not exactly a routine day in the suburbs. Something welled up in me then, an old excitement I hadn't felt since leaving MicroLine—a rush that came from involvement in events much larger than oneself—but it didn't feel healthy, so I tried to ignore it, hoping the feeling would go away.

"That agent you sent to MicroLine to look into my background He gave the impression I was working for you."

Fisk tossed me a grudging nod. "You found out about that, huh?"

"I'm not working for you people, Fisk. It'll cause trouble if they think I am."

"Nobody said you were. It's a slip up. Don't worry."

"It has to be taken care of."

"And it will be. You have enough to worry about."

"You're right. I do. The goddamn dog started barking last night around four and wouldn't stop. I almost called the police."

"Boyd, you're not living next to Hannibal Lecter. Moreno's a killer, but he's not a psycho. He's a businessman. It's like with the mob. Don't screw with him and he won't bother you. He wants to blend. Guys don't blend by knocking off neighbors."

"But I am screwing with him. The FBI has cameras in my trees."

"Yeah, well, he doesn't know that."

That logic didn't make me feel any better. "I want a phone number where I can reach you guys. In the middle of the night, if necessary."

Fisk shook his head. "You start making calls in the middle of the night and your wife will get suspicious."

"Yeah...well, how can you protect us if I can't reach you?"

Growing impatient, Fisk amped his volume. "Moreno isn't going to break into your house and kill your family."

Carter stopped counting and looked up at me. "I want to go, Daddy."

"We'll go soon, buddy. Keep counting." Dropping my voice to a hiss, I shot the FBI man a glare. "Thanks, you scared my son."

"That's what I'm talking about. You freak out and your kids are going to notice. Your wife, too. Then questions start, and questions require answers. This isn't going away, Boyd, but it won't last forever, and no matter how isolated you feel you're not alone."

Carter said, "I'm tired of counting, Dad."

"Just count ten cans and put them in the cart for Hondo."

Special Agent Fisk said, "So what's he doing?"

"Who?"

"Moreno."

"I thought you were watching."

"Well...my team is." Fisk lifted his hands. "Don't worry. Even with the cameras, you see more than we do. You hear things."

Grabbing a quick breath, I tried to relax and recall what I knew. "He got up this morning at seven and mowed the lawn," I said. "Probably a little early for most of the neighbors—he'll hear some complaints—but hey, it's still brown and dead, but the grass looks better. That'll earn him good-neighbor points. I left shortly after that and came here. Obviously, you know that, because you followed me, which means you really are watching. I'll sleep better tonight, I guess."

Carter brought Alpo to the cart, two at a time, and dumped the cans on top of the corn.

"He's coming over tomorrow for a barbecue."

Special Agent Fisk eyed a woman pushing a cart toward us, kept his body language casual—two guys chewing the fat about the Dodgers or Lakers, maybe weighing the finer points of gas versus charcoal—but he was clearly pleased.

"That's good. That's what we want. Keep things neighborly, make him feel at home, and let us do our job."

"Do it fast," I said.

"Don't worry. We intend to."

I looked at Carter. The Alpo was loaded, and we were good to go. I reached down and took my son's hand. Then Fisk offered me a business card.

"What's this?"

"I want you happy, Boyd. It's a cell number, in case there's trouble. You might get my voicemail. Just leave a message and I'll call back."

"Or call in the cavalry?"

"That too."

"There'd better not be trouble, Fisk."

The agent managed a nod, then said, "One more thing. If Moreno starts to trust you, there's something we need. If you can get it for us, it'll help close this ASAP. Your family can get back to a normal life."

"And that would be…?"

"Find out what kind of cell phone he uses and get the number."

MICHAEL HARBISON

Chapter Ten

Halfway through the barbecue, Moreno approached my deck with a beer in each hand, wearing a suave *I've come to steal your wife* grin only Latin men can muster. Seven families overfilled my yard with loud conversation and gnashing teeth, and the endless current of chicken and beef flooding my grill produced enough smoke to prompt a stage three smog alert. Corn on the cob was next. Thirty ears wrapped in foil. Moreno poked the corn with a long finger and nodded.

"Hello, Jack."

"Charlie, glad you made it."

He glanced at the tables and grinned. "Yeah, I wanted to meet everyone. Sorry I'm late. You know how moving is. Still unpacking. Sprinklers aren't working, and everything needed watered by hand. It's a big yard."

He handed me a beer. Sweat dotted the bottle, and little beads of my own broke out as Moreno moved closer. A thick marine layer had invaded the Inland Empire during the night, piled clouds against mountains, banishing the sun. Nonetheless, despite the cool marine air, standing beside the Mexican, I perspired as if I'd just swallowed a bucket of jalapeños.

Moreno pointed at the beer. "Mrs. Boyd said you could use that. I think she was right. You look hot. "

A spit of flame shot from the grill. I lifted my spray bottle and tamped it down. "Call her Abby."

"Of course." Moreno smiled. "Can I help? Perhaps you need to circulate among your guests. I'm an excellent cook."

Most of the neighbors were on their second helping of food. A few worked on a third. I rolled my shoulders and turned the corn. "I'm okay," I said. "Abby's the cruise director. I work behind the scenes. These people like to eat, so the grill keeps me busy. That way I avoid hearing the same story ten times."

Moreno surveyed the tables and said, "Americans have the privilege of being fat."

I flipped more corn. "Privilege?"

He sipped his beer and nodded toward the tables. "It's a rich country. People overeat, get fat, then join gyms or go to doctors for liposuction and body sculpting. It all takes money, so that makes it a privilege."

Never thought of it that way, but he had a point. I surveyed my neighbors, spotted five or six who could shed twenty pounds— Mrs. Green from two houses down had at least a hundred to give— and felt my patriotic hackles flare a bit. I sipped more beer and squinted at Moreno.

"You telling me there are no fat people in Mexico?"

His response took several beats, so I figured I had scored a point. Then he grinned. "What makes you think I'm Mexican?"

Dripping butter ignited, and a spit of flame shot from the grill. The blast singed my hand. Moreno stepped forward, grabbed the water bottle from me and sprayed the fire. When the flames died, his brown eyes dug into mine, carving a long, deep trench I hoped wasn't the start of a grave.

Shit!

He never said he was Mexican.

The only way I knew was through Fisk. FBI Special Agent Fisk, who at that moment probably watched on surveillance monitors as I tried not to crap my pants.

Carter ran up onto the deck then and bought me some time. "Dad, can I take Donny and Michael up to my room?"

With effort, I looked down at him. "What for?"

"To play Nintendo."

"No, play outside."

"But they're bored, and the girls keep following us."

"Find something to do then. I don't want you guys in the house."

"Daaaad!" Carter slumped against me. Then he said, "Uncle Ransom's here," and ran away.

I turned the corn and glanced back at Moreno. He took a long drag from his beer and swallowed. His lips gave a funny twitch. There was only one way out.

"My apologies," I said. "Guess I'm just another bigoted Anglo thinking anyone with a good tan who speaks Spanish is Mexican. Sorry about that."

Moreno tapped a nail against his bottle, then slapped my shoulder and smiled. "Relax, Jack. I'm pulling your leg. I'm Mexican. Half American, too, but one-hundred percent Mexican."

My chest loosened a notch. Air seeped in, and breath-by-breath, red flecks of oxygen debt left my vision. For sixty seconds, I guzzled beer, turned corn, dripped sweat, and tried to smile. Then Abby approached the deck with another platter of uncooked meat and two fresh bottles of brew. She handed us each a beer. I chugged mine in one endless gulp.

"Whoa, cowboy," she said.

Wiping sweat, I tried to smile. "Been cooking a while. I'm hot."

"You're not finished either, so don't get drunk." She forced a smile. "Your brother's here, by the way."

"I know."

Moreno looked at Abby and flashed his teeth.

"This is a nice thing you do. Have your neighbors over for a fiesta."

Abby returned his smile. "We get together one Saturday each month during summer. It was Jack's idea. You know, once the foreclosures started, things kind of fell apart. Neighbors disappeared in the night. It got creepy, waking up to find an empty house. Jack figured that if we got together, we'd know who was in trouble and who needed help. I'm not sure it's worked out that way, but it keeps us talking."

I frowned at the platter of raw meat she held—some kind of steak I didn't remember buying—spiced up and ready to burn.

"More meat, Ab? Half these people are going to die of a coronary before they leave our yard."

She threw me a hard look. "Charlie brought it."

I looked at Moreno and prepped another apology. The killer stepped close and reached for my tongs.

"*Carne Asada con Cebollitas*," he said. "A family recipe. You gotta be Mexican to cook it right, so with your permission, I'll teach a bigoted Anglo how it's done."

*

Moreno seared the last cut of beef and placed it on the platter as Dave Manker, a neighbor from across the street, bounded onto the deck and made a face. Dave almost tottered into the grill but righted himself. Since walking through my back gate, he had consumed four beers, and his lean body wasn't processing the alcohol well. He eyed the *carne* and shook his head.

"Christ, Boyd, that's a lot of dead cow. You're gonna kill somebody."

Manker ran half-marathons every month and, on a bad day, could box twelve rounds without breaking a sweat. Far as I knew, the guy's only weakness was oversized ego, and from the way he eyed Moreno, our neighborhood jock had sniffed fresh competition in the machismo department. He shot an open hand at Moreno and grinned.

"Dave Manker. You must be the new guy."

"That's right. Charlie Moreno."

They shook, and Manker's lips twitched into a slanted smile as he noted Moreno's handshake. I had spent enough Sundays jogging alongside Dave to know he would take a loose grip as a sign of weakness.

"Welcome to the neighborhood." Manker pumped hard. "You sure jumped on the yard early yesterday."

Moreno swallowed beer and nodded. "Sorry if I woke you."

"You kidding? I was up before that. Start each day with a five mile run." Manker dropped a hand along his flat stomach and then pointed at Kate and Ken Sawyer. They lived next door to him and were neck deep into a second bottle of Pinot. "Doubt they were up, though. You should see their recycling bin. Thing rolls to the curb like a damn safe."

"The sprinklers aren't working, so the soil is very dry," Moreno explained. "I mowed early to keep the dust down."

Manker nodded. "No problemo, my friend. The sooner that place shapes up, the better." He turned to me. "So where you been hiding, Boyd? Haven't seen you jogging this week. Your dog, either, come to think of it. You get tired of playing entrepreneur and get a real job?"

I gave Manker the finger.

Dave laughed and faced Moreno. "Boyd usually works half days. He's got time on his hands. Get him to fix your sprinklers."

Moreno frowned. "You shouldn't insult your host."

Manker slapped Moreno on the shoulder and laughed. "Host. You hear that, Boyd? Now you're Martha Stewart."

Abby returned to the deck then, took the steaming *carne asada* from Moreno, and started toward the tables. Manker reached out and stopped her.

"Hey, Ab, when are you gonna send your husband back to work? He's getting soft. I'll bet he spends all day watching soaps."

Abby flashed a shoot-me-now grin. She disliked Manker but was too polite to exclude him from the party. Everyone came or everyone stayed home; that was her rule. I noted Manker's hand on her shoulder. How it rubbed small circles on her pale skin and turned it red like sunburn. Dave had a rep for cruising neighborhood women—married, single, whatever—and had offered to take Abby and the kids for pizza more than once when I was away on business. Standing in the smoke, watching him touch my wife, I bit my tongue until Abby bunched her shoulders and his hand fell away.

"Jack's right where I want him," she announced. "Barefoot and holding a pair of tongs. If I could get him pregnant, I would. Keep him home permanently. Honestly, Dave, I don't care what he watches as long as dinner's ready by five."

I lifted my beer in salute. "Thanks for the support, hon."

Manker shook his head. "Fuck. Why can't I find a woman like that? I can cook."

Moreno glared at Dave. "Children are around," he said. "You should watch your language."

Dave lifted an eyebrow, wobbled on his feet, and then frowned. "Who is this guy...the pope?"

A sharp breeze swirled the smoke and swayed the trees. I looked up, searched for anything that resembled a camera, hoped Fisk or one of his boys might swoop in for a rescue, and then glanced back at Moreno. The Mexican's lips gave that funny twitch again.

"He's right, Dave. Learn some manners," Abby said and then looked at Moreno. "Women like polite men."

She left the deck.

I gave Moreno a crisp nod.

He nodded back.

Then the words leapt from my mouth, fired like a bullet with no chance of recall. Special Agent Fisk had instructed me to be a good neighbor—Moreno had received an invite to the barbecue, so that base was covered—but I was about to cross a line that separated neighbor from friend, and I knew already nothing good would come of it.

"I can help with your sprinklers," I said.

Moreno began to protest.

Manker chuckled.

"Dave will, too," I said. "Since it was his idea."

Manker sniffed a challenge, unkinked his neck a few times and then shrugged. "Sure…why not? How hard can it be?"

Moreno lifted his hands. "Not necessary, gentlemen, thank you. I bought PVC yesterday. All I have to do is dig trenches. To be honest, if I had known the condition of the yard, I would have fixed things before moving in."

Manker shook his head. "You bought that house without seeing it first? You must be nuts."

Moreno responded curtly. "My company purchased the home."

"Your company bought you a house? What kind of business does that?"

"I sell concrete," Moreno declared without hesitation. "My employer owns the home. I'm merely a tenant until my assignment here is finished."

I couldn't stop myself. "And how long will that be, Charlie? Until you finish your assignment?"

"Depends," he said.

Manker raised his eyes and swallowed some beer. "Shit. I wish my employer would buy me a house."

Moreno's lips gave that strange twitch again. "What kind of work do you do?" he asked politely.

I faced the grill, watched charred bits of meat drop into the flames, and uttered a silent prayer.

Keep your mouth shut, Dave. Keep your mouth shut, Dave. Keep your damn mouth shut, Dave.

Manker drained a last sip of beer and flashed a broad grin.

"Me?" he said. "I'm a cop."

Ten minutes later, Moreno and Dave left the deck to mingle, leaving me alone with the smoke and fire. Soon after, my brother exited the house and crept toward me across the grass using a paper towel to clean his hands, glancing over his shoulder as if someone were following him. Ran was long and lean and walked with a forward tilt as if he fought a headwind all his life. For the most part, he had. During a stint in Pelican Bay, he had packed on thirty pounds of prison muscle in order to survive. The bulk was gone now, consumed by the long days he worked at Devlin Auto Body and however he fought his demons at night. Hands clean, he stepped onto the deck, peeled off his sunglasses, and tossed me an envelope.

"What's this?"

"Is that your station wagon in the driveway?"

"The Outback? It's not a station wagon. It's an SUV."

Ran stretched his six-foot frame and winced. "Maybe for a midget."

"What's in the envelope?"

He smoothed his clean jeans and freshly ironed shirt as Abby stepped from the kitchen and moved toward the tables. "How are the kids? I didn't see them."

"They're around."

"Everything good?"

"Sara's personality changes every other heartbeat. Carter's doing okay."

"He must be what…five now?"

"Six."

"Jesus, they're getting big." Ran shook his head and looked around. "Yard looks good. I forgot how nice it can be. Flowers and grass, trees not choked to death by concrete."

"Takes more effort than it's worth sometimes," I said.

Ran gave a weak laugh. "You sound like Dad. Remember that spring we begged him to plant grass so we could play ball? He said a lawn wouldn't grow—smog would kill it, or some bullshit—so we bought that hose with our lunch money and watered until weeds sprouted."

I recalled our house in Fontana, not far from Kaiser steel mill. How the place became an eyesore after Mom died. The way flowers withered in the Santa Ana winds, ignored by the old man, as if without her light in the world having them eat sunshine was too much to bear. Marty and Janis had moved next door a month after Mom's funeral. Days later, my father had left town on business, and I'd decided to replant the lawn. My efforts caught the eye of Marty Goodman. He had been in his late forties then, strong and broad, fists like boulders, and with his help, green shoots of rye soon poked from the dirt. Coming back from his trip, my old man had tramped over the nascent lawn, dumped his suitcase in the living room, and opened a bottle of Stoli, then played side two of *The River* for six long hours. Every so often, listening to Springsteen, he would come up for air, look out at the grass, and then pour another drink. The next weekend he had spent three hours ripping the sprinklers out of the ground.

Ran shook his head. "Dead grass and dry rocks...that was the old man's idea of landscaping."

"Yeah, well, he's gone now, so you can let it go." I opened the envelope and spotted ten hundred dollars bills. "What the hell is this?"

"I don't need you paying my rent. That's your money."

"Your landlord said you were three weeks late."

"That Vietnamese broad? She's the manager. My kitchen's knee deep in roaches. I was holding rent until they gassed the place. The law says that's my right. Like a bargaining chip. Only now, my big brother paid, so the landlord's got his money and I'm living with bugs for another month."

Ran had a thing about cleanliness, damn near obsessive-compulsive. Seemed to pick it up in prison—I never remembered him that way as a kid—a means of turning the utter chaos of cell life into some kind of order. I once asked him what the hardest part of prison was. Staying awake during the day, he'd said. Reading shitty books, pumping iron in the yard, listening to your cellie's bullshit stories for the hundredth time, anything to stay awake. Because if you slept during the day, you might have trouble sleeping at night, when everyone else was lights out. And alone in the dark, with nothing to do but contemplate your fucked-up existence, was nowhere you wanted to be.

I held out the envelope. "Pay for an exterminator."

"I have money. Besides, looks as if you need the cash." Ran glanced at the tables. Enough food to feed an army of defensive linemen, wine, beer, the works. "Do me a favor. Stop riding to my rescue without being asked."

"Try calling me more often. Then I'll know what's up with you."

"Yeah, I could do that." He nodded toward Abby as she circulated among the tables and approached Moreno and Dave. "She looks happy. Life must be good."

Dave wrapped an arm around Abby's waist and pulled her close. Moreno looked annoyed. Abby disentangled herself and shot me a look. It struck me that if I had a gun at that moment, and only one bullet, Dave would have been my target of choice.

"Things are great." I tucked the cash into my pocket, hoping Abby didn't notice, and then looked at my brother. "You went to see Marty."

It was more like an invitation than a question. After a long hesitation, Ran accepted. He thumped his chest. "You believe that old bastard's still breathing?" He looked at his hands then, found some piece of dirt or grease under one of the nails, and picked it out.

"How'd you hear about Janis dying?" I asked.

Ran scratched his head and shrugged. "Woke up one day and the article was in the newspaper."

"You read the *High Desert News* on a daily basis, do you?"

"Depends if I'm running late for work."

He had probably Googled Janis's name. I'd done the same through the years. Less and less over time, but when you send a woman to prison for two decades, a feeling of responsibility comes as part of the bargain.

"So where'd you get the baseball card?"

Ran shrugged. "Been saving it for my memoirs. Might have one of you, if you want?"

"No thanks."

"Anyway," Ran said, "thought Marty would like to know she was gone. He can die a happy death now, and that'll end it."

I watched Moreno and Dave talk with the neighbors. Their antagonism seemed to have passed, and a momentary feeling of confidence raced through me, as if having Moreno's attention diverted onto Dave had constructed a moat around everything I held dear. Then I glanced at Ran and that confidence died.

"That won't end it," I said.

Ran shook his head. "Probably not, but one can hope." After a moment, he added, "Speaking of happy deaths, I hear Jane Selig brought some business your way?"

"Yeah, Devlin referred her."

"We need to talk about that."

"Okay," I said, "talk."

"Danny's worried about her. Afraid she might hurt herself. He'd like a head's up if you find info on the drives."

"What sort of info?"

"Pretty much anything."

*

An hour later, things wound down, guests left my yard, just a few adults and a handful of kids lingering behind. When the crowd thinned, I took a seat at an empty table and ate some carne asada. Moreno sat a few tables down, talking to Kate Sawyer and sipping beer. Halfway through a mouthful of meat, I watched Abby leave the kitchen and walk toward me.

"That went okay," she said and sat down.

91

"You look tired."

"I can handle it." Her eyes drifted toward Moreno. "Charlie's fitting in."

"Yeah...I guess he is."

"What do you think of his carne?"

"Too spicy for me."

"Then why are you eating it?"

"Don't have much choice. It's all that's left. Our neighbors eat like mules."

I swallowed the steak as a loud bang echoed from the side of the house near the trashcans. Donny and Michael, followed by my son, ran toward the far side of the house. They were older than Carter was, in trouble at school and around the neighborhood, and I wasn't thrilled about them playing together.

"Carter seemed to have a good time," Abby said.

"He whined for half an hour because I wouldn't let them play in his room."

"Would that have been so bad?"

"Only for our furniture. Boys need to be outside. Besides, I think Donny steals things."

"That what you and Ran did when you were kids?"

"Steal things?"

"Play outside."

"Most of the time. Dad liked to drink in peace."

Abby picked a piece of steak from my plate. "You never told me Ran was coming."

"I forgot. Did you even talk to him?"

"Come on, Jack, I barely had time to talk to anyone. Did you talk to all of our guests? Now that you have the chance, I notice you're here at this table eating alone."

"Ran likes you, Ab. You should be nice to him. He's family."

"I do my best."

"Give him a chance."

Abby said nothing as she grabbed another piece of meat.

"You're wrong about this," she said in a low voice. "It's pretty good, but it's not a family recipe. They sell it at Stater Brothers."

Charlie Moreno left Kate Sawyer then and stopped by our table, firing off another world-class grin. "Thanks for the meal. It was a pleasure meeting the neighbors."

"You're going?" Abby asked.

"A lot to do in the house. Limited time. I have to go back to work on Monday."

"Let me wash your platter."

"No need," he said. "I'll get it later, or you can slip it under the fence." He held out his hand and we shook. "See you soon, Jack."

Then he left.

"You guys seemed to hit it off," Abby noted.

Pushing away my plate, I said, "Oh yeah? I didn't notice."

"What are you talking about? You huddled around the grill like a bunch of cavemen. You seemed to get along."

"He lied about his meat."

"What do you expect? He just moved in. He was trying to impress us."

"I have to admit he's different than I expected."

Abby shot me a look. "What were you expecting?"

Before I answered, more bangs echoed from the side yard, followed by the snap of splintering wood. Wiping my hands, I headed over, prepped for a stern lecture and some hard looks. Our fence made two long alcoves that ran along either side of the property. One was for trashcans, and I didn't mind the kids playing there, but the other was near the front gate, next to a sliding glass door that led to the family room, and space was limited because of our chimney. All I needed was for some kid to break the glass, or worse, fall through and gut himself. Lungs filled with enough air to chew some serious butt, I turned the corner and spotted blood.

Donny and Michael rolled in the gravel near the chimney. Michael's lips and nose leaked red as Donny pinned him, straddled his chest, and threw punches with assembly line precision.

"Take it back! Take it back."

Michael may have wanted to take it back, but I doubt he could have spoken through all the blood.

"Hey, you two," I shouted. "Knock it off."

The boys froze.

Charging forward, I reached out and yanked Donny to his feet.

That's when I noticed them. Standing in the corner, shielded from view by the chimney, Moreno and my son. Moreno's hands resting on Carter's shoulders, holding him in place, both of them watching the show as if the flying blood were nothing but red paint.

Moreno looked at me then and shrugged. "In my experience, Jack, sometimes, it's better to let boys fight."

Chapter Eleven

Next morning I woke to the sound of an implement breaking dry ground. I pushed the sound away, convinced it had followed me from a dream about my dead mother. Two minutes later, the sound came back—a rhythmic *thump, thump, thump*, which after the dream sounded like the prepping of a grave.

Moving to the window, I pushed the curtain aside and glanced down at Moreno's front yard. In the field of dirt and burnt grass, Dave Manker swung a pickaxe, buried the point into the soil and then flexed his pectorals like a lowland gorilla searching for a date. Behind him, a foot-deep laceration, bordered by mounds of soil, ripped the yard in half. Moreno stood next to the mounds, hacking a piece of PVC with some type of knife. From my angle, the blade seemed to plunge into Dave's throat, and I watched for several beats as Moreno appeared to sever my neighbor's head.

Footsteps moved on the hardwood behind me. Abby walked into the room carrying an armload of laundry. Socks, underwear, tee shirts, a few towels. I could handle washing and drying, but folding and ironing were magical abilities beyond my ken and fell to my wife. That morning, she looked tired of the routine.

"About time you woke up. Your buddies next door started without you."

I sat on the bed and felt the corner sag. "They're not my buddies."

Carter ran into the room and jumped onto the bed. Hondo followed close behind. My head pounded, the beat synchronized to the thumping axe as my son grabbed a towel and draped my shoulders.

"Now you have a cape, Dad."

"Great."

The bed became his trampoline. "Super...Man...Super...Man."

"Give it a rest, Son."

"Super! Man! Super! Man!"

Abby closed the drawer, came over, and sat beside us. The bed sagged lower.

"What's wrong with you?" she asked.

"We need a new mattress."

"I like it soft. What's wrong?"

"Hangover...and a loud kid." I looked at Carter, tried to delete the memory of him standing next to Moreno as his bloody friends pummeled each other, but the effort failed."Go build me something with your Legos. Make a bridge, or a building. Something big and complicated."

He hopped off the bed and ran from the room. The dog followed.

"That's it?" Abby wondered aloud. "A hangover?"

"At the moment, that's enough."

She reached into my hair and grabbed a handful. "You're a terrible liar, Jack. You have no poker face."

If that were true, I'd probably have felt much better about myself. I wanted to tell Abby about Special Agent Fisk and Charlie Moreno. But what then? Hit the road until things blew over? No way. The kids had school. I had clients. Thinking through the problem, only two options made sense: give the FBI time to work, or give Moreno a chance to finish his job and leave the neighborhood. Either way, to ensure domestic tranquility, Abby had to remain in the dark.

"I need an Advil."

"Headache?"

"More like a Caltrans crew jackhammering my brain."

"Not to add to your problems," she said, "but this was in your jeans." She lifted the envelope Ran had given me, flashed the Ben Franklins, and tossed the money onto the dresser. "Want to tell me about it?"

"Not really."

"Well, try anyway."

I draped the towel over my shoulders, waited a few beats, and decided to go with the truth.

"Ran was late with his rent. I wrote a check."

Hearing my brother's name, Abby found a less-than-perfectly folded shirt in the pile of clothes, unwrapped, it and smoothed out the wrinkles.

"So we have money for your brother's rent but not for Carter's education? You won't consider The Phoenix Academy, but giving your brother cash is no problem. That's not acceptable, Jack."

"Come on, Ab. There's a difference between lending money for rent and paying for private school, and you know it. Besides, money isn't the only reason I don't want Carter going to that place."

"You should have told me."

"Ran gave the money back."

"Then why hide it?"

"I figured you'd be pissed, and I was right. You're not exactly rational when it comes to my brother."

"He's not our responsibility."

"Yeah, well, he's mine."

Before her death, my mother spent most of her time in bed watching TV. She liked soaps, how dialogue flitted from one crisis to the next, as if each second mattered, a constant stream of voices clacking at low and constant volume as if a tight cluster of friends had surrounded her bed. Most days after school, I led Ran down the hallway toward her room to give her a kiss and say hello, but he usually broke free long before we reached the door. Then I would go in alone, catch the strange fruit odor coming from her skin, and watch TV while she fought to breathe. Excessive cell growth of the respiratory system. Small cell lung carcinoma. Terminal cancer. Whatever you called it, one day near the end, she had reached out and touched my wrist, her fingertips no longer appendages of flesh but more like pieces of hard, lifeless stone. "Take care of your brother," she'd said. Thinking nothing of it, I'd nodded. Then she had looked at the TV screen, watched the actors, and said, "It'll end in tears. It always does." At the funeral two weeks later, Ran had stood beside me, staring into the hole, pulling away every time I grabbed his hand.

"He doesn't deserve you," Abby said.

"Deserve isn't part of the equation. He's my brother."

"You spent years putting people like him in jail. I never heard you make excuses for them. Why should your brother be judged differently?"

"I'm not judging anyone."

"Well, it feels like you're judging me."

Maybe that was true. Abby and Ran never connected after I met her at Cal State Fullerton, and at that stage in the game, the fault had been my brother's. Not that his behavior affected Abby directly. Even then, he loved her, and when his temper blew it blew in some other direction, but I spent so much time fixing wreckage from Hurricane Ran, her opinion of him grew indelible, a tattoo that had seeped into bone. What else could I expect? She knew my brother's deficiencies, but out of context. Now all she saw was an ex-con who worked at a possible chop shop. I saw a kid whose mother died young and left him in the hands of a bastard father—not just a drunk, but an abuser with a taste for total domination. From what I knew, my Dad had gone off to Vietnam one man—no combat, a medical supply clerk in Saigon—and come home another, as if halfway through his tour a parasite crawled inside and consumed the guy everyone loved. Back home, the drinking started. I was born that year, my brother four years later, but somehow my mother kept Dad in check. He had never wanted kids. It must have been some kind of deal between them; she waited for him to come back from the war and, for a reward, got the kids she wanted. When she died, home life became a free-fire zone. I was seventeen by then, too old for the old man to target, so his energy focused on Ran.

"He's my brother," I said, putting it as simply as I could.

Abby plucked the towel from my shoulders. "You're not really Superman. You can't help everyone."

"Yeah, well, I have to try."

She got up to leave. I put a hand out and stopped her.

"There's something else, Ab."

"What?"

"I went to MicroLine after you told me about the email."

"Leila?"

"Yes."

"And?"

"She's no longer working there. Reed wasn't there either, so I didn't find out anything."

"Then why are you telling me?"

"I didn't want you to think I was hiding things if you heard about it later."

"Are you hiding anything?"

My face went hot.

"We've been through this a hundred times. I never touched Leila Krebs. I told off-color jokes. But it wasn't sexual harassment, and it sure as hell wasn't an affair. If you don't believe me by now, I'm not sure what more I can say."

Abby twisted the towel into ropey knots and looked as if she wanted to wrap it around my windpipe. "If I thought you were lying, Jack, I'd be gone already."

She walked away then.

My head pounded.

Outside the window, the *thump, thump, thump* continued.

I was halfway dressed when Carter stepped into the room carrying my cell phone. Hondo followed close behind, and both of them crawled up onto the bed. Within half a second, the dog began to snore.

"Phone call," Carter said.

"Who is it?"

"Uncle Leland."

I took the phone. "Hey. What's up?"

Leland Reed laughed. "You hear that? Carter still calls me Uncle Leland. I love it."

"Well, he thinks Hondo's his brother, so don't get too excited."

On the bed, kid and dog smiled as a dull, rhythmic roar, accompanied by the screech of birds, rose from the phone's receiver.

"Where are you?"

"Cabo. Off the coast. Been working in San Diego, staring across the border so long, thought I'd give Mexico a try for the weekend."

"Surfing?"

"Fishing. Marlin, or maybe it's tuna. I love Mexico. The sun is hot, the beer's cold, and the *senoritas'* favorite word in English seems to be *yes*."

"Sounds great," I said.

"Fly down and join me. It'll be like old days. Nah, that won't work. I'd be leaving for SD by the time you got here. We'll do it some other time."

"Sure."

"What's up? You sound out of it."

"Hangover."

Reed laughed and then yelled at someone in Spanish. After a quick response, he resumed speaking to me. "That's right...the great suburban barbecue. Sorry I never responded to the invite. Work's kicking my ass. How was the party? Anyone from MicroLine show up?"

"Nope. Just neighbors."

"Sounds great."

"Not really. I overcooked the chicken and nearly sparked a riot."

Reed laughed again. Some kind of commotion rose in the background, trailed by a blistering whirr that sounded like electric current humming through wire. "Hey man," he shouted, "I gotta split soon. Hooked another fish. I called because Singh told me you stopped by the office. Rezko gave you a hard time, I heard. Don't worry; I've dealt with that. But Rez doesn't like you. Best stay away until I get back in town and we straighten some things out."

"What things?"

"Come by next week. We'll talk it over."

I looked toward the window. Outside, the thumping continued. Refocusing on Reed, I tried to decide how much to tell him. "Screw Harvey. I was looking for you."

"Uh oh. Must be bad news."

"I heard a rumor."

"Yeah?"

"That you're looking to sell MicroLine."

"Don't listen to rumors."

"Normally I wouldn't, but a new owner could invoke the no-compete clause and force me to close my shop. If there are any surprises coming my way, I'd like a heads up. There's enough on my plate at the moment."

"Relax. I'm not selling."

"Maybe the board of directors sees things differently."

"It's my company. They see things the way I tell them to. Look, Vector made an offer. I turned them down. End of story."

"And I can take that to the bank?"

"You can." On Reed's boat, the commotion grew intense four or five Spanish speakers talking at once. "Is that all you wanted?"

An urge to tell him about Fisk and Moreno shot through me, but the hum on the boat was growing stronger, and Carter was on my bed, eyes and ears wide open. After meeting Fisk at Costco, I kept waiting for my son to ask about the FBI man, but he never had. Better not push my luck.

"There are some other things," I said. "They can wait."

Reed laughed. "Manny's afraid you want your old job back."

A few beats passed. I couldn't let it go. "Running the SHU?" I asked.

Reed waited before responding, silent for a long while, the only sound coming from the ocean and the birds. Then he released a long sigh. "Look, I know the bunker was your idea, and it must kill to see a goofball like Singh running the show, but it would have happened sooner or later. Leila convinced me you were right. I couldn't pass it up. Anyway, we took things a bit further than you envisioned."

"Meaning what?"

"If everything falls into place, we're going for SCIF approval."

"Seriously?"

"It'll be good for business."

SCIF stood for Sensitive Compartmented Information Facility, and the term described any location secure enough to meet government requirements for handling classified information. A SCIF might be an entire building, or just a single room with beefed up security. I paused as the news settled. With terrorism the government's top priority, a SCIF would set up MicroLine as a top bidder for national security work. It would also make the company a more tempting acquisition target.

"The SHU was my idea. Kind of a coincidence, the timing and all. I leave and you implement my plan."

"Like I said, we took it further. And we don't call it the SHU."

"You should have told me."

"I thought you'd be pissed."

"You were right."

Reed sighed again. "Tell you what. When I get back in town we'll discuss some kind of finder's fee."

A few beats passed. "Okay, but you can keep your money. I want something else."

Reed chuckled and the tension burst. "That was fast. I hesitate to ask."

"Rescind the non-compete clause in my contract. That way my business is covered no matter what happens at MicroLine."

"I already told you I'm not selling."

"And I believe you, but that doesn't mean I trust the board."

Reed blew into the phone. "This doesn't have anything to do with the FBI, does it? They came in asking questions about you. Mitch Rojas in legal thinks you're working for them, which means you're violating your severance deal. He wants me to cut you off at the knees. You know, if the wrong people hear about it, friend or no friend, there's nothing I can do."

"I'm not working for the feds," I told him. "They're not my clients, not even close. They were looking into my background, but it's regarding something else."

"Not your brother, I hope."

"No."

"Want to tell me about it?"

"Not at the moment, but maybe soon."

"So for now, you want me to trust that you're not stealing my business and, in addition, release you from any legal obligation not to do so?"

"Something like that."

"Anything else I can do for you? Buy you a new house? Get you a Ferrari?"

"Yeah, you can find out why Leila Krebs is sending email to Abby."

The ruckus on the boat grew louder. "Leila sent email to Abby? That can't be good."

"It's not."

When Reed spoke again, he sounded distracted. "Leila's no longer working for me, or I'd ask her."

"Any idea how I can reach her?"

"Sure. Try responding to the email."

"Already did that. No reply."

"Well, Singh could probably get her address and phone number from human resources, but you never heard that from me."

"Thanks," I said. "That might get Abby off my back. Believe it or not, I got enough to worry about at the moment."

"Yeah, me too. Like what to do with all this fish."

"When you coming home?"

"I'll be in San Diego another week. This Hartmann-Rydell thing is dragging ass." Reed paused as another burst of Spanish sprayed the background. "Hey, I gotta go. See you soon."

He cut the connection.

Listening to the falling axe outside, I looked down at my son and finished getting dressed.

Chapter Twelve

Dave Manker offered an open hand, so I reciprocated and shook, careful to squeeze tightly and look him in the eye, hoping my sleeveless black tee shirt didn't make my arms look flabby. Around the neighborhood, most people were at church, in bed, or eating breakfast, so beyond Moreno's yard, the street was quiet. Moreno's blue Ford Taurus—a sedate choice for a professional killer—sat parked in the driveway with a fresh dent along the left side and tubes of PVC pipe resting on the hood.

"Sorry about yesterday," Manker barked. "Too much beer and I get loopy. Charlie says I was out of line. I don't remember, but what the hell? At least I'm man enough to apologize."

"No sweat." I released Manker's hand and addressed Moreno, who held a hacksaw and a foot-long piece of PVC. "So what's your plan?"

Moreno eyed me a few beats, then surveyed his front yard, which, despite the dead grass, managed to look even worse with two scars running through it. As I waited on an answer, Manker continued hefting the axe, digging a third trench to link the others, forming an H pattern. The hard clay soil had Dave lathered in a good sweat. Unlike the past few days, the air was warm and strong and autumn sun hinted at Indian summer.

"Dave is doing most of the real work," Moreno said. "He's the man with the plan. You better ask him."

"You ever swing a pick?" Manker asked.

I shrugged. "Once or twice."

"Take a shift. I'll measure pipe, and Charlie can cut. With three of us, it'll go fast. This place will stop looking like shit, and our property values will shoot up twenty grand."

Handing over the pickaxe, Manker addressed Moreno. "You got a longer measuring tape?"

"In the garage. There's a tool box by the door."

Manker stepped out of the trench and walked to the open garage. When he was beyond earshot, I lifted the axe and swung.

"Twice a month I get the same apology from Dave," I said. "Booze turns him into an ass. Thanks for setting him straight."

Moreno looked toward the garage and shrugged. "Alcohol changes everyone. Some men get happy; others get mean."

"Dave just gets stupid."

Moreno's teeth flashed like bits of cream in coffee. "Where I come from in Mexico," he said, "there's a tribe called the Tarahumara. Much of their culture revolves around drinking alcohol, a drink called *tesguino*. They hold no one responsible for what they do under the influence of *tesguino*. Assault, rape, even murder is forgiven."

"No kidding."

Moreno nodded. "I knew a girl, she was Indian, and her father got drunk one night and killed a state policeman with his car. *Tesguino* pooled from the man's skin, so everyone in town held him faultless. In the morning, they took the cop to the mountains and buried him without telling anyone. He simply disappeared, the killer was forgiven, and life continued."

My mouth went dry. "Then I guess Dave's forgiven," I said.

Moreno nodded and grinned. "At least he didn't kill anyone."

I swung the axe into the dirt and wished for gloves. After a couple more swings, sweat beaded into fat drops that ran down my face until I tasted salt. As each thump vibrated up my arms, a burst of light popped in my head like a flash bulb freezing an image.

Thump.

My dead mother's grave.

Thump.

Four decapitated Mexican cops, eating their cocks.

Thump.

Jack Boyd and Dave Manker buried alive in Charlie Moreno's front yard.

Moreno grinned in my direction. "I owe you an apology as well," he noted.

I took a break, wiped more sweat, and lowered the axe. "Why's that?"

"Yesterday…the two boys. I should have stopped the fight."

I leaned back for another swing, gave it everything I had. The pick barely pierced the earth, and twin lightning bolts traveled up my spine. "Maybe you were right, sometimes it's better to let them fight."

"Your barbecue wasn't the venue for testing my opinions on childrearing, and your son was watching. Maybe with their parents' permission, the boys could have been given boxing gloves and allowed to settle things. But not in your backyard. I made a poor choice."

I took another swing and shrugged. "Forget it. My brother and I did it that way. When we argued too much, my dad grabbed gloves and took us to the garage. Gave us three rounds to work things out. After that we let go, or we had to fight without the gloves."

Moreno nodded. "My father liked to say violence cured all problems because escalation involves pain, and eventually, the pain is too great to bear."

Burying the pick in the soil, I wiped some sweat. "I see his point."

For the next few minutes, we worked in silence. Moreno cut pipe while I dug. After three or four axe swings, I rested and watched him as he worked with the knife. Sawing back and forth, he looked mechanical, ropes of muscle crawling up his arms, twitching with the heat of an electric knife carving into cooked flesh. As I watched, the PVC morphed into sinew and tendon attaching a head to a neck. He bent over, grabbed some fresh pipe, and his lifting shirt revealed a scarred back. Seizing a quick glance, I couldn't tell if the marks were burns or lacerations. Then he caught me looking and grinned.

"Dave's right," he said. "With three of us working, this will go fast. He likes to work, our neighbor."

"Mostly he likes giving orders."

Moreno resumed his cutting and shrugged. "Most cops do. It's bred into them."

Not enjoying the shift in conversation, I lifted the axe and swung. Talk of cops and violence made me think of Special Agent Fisk and the cameras in my trees, ruining the illusion that I was outside on a Sunday morning, helping a neighbor with his yard. Still, I didn't want to leave Moreno with the wrong impression.

"Dave's not that kind of cop," I said.

His lip got that strange twitch. "In my experience, all police are the same. The Mexican police ruined my father when he refused to pay their bribes. I came to hate them." His tone was cold and tactical, as if he had noticed a spider on his kitchen floor and was discussing how to kill it. "They closed his business. He started drinking, forced me to leave my mother. We went throughout Sonora and Chihuahua, making little money and spending what we had on booze."

Maybe the story was true, maybe just an elaborate part of Moreno's cover, but thinking of Special Agent Fisk, I tried to respond like a good neighbor.

"That sucks," I said.

He pointed toward the garage. "Dave tells me your father was also an alcoholic."

Making a mental note to kick Dave's ass, I nodded. "My dad drank some," I said. "He had things rough."

"After your mother died, you mean?"

Another swing. The axe bit into the ground, and I let it rest there. "Here's a news flash," I said. "In case you haven't noticed, Dave gossips. Better watch what you say around him."

Moreno sawed and nodded. "Knowledge is power, and power is nothing unless it's used. Cops love to be in control."

"Like I said, Dave's not that kind of cop."

Moreno nodded and his demeanor grew formal, as though he had offended me. "You know him best, of course."

"What I meant to say was that Dave's a school district cop. He patrols a junior high school in Abby's district. His car has lights and a siren, but he's just a security guard. He tells people he's a cop because he likes the way it sounds, but he's not LAPD or anything like that. He guards little kids."

Moreno grinned. "I admit that sounds less impressive."

Manker emerged from the garage then, holding some kind of camouflage jacket. My hands throbbed, so I climbed from the trench and dropped the axe as Dave stepped forward and screwed up his face.

"You're quitting, Boyd? I dug for more than an hour."

"I'm a wimp. Charlie was telling me about corrupt Mexican cops."

"Yeah?" Manker shook his head. "I hear people get jacked down there all the time. Pretty bad, huh?"

"The worst," said Moreno.

"Charlie thought it might be the same here. So, Dave, you ever hit the school kids up for a bribe? Raid the nurse's office for drugs?"

Manker frowned. "Screw you, wiseass."

Pointing at the PVC, I said, "Tell you what. I'll measure. You swing the axe. Where's the measuring tape?"

"Couldn't find it." Dave faced Moreno and lifted the camo jacket. "You were in the military?"

Moreno gave a sharp nod.

"American or Mexican?"

"Both, two years in each."

"Really?" Manker said. "Didn't even know that was legal. What if we'd gone to war with Mexico?"

"That possibility never crossed my mind."

Dave shrugged and looked at the jacket. I guessed where he was heading and felt a little sick.

"Twice a month guys from the neighborhood patrol the park. You know, looking for troublemakers—gangbangers tagging trees, homeless weirdoes lighting fires. You should come along. We could use another pair of eyes. Especially someone trained."

"Perhaps I will."

Dave turned to me. "What do you say, neighbor? Think he'd be good for the squad?"

Two years ago, a fire had originated in the park, burning close to our homes, and afterward the police had sanctioned the walks as a kind of Sierra Club Neighborhood Watch. For most guys, patrols were an excuse for an evening hike capped by bullshit sessions in Dave's garage. No one except Dave took them seriously, but I saw his mind working, figuring Moreno might amp up the testosterone level and get the guys focused. Picturing a rolling field of dead gangbangers, I shrugged.

"That's up to Charlie, I guess."

Dave shook his head. "Boyd lacks killer instinct. His idea of catching bad guys is making noise so they run away. I tell him to unleash the beast a little. Do him some good." He looked at Moreno. "Next patrol's Thursday night." Manker nodded as if that settled things and tossed the jacket onto a shrub and picked up the axe.

I went to the garage and looked for the measuring tape.

The toolbox rested next to a door leading into the house, lost in a landscape of moving boxes that turned the garage into a series of deep canyons. Dead air filled the gaps between canyon walls, smelling of cardboard and dust. Some boxes looked empty, some full. I poked around, wondering what gear a professional killer brought to a new neighborhood. Surprisingly, it looked like the shit in my garage: old dishes, stained Tupperware, Christmas ornaments, and faded pictures. Lifting flap after flap, I saw no machine guns or hand grenades, no heads in jars of acid, and no severed penises.

Moments later, lifting the measuring tape from the toolbox, I stumbled into a stack of boxes. One fell and spilled picture frames onto the concrete. The glass didn't break, so I squatted and put the frames back into the box. That's when I spotted the cell phones, buried under pictures at the bottom of the box. A dozen smart phones. Web access. Camera. The whole nine yards. Judging from their condition, someone had pounded them into oblivion with a hammer. Recalling Fisk's request for Moreno's number, I grabbed a phone, peeled the back, and glanced inside. The SIM card—the Subscriber Identification Module where data resided—was gone. Moreno had also stripped the battery. The phone was a corpse, so I dumped it back in the box.

"Find what you need?"

His voice barely moved the air, but Moreno stood a few feet away, having crept up on me like a deep chill after a hard run. The Mexican held a piece of PVC in one hand and a hacksaw in the other; the saw's shark-toothed blade coated by a fine layer of rust the color of blood.

Lifting the measuring tape, I managed to swallow. "Knocked over your boxes," I said. "Thought your pictures broke. No harm done, though. Sorry about that."

Moreno stepped closer. I stared at the saw blade and wondered how quickly he could lift my head from my shoulders. Instead, he bent down and scooped up the last picture. The image showed a boy, standing next to a sway-backed horse in a field. The image quality was poor and grainy—a notch below Polaroid—and the boy looked unhappy. Moreno winced, as if the photograph had dislodged a painful memory that was passing through his bloodstream, and then glanced at the phones.

He grinned. "Like you said, no harm done."

I kept cool and pointed at the picture. "That you?"

Moreno looked down. The boy had one hand wrapped in the horse's mane, while the other clutched the reins and held the animal in place. "My father as a young boy," he said.

"Looks tough," I noted.

"He was, but the boy grew into the worst kind of man."

A few beats passed. I glanced down at the saw blade. Out in the yard, Dave Manker continued digging and the *thump, thump, thump* mimicked my racing heart.

"What kind of man was that?" I asked.

Moreno tossed the picture into the box and shrugged.

"Very foolish."

*

Tuesday night, coming home from work, I made a foolish move of my own. Turning onto our street from the south, I spotted Moreno's Taurus backing out of his driveway and then heading north toward the mountains. Tired of passivity, of Fisk holding the intelligence cards, recalling what the Mexican had said about knowledge being power, I decided to get a little intel of my own.

Until that moment, despite Moreno's appearance, suburban life progressed in the normal fashion: work, school, too much bad television at night. To be honest, beyond a slowly spreading dread carried like a bomb in my stomach, his arrival had changed nothing. Work at DRI continued. Abby complained about school. Sara's nose hovered an inch above her phone screen, and Carter's future gave me endless nightmares. Normal suburban life, creeping along under abnormal conditions.

Like every other guy on the street, Charlie adhered to a schedule, leaving in the morning and not coming back until dark. His activity between those benchmarks remained a blank, but I trusted Fisk, believed the FBI was doing its job, and felt reasonably safe. Whenever Moreno and I crossed paths, we exchanged greetings and continued with our separate lives, an unremarkable occurrence enacted daily in every suburb on earth, and one promptly forgotten had my neighbor not been a professional killer. If any strangeness accompanied his settling in, it was the seamlessness of his fit within the community—the moving van drove up, dropped him off, and within a matter of days, he became the perfect neighbor.

When his Taurus reached Padua Avenue at the edge of our housing tract, he turned south and drove toward Interstate 210. I kept my Subaru far behind—no more than a prick of headlights in his rearview mirror—then flouted the hands-free law and called Abby on my cell phone.

"Where are you?"

I cleared my throat and prepped a lie, hoping she hadn't seen me drive down the street.

"Working late. Swamped all day. There's some kind of cheating scandal at the colleges. They have us searching the drives."

That part was true. DRI's customer drought had ended. An academic scandal had broken out at one of the colleges—ten cheating kids facing expulsion—and the forensic work had come our way. The school issued each student a laptop upon admission, and legally, that was no different from a corporation providing an employee with a work computer. There was no right to privacy, so the administration had us digging into everything. So far, it was all porn and illegal downloads, but some drives had encrypted files stashed into the slack space between sectors, and Fisher took their recovery as a personal challenge. While he dove into that, I was handling DRI's other customers, including Jane Selig, whom I had informed of a delay in examining her husband's hard drives.

"How much longer?" Abby asked.

I took a beat to answer.

Following Moreno all night was out of the question. This was about curiosity, maybe regaining a feeling of control and not relying on Fisk to spoon-feed me information whenever we crossed paths at the grocery store. Besides, I had gleaned my suspect tailing skills from *Magnum PI*, not real training, and if I followed too long, Moreno would spot me. If he drove to the closest movie theatre, bought a ticket and an extra large popcorn and soda, I'd heave a relieved sigh and sleep better that night. If he headed south on the freeway to Mexico, I'd turn around and drive home none the wiser.

"I'll wrap things up soon. Don't hold dinner. I'll eat later."

"Don't worry, it's leftovers. Carter had mac and cheese. Sara went to the movies with some friends."

"On a school night? What friends?"

"Relax, Officer Dad. She finished her homework. School's just getting started this semester. I figured it's better to give her a little freedom now so we can clamp down later in the year when it's really needed."

My wife, the academic tactician. "Sounds pretty smart. You learn that at school today?"

"I learned a lot of things at school. We had an in-service on restraining unruly students. Don't work too hard, and I'll show you some of my moves after the kids go to bed."

"Sounds educational. Save me some of that mac and cheese, okay?"

I said goodbye and cut the call.

Moreno had just crossed Baseline Avenue and turned into the lane that led onto the eastbound 210. I pressed the gas and sped up, making sure I caught the light.

*

Moreno changed freeways once, transitioning south onto the I-15, then got off at Foothill Boulevard, driving into the parking lot for Victoria Gardens. The place was an open-air mall built to look like an Italian plaza in Rome or Venice, evoking a sense of foreign travel as consumers racked up credit card debt, thereby ensuring they'd never visit the real Venice or Rome. Prices were marked up accordingly. Moreno bypassed all that and headed toward the eastern border of the complex, near the freeway, parking in the oversized lot for Outdoor World.

I found a spot at the opposite end of the lot and watched as he entered the store. Through the windows, the place looked aircraft carrier big, offering two dozen of every implement one could possibly need to conquer the great outdoors: boats, trailers, tents, backpacks. A restaurant with a giant shark hanging from the rafters sat alongside the shopper's paradise. For a Tuesday, the place hummed, people milling about like zombies in a George Romero movie, searching for low prices.

I got out of the Subaru and went inside.

Moreno climbed the stairs to the upper level as I entered, sweeping past the gaze of a stuffed big horn sheep, focused on his destination. At least a hundred people roamed the showroom, conversations humming, and I wasn't concerned about him spotting me. As long as I kept the Mexican in sight, I figured I could melt into the crowd. Drifting to a display containing pheasant-flavored dog treats, I waited until he reached the top of the stairs and followed.

My senses kicked into overdrive when I got to the second floor.

Moreno had disappeared.

I scanned left and right. Back down the stairs. Even clocked the elevator.

He was gone.

Then I saw a triple-chinned guy walking out a double door near the back. Before the door closed, I spotted Moreno inside, slipping into some kind of orange vest. The door sign read GUNROOM. The big guy walked toward me. I reached out and tapped his shoulder as he passed.

"Hey, what's in there?"

The guy cocked a manic grin, as if coming down from a potent Twinkie high. "Shootin' range. If you never pulled the trigger, brother, you oughtta give it a try. It's a blast."

He laughed at his joke and walked away.

That made sense.

Moreno hadn't come for a boat, tent, or pheasant-flavored dog treats.

He'd come for target practice.

*

Near seven-thirty, I watched from the Subaru as Charlie left Outdoor World. After thirty minutes in the gun range, he had entered the restaurant, ordered what looked like a plate of chicken, and spent twenty minutes eating alone. My stomach started grumbling, so I bought a Cliff Bar—dry as a week-old dog turd— and went back to the car, repositioning so I could see him through the glass. Moreno ate slowly, over-chewing his food, glancing at his watch periodically to check the time. Once the chicken turned to bones, he paid the bill and went to his car. Back on the I-15, we headed south and transitioned onto the westbound San Bernardino Freeway. Like a surgeon's knife, he was carving a circle around the heart of the Inland Empire. Five or six car lengths back, I found myself bored with the itinerary. Whatever I had expected of Moreno's activities, other than blasting away at the gun range, his life seemed no more interesting than mine did, and it damn near put me to sleep.

Alongside the freeway, Ontario Airport glowed. MicroLine sat beside it, another beacon in the night.

Moreno passed both, moving closer to home. Then, at Central Avenue, he pulled a surprise exit and headed south toward Chino. Five miles later, on the other side of Mission Boulevard, he turned into a jammed parking lot.

A building with no windows sat on a busy street corner. Next to it, a flashing neon sign shouted LIPSTICK PALACE -

GENTLEMEN'S CLUB. Moreno parked and went inside. After five minutes searching the street for a spot, I pulled into the lot and parked far from his Taurus.

From outside, the strip joint had the dimensions of an oversized firehouse. No way could I go in. Even dark and seedy, the place was too small, and Moreno would have a good chance of spotting me. It was time to go home. I had learned what I could from following him, and that wasn't much. Despite his odd career, the Mexican seemed like most other guys I knew. He took his job too seriously, had multiple appetites, and didn't use a map to find his way around. The rest I would leave to Fisk.

I started the engine and prepped to pull away.

Fingers rapped my window then.

My heart did a back flip.

I glanced outside, drained a sigh, then rolled down my window and looked at my brother.

"Don't tell me," he said. "Midlife crisis?"

Ransom was rubbing his hands together, wiping a line of grease he had apparently missed before leaving work.

"Jesus…Ran…You scared the shit out of me."

His face glowed red and blue in the neon, and the forced smile he wore made him look like a bruised clown. He glanced over his shoulder, then back at me, cocking his chin at my wedding ring.

"You and Abby having problems?"

"What? No, things are fine."

"Really? Then what the hell are you doing at a strip club?"

"I'm working."

Ran nodded at the lie, but he wasn't buying. "Since when do you creep around strip clubs for work? That's PI stuff. You know they have cameras on all four corners of that building." He nodded toward the club. "They see you hanging around out here, they're going to call the cops. Too many dudes whip their skippies in the parking lot. It's bad for business."

I cleared my throat and looked toward the door. "A client had us pull coordinates from her husband's navigation system," I said. "She wanted pictures to go with the coordinates. She's gearing up for a divorce."

"Uh huh. Where's your camera?"

I held up my cell phone, scoring a point.

Ran nodded.

I looked up at him, defiant. "So what's your excuse?"

He unkinked his neck a few times. "Not many girls line up to date guys like me...The nights get long."

"You plan on finding one in there?"

He grinned. "My past doesn't matter here. Only my money."

"You come a lot?"

Ran shrugged. "Best gentleman's club this side of Vegas. Every lonely guy within a hundred miles probably makes the pilgrimage once a week. Put your camera away and come inside with me. I'll buy you a beer."

I glanced at the door again, half expecting Moreno to burst out lifting his gun, and shook my head. "Better not. The client's husband might be inside."

"Oh yeah, I forgot. The client's husband."

I thought back to the barbecue, trying to recall if Ran and Moreno had met. I hadn't introduced them and doubted Abby had. My brother had mostly skulked around the kitchen, eaten food and sipped beer, not staying that long. Moreno could have seen him, though. Maybe enough to recognize him when Ran walked into the club. We didn't look that much alike—my hair was dark and short, my brother's long and blonde—but there was some family resemblance, mainly around the eyes. If Moreno paid attention, that could mean trouble.

"Do me a favor, will you?"

"What's that?" Ran asked.

"Skip it tonight. Go home."

"Don't tell me. You're no longer content interfering with my financial affairs. You need to save my soul now, too?"

"That's not it. Like I said…the client."

Before he could respond, my phone rang. I saw from the display that it was Abby, held up a finger to my brother, and answered, expecting a deserved ration of shit for being so late. That wasn't how things played out.

"Sara just called."

Abby sounded breathless, a few ticks north of full-blown panic.

"What's wrong?"

"She and Scott went to get something to eat after the movies. She says there's a guy following them."

"Call the police. I'm on my way."

*

Scott Hinton was the kid Sara liked. Tall, thin, a good baseball player. They had been out a few times in groups, but I wasn't happy about the situation. For me, fifteen was too young to date, so we'd come to an arrangement. We checked Sara's location using her cell phone's GPS, and as long as the phone stayed where she told us they'd be, we allowed them to go out in groups. It was an imperfect plan—she could always hand the phone off to a friend—but so far, the arrangement had worked. Dating with training wheels, we called it, and even now, with Moreno next door, the thought of teenage boys circling my daughter like hungry sharks seemed no less of a threat.

Speeding up Central Avenue, eyes darting between road and screen, I noted the beating red dot on my cell phone display showing Sara's location near the theatre in College Heights.

The dot wasn't moving.

By the time I got there, the cops were driving away. Abby stood with Sara in the shadow cast by the theatre's marquee, watching me run toward them. When I got close, Sara looked away, her face a mask of embarrassment, no doubt wondering how many of her friends stood nearby watching the show. Not giving a damn, I wrapped her in a hug.

"That took a while," Abby noted.

"Sorry. They're doing construction on Garey," I lied. "I should have used Towne. Where's Carter?"

"Liz is with him."

I nodded and then looked at my daughter. "What happened?"

Sara pushed me away. "It's no big deal, Dad."

"Then why were the police here? Where's Scott?"

"He went home."

"What happened, Sara?"

"This creepy guy was following us. He didn't say anything; he just went everywhere we did and sort of hovered in the background. I told you, it's no big deal. I want to go home."

I nodded. "Okay, sure." I looked at Abby. "She can ride with me. We'll see you at home."

Abby left without saying anything more. I walked back to my car with Sara. "What did this guy look like?"

Away from the theatre and her friends, she loosened up and gave a description. As she did, a man's image coalesced in my brain, and I conjured a name to go with it.

Fisk.

When we got home, Sara went into the house and I stayed in the car and made a phone call. The FBI man answered on the second ring.

"You're following my kid now, Fisk? What the fuck?"

"It wasn't like that, Mr. Boyd."

"Then how was it?"

"I had just gotten off surveillance and stopped by to grab a burger. You know that place in the Packing House. Fourteen bucks for a goddamn cheeseburger. Six bucks more if you want fries—"

"Why were you following my daughter, Fisk?"

"I was doing you a favor."

"What?"

"I have two girls, both of them in college now, but I went through the same thing you're going through. All dads do, you know. That kid your daughter's seeing…he's a punk."

"Excuse me?"

"They walked past me while I was eating. At first, I didn't recognize your daughter. Then I did. Anyway, that kid she's with? He goes into the music store and right through the glass I see him stuff a CD down his pants."

"What?"

"More than one, actually. Bold little shit peeled the security tags off and filled his pants."

"Did Sara know?"

"She was up front, looking at posters. I don't think she saw him."

"Goddamnit."

"There's more. You're probably going to like this even less. The kid has grabby hands. He was touching her on her rear end, every other heartbeat. I just sort of followed them around awhile, giving the kid the stink eye, trying to back him off. Figured as long as I was down there getting some food, I could help you out. I didn't mean to scare your daughter, and it won't happen again. Usually I never eat in a subject's home territory, but today was a long day."

I took some deep breaths, let the tension seep out, and then said, "I don't want my kids involved in this, Fisk."

"I know. They won't be."

"I mean it."

"Don't worry. It won't happen again."

His contrition seemed genuine, and as much as I wanted to rip into him, I was glad for the information on Scott Hinton. So armed, I might plan a little surveillance of my own, and I'd definitely converse with Sara about shoplifting and inappropriate displays of affection. If those tactics failed, well, Scott could always accompany me on a long, quiet drive into the desert.

I didn't know what else to say. Part of me was relieved. The good news was, with Fisk in town, he couldn't possibly have seen me tailing Moreno. But then if he hadn't been on Moreno, who had been, and what had they seen? I decided on a little test, probing the flow of information, gauging the degree to which Fisk could be trusted to share what he knew.

"You were tailing Moreno tonight?" I asked, knowing he had not been. "That's why you're around town?" I figured Fisk would lie, deflect, or tell me it was none of my damn business.

"Not tonight," he said, sticking with the truth. "It's related, but something else. Look, Mr. Boyd, we can't be up on the guy 24/7. You have any idea how many man-hours that requires? My ASAC would never go for it. These days, unless your name is Abdul Bin-Fuck-Nuts, you don't rate full-time surveillance. Don't get me wrong, we're watching, but we can't follow him day and night. You know what L.A.'s like. This place is too big. It's not a city, it's a goddamn country."

Abby opened our front door then and stared out at me. The hint was obvious. My workday had been long enough.

"I gotta go, Fisk."

"Sure, Mr. Boyd. And again, I'm sorry for scaring your girl."

I cut the call.

After that, things didn't go south again until Thursday night, when Moreno and Dave set the homeless guy on fire.

Chapter Thirteen

Halfway through lunch at work—pastrami on rye with mustard—my phone rang. It was Dave.

"Boyd, I'm pleasantly surprised. Your slacker ass is actually working today."

"What's up? I'm busy."

"Charlie's in for tonight," he said. "Just wanted you to know."

"In for what?"

"Patrol night. Moreno's meeting us in the parking lot at six."

A groan forced its way up my throat. "Not a good night for me, Dave. I'm swamped, and things are getting worse here by the minute. You'll have to count me out."

Manker blew into the phone. "Bullshit. Come on, Boyd. It's your night. Twice a month isn't asking much. Besides, if I let you off, how long until Ken and Danny bow out? Pretty soon no one will go."

Ripping into the pastrami, eyeing the clock, I talked and chewed at the same time. "Is that such a bad thing, Dave? Are the patrols necessary? We haven't seen anybody up there for a while."

Dave gave an exasperated groan. "Because they know we're around. We stop patrolling, how long until they come back? Losers are like a virus, Boyd, you gotta be vigilant. Who knows? Another fire starts, and I might not be around to help tamp down the flames."

Dave had once attacked a wildfire burning near my house with a garden hose. David versus Goliath, for real. What could I say?

"Okay. I'll be there."

Dave chuckled. "Knew I could guilt you. Charlie's coming straight from work. Bring an extra flashlight and meet us in the parking lot at six. No whining, either. Twice a month, Boyd. Nobody ever died doing something twice a month."

*

Ten minutes after six, I pulled into the College Heights Wilderness Park and saw them waiting by Dave's truck in the parking lot. Behind the park, the sun had recently set and the foothills wore a dim red crown of clouds and smog, daylight's last faint glow moving toward darkness.

Ken Sawyer and Danny Chin wore bright-colored hooded sweatshirts covered in reflective tape. Dave and Moreno had opted to dress in black. Standing beneath the orange glow of the sodium vapor lights, the four of them seemed to cast a single deep shadow.

"About damn time, Boyd."

Grabbing my flashlight and closing my car door, I nodded at Ken and Danny and then looked at Dave and Moreno.

"Sorry. Like I said, work's crazy right now."

"No harm done," Moreno said. He'd uttered the same phrase when he'd caught me snooping through the box in his garage, and I fired off a quick glance to see if he was messing with me.

His eyes were on Dave.

Dave squatted down in the dirt. "You missed the briefing, Boyd." He picked up a stick. "We're gonna change things up tonight."

Over the past eighteen months, we'd developed a routine for what Dave called our patrols. Starting at the park entrance, moving as a group, we walked the five-mile loop on the fire trail, heading up Johnson Canyon and coming down Corral, making a climb of around five hundred feet. We carried two-way radios, had cell phones in case we needed to call the police, and moved fast. For desk jockeys, the trail was steep, and most nights the guys worked up a good sweat just leaving the parking lot. That said, no matter how quickly we marched, Dave bitched about our lack of speed.

"Thought you had these missions down to a science, Dave. Why the tactic shift?"

He used the stick to draw something in the dirt. I clicked on my flashlight. "Charlie had some ideas. Things he picked up hunting terrorists in Chapass."

Moreno's upper lip twitched. "Chiapas," he corrected. "A state near the Yucatan. We conducted operations there against Zapatista rebels. Not everyone considers them terrorists."

Dave grinned. "Yeah, well, I'm sure that didn't stop you from drilling a few."

Moreno didn't respond.

Dave pointed his stick at me. "Change number one, Boyd. We're going in dark, so turn off that damn flashlight."

I clicked off the light and glanced at Ken and Danny. They both shrugged. "Dark sounds like a bad idea," I said.

Dave pointed the stick at Charlie. "This guy has experience hunting men, so I'm deferring to him."

Moreno looked embarrassed. "Flashlights give away your position. Take away the element of surprise."

"I thought that was the idea," I said. "Anyone up to no good sees us coming and leaves the park...Anyway, it's usually just a few homeless guys and some deer."

"Yeah, and what happens once we leave?" Dave asked. "They come right back."

"Deer are supposed to live in the park, Dave."

Ken and Danny laughed.

Dave frowned. "I'm talking about the winos, asshole."

"How the hell are we supposed to see?" I asked. "You walk off that trail in the wrong spot, and you're falling hundreds of feet. Not to mention the snakes."

"Your eyes will adapt," Charlie said. "Takes about thirty minutes for both cones and rods, but you'll be surprised how much you see. I promise."

Dave tapped his stick on the ground. "Charlie's right. If we go dark, they won't see us coming. They'll never know when we're out here, and even if we're not on patrol, they'll be wondering if we're lurking around the corner. We should have thought of this sooner, Boyd. We'll take the flashlights, but they stay dark unless we find something. Understood, ladies?"

Ken and Danny nodded. After a moment, I joined them.

"Okay, Boyd, don't freak out on me," Dave said, "but here's change number two. Tonight, we split into groups."

*

Halfway up Johnson Canyon, I caught my breath and looked at the city below. Despite the sea breeze, sweat burned my eyes, turning College Heights into a wavering mirage of light and bottomless shadow. I spotted my house, lit at the edge of the park, set off by the darkness of Moreno's place like a distant galaxy perched alongside a black hole. Dinner would be over, Carter ready for his bath. Standing there, I longed for that normalcy but realized my family was probably safer with me up here. As long as Moreno was in sight, he couldn't hurt them.

Then a permanent end to my problem came to mind: the Mexican slipping off the trail in the dark, tumbling down the canyon walls. It wouldn't be difficult. A close pass, a quick push. Then I thought of Special Agent Fisk, wondering if his men were close by, watching me contemplate murder.

Seconds later, Moreno came up behind me. "Everything okay?"

"Fine," I said. "Just resting."

"Dave sets a fast pace."

"He's trying to impress you."

"Dave seems too full of himself to care about the opinions of others."

"Usually, I'd agree, but you're an ex-soldier, and in Dave's head, these patrols are military operations. Most nights, he acts like the Taliban might pop out from behind a rock."

Moreno nodded. "He asked if I thought he should carry a gun."

Swallowing air, I noticed the wind grow colder. "What did you tell him?"

Moreno shrugged. "Guns are pointless unless you're ready to use them."

I resumed hiking.

Moreno was right about one thing—my eyes adapted to the darkness. We had been going forty minutes, covered almost two miles, and I had no problem staying on the trail. Back in the parking lot, before we split, Dave instructed Ken and Danny to head up Corral Canyon and meet us near the summit benches. Once there, we could exchange information and then descend in the opposite direction before meeting at the parking lot. The entire circuit would take about ninety-minutes. Despite my misgivings at splitting up, Dave's idea made sense, as it turned a single patrol into two separate sweeps of the park.

Picking my way up the hillside, I felt Moreno close behind me. He seemed to move without exertion or sound. I listened hard but couldn't even hear him breathing.

"Why are you out here, Jack?"

His voice was so close I nearly stumbled. Two more strides, then I forced an answer.

"Dave's right. People come out here, start trouble. The patrols help. With our houses up against the park, it makes me feel safer."

"That makes sense, but why not let the police handle it?"

"Just want to be involved, I guess. We went through ten weeks of civilian training at the department. Dave organized everything, so I decided to tag along. I don't play softball, and my knees can't handle football anymore, so this is something I do with the guys from the neighborhood. Plus, like I said, it keeps my family safe."

"You like the excitement."

"A little, I guess."

"Somehow, the fact this was Dave's idea doesn't surprise me."

"Yeah, I guess not."

"Another chance to play cop and bark orders. Doesn't seem your speed, though, running behind Dave, taking orders."

"A week in the neighborhood, and you know me that well, huh?"

"Maybe."

Glancing up the trail, I spotted Dave near the saddle, his shadow a black patch against the lamplit sky to the west. In Los Angeles, true darkness never falls; even at midnight the sky retains a permanent, streetlight tint.

I kept moving toward Dave as I talked. "Two years back, fire swept the foothills. Near two in the morning, police ordered us to leave our homes. Embers flew. The hills glowed like one of those disaster movies. The wind blew hard from the northeast, so our house was first in line to burn. I packed Abby and the kids into the car and got ready to leave. Then Dave crosses the street dragging two lawn hoses, runs into my backyard, and starts spraying my trees. Eventually the wind shifted and drove the fire west of our house, but I never forgot Dave standing there, using a garden hose, trying to save our home. So yeah, he can be an ass, but I owe him. And, Charlie, no offense, but after a few days in the neighborhood, you don't know shit about me."

I stopped and turned around.

Moreno wasn't there.

Glancing down trail, I spotted him thirty paces back, standing at the edge of a drop-off, peering into the canyon. After a minute, he rejoined me.

"Sorry, I had to urinate," he said.

I wondered if he had heard anything, then hoped he hadn't. The less he knew about my life the better. Two minutes later, we reached the saddle, and Dave could barely contain himself.

"About damn time," he growled. "Ken and Dan found someone."

*

From the fire road in Corral Canyon, we looked down on a canopy of oak and dense brush lit by the periodic flash of firelight. Other than the flame, nothing was visible beneath the trees. Ken and Danny stepped back from edge, we congealed into a huddle, and Ken spoke in a hushed tone.

"One guy. Looked like Walking Dead. We spotted him down the trail and followed him up. Just before we called you guys, he broke off trail and headed in there. Seems to be alone, but a dog was barking, so I'm not sure."

Walking Dead was a homeless guy who frequented the park. He moved in low gear with a perpetual slouch and smelled like a corpse, hence the name. *In there* was a side canyon packed with chaparral, decomposed granite, and poison oak. We passed it regularly, and the entrance formed a tight slot barely thirty feet wide. Up canyon from the entrance, things opened up but the walls remained steep, so it made a perfect spot to camp and smoke weed or whatever else people like Walking Dead did up here for kicks.

"You want me to call in the cops?" Ken asked Dave.

Moving to the edge, Dave looked down, then glanced at Moreno. The movement was almost imperceptible, but the Mexican's head shifted from side to side.

"We'll handle this alone," said Dave. "You guys head back down the trail and watch the entrance. We'll drop in from above and sweep down the canyon. He won't have any place to run. If he comes out at your end, stop him. Shouldn't be hard. The guy's a bag of bones."

Ken and Danny turned and moved down the fire road.

I grabbed Dave by the shoulder. "We need to call in. The police can be here in fifteen minutes, and we'll sit and watch him until they arrive. There's no reason to go Charles Bronson here. This isn't how we do things."

Dave opened his jacket, flashed the butt of a revolver jammed into the waist of his pants, and shot a grin. "Tonight it is." He looked at Moreno. "What do you think, Charlie? Shall we drop in and say hello?"

*

The dog heard us first and gave off a single, high-pitched bark that sounded more excited than threatening, so we kept moving forward. Through the trees, the flames burned stronger, producing a screen of smoke that floated on the wind and stung my eyes, reminding me of camping trips Marty took us on after my mother died. We moved in single file, winding along the course of the dry streambed, Dave first, then Moreno, me bringing up the rear. Moving along behind them, imitating their low combat crouch, I felt resigned to fate, as if riding the leading edge of a flash flood about to tear through the canyon.

The dog resumed barking.

Then a bundle of rags shifted near the fire and a human head popped up.

A bad smell moved toward us.

"Hello by the fire," I yelled.

Dave cocked his head in my direction, shot me twelve-gauge look.

"Well done, asshole. There goes our surprise."

The dog was going nuts by then.

Cover blown, Dave rushed forward, ducked oak branches and hopped boulders until he reached the edge of Walking Dead's camp.

Moreno and I followed.

"Well, well," Dave said, taking in the fire and strewn trash, shifting position to cut off Walking Dead's potential escape. "What do we have we here?"

Walking Dead's eyes darted from body to body, sizing up the opposition.

Then he released his dog.

Bounding like a brown bullet, the mutt shot at Dave and latched onto his arm, launching off the ground as it chomped. Startled at the lost advantage, Dave nearly fell over, hands already reaching toward his waist.

Sensing an opening, the dog let go of Dave's arm and leapt for his crotch as Walking Dead grabbed his meager possessions and pulled a hot stick from the fire.

"Kill 'em, Bean. Kill 'em!" the old guy screamed as he hurried away.

Chaos ended with a bang that came so fast, it barely registered as a gunshot. A loud pop—more like a snapping branch or a log cracking in the fire—accompanied by a yelp. Walking Dead's canine companion woofed away into darkness. Beats passed and nobody moved. Fresh smoke polluted the air, this time carrying the chemical tint of cordite.

"Jesus Christ, Dave! You shot the dog."

Dave stared at the gun as if the bullet had leapt out unaided by his trigger finger. "Fucking thing just went off."

Moreno stepped forward and grabbed the weapon, flicked on the safety, then tucked it into his waistband. Somehow, with the gun in the Mexican's hand, I felt safer.

"You shot my dog." Walking Dead lifted the burning stick, lunged toward Dave, and missed. "Bean," he yelled into the trees. "Bean, get back here."

Something rustled, but the dog stayed hidden, and by the blood smearing Dave's shoes, it had probably crawled off to die. More rustling, then a faint whine, then nothing. Unmoved, Dave checked his damaged arm and grew angry.

"Stupid crazy shit," he muttered. "Why'd you sic that goddamn dog on me?" He glanced at Moreno, then at me. "Thing probably has rabies. I'll get sick."

Walking Dead turned and ran.

Dave was on him fast. Taking four long strides, he skirted the edge of the fire and grabbed a handful of rotten clothes. A loud rip signaled tearing fabric, and Dave lost hold. Sensing opportunity, Walking Dead swung his burning stick, but Dave lifted his wounded arm and blocked the blow, then punched Walking Dead in the face.

Moreno stopped me as I tried to intervene.

Dave threw another punch, tagged the homeless man in the stomach.

Walking Dead vomited.

Dave stepped back from the spray.

Drooling, the old man started running again. This time toward me. Moreno let go of me and approached the fire. Walking Dead brushed past him, still moving in my direction.

Dave yelled, "Stop him, Boyd!"

I tried stepping out of the way, but Walking Dead mistook my intention and, seeing me as the last barrier to freedom, threw a punch. No one had hit me since the tenth grade, and when the blow landed in the center of my chest, it hurt like hell.

"Stop him, Boyd."

So I did.

Pumped on adrenaline, I grabbed a handful of Walking Dead's matted hair and yanked. The old guy tipped backward, skidded on loose rocks or dead oak leaves, and fell hard. As he went down, I caught a glimpse of his face in the firelight.

Not threatening, just wasted and terrified.

Dave was there in two seconds. "Hold him down," he ordered.

Pressing the man's chest, I held him while Dave thumped. The beating went on for thirty seconds. Dave pounded the man's face at first, but that hurt his hands, so he switched to body blows. I stopped counting after a dozen. Toward the end, Walking Dead made no sound, just gasped air, blowing rot into my face until I grew so accustomed to the smell I no longer knew whether it came from him or from something deep inside me.

Then Dave finished and I let go.

Walking Dead rolled to his side and issued a wet groan.

Dave shook out his hands and kicked the old man. "Get your skeletal ass out of my park. You can't stay here."

Moreno spoke from beside the fire. "He looks cold."

During the beating, I had lost track of the Mexican. Now he stepped away from the flames and moved toward us, carrying a burning tree branch.

"He can go to a damn shelter," Dave said. "Like normal losers."

Moreno gazed down at Walking Dead and handed Dave the torch.

"Maybe you should warm him up."

Dave grinned and the old man started to scream.

Chapter Fourteen

Friday at lunchtime, sunlight painted hard streets in downtown Los Angeles as I stepped into the restaurant and spotted Les Suarez in a booth opposite the bar. The lunch crowd, most dressed for business, was at high tide, the noise level two octaves below crescendo, and Les wore a blue suit and red tie. Walking across the penny-tile floor in cargo shorts and a luau shirt, I felt like a hobo. Thinking of hobos, my mind went to Walking Dead, and as my feet tapped, I kept seeing Dave lowering the torch until the old man started to scream.

That morning, after seeing a client in Westwood, I had called Les and suggested we meet for lunch. You crave French dip in downtown L.A. and there are two real options: Philippe's on Alameda, not far from Union Station, or Cole's a bit farther south, tucked beneath the Pacific Electric Building at Sixth and Main. Both joints were good, but preference came down to a single question: Did you want the *jus* on the bread, or on the side? I preferred the *jus* on the side, so we met at Cole's.

L.A.'s future district attorney sat in the red leather booth, sipped a beer, and gazed at two pictures of burlesque dancers sporting huge breasts, hovering next to one of gangster Mickey Cohen flashing an oversized grin. The *gentleman gangster* had grown up a few miles away in Boyle Heights and, like the cartels, had not been shy about publicity, chumming with the Rat Pack, Marilyn Monroe, even appearing on the Merv Griffin Show. Hard as I tried, I could not imagine Charlie Moreno talking to Merv Griffin. Not for a second.

Suarez nodded.

"You're late," he grumbled as a waitress hurried over.

I ordered a beer and a beef dip and then glanced at the pictures.

"You a fan of Cohen's?"

"My grandmother lived down the street from him when she was a girl."

"Friend of the family," I noted. "That won't be good come election time."

Suarez gave a shrug. "Less complicated days," he said. "When the Outfit ran Los Angeles, at least you knew where to point the finger. Now you have a thousand street gangs and no one's in control. It's the Wild West, and the black hats are winning."

I looked out the window. Cole's was half-submerged below ground level, so people on the street looked extra tall, and for the duration of lunch, Los Angeles became a city populated by giants.

"What can you do?"

"Keep fighting the good fight." Les gave my wardrobe the once over. "You're dressed for success, I see. Clients don't mind you showing up like a cabana boy? With that getup you could sell sunscreen in Venice."

"Part of my persona. I'm supposed to be a tech nerd, but the luau shirt is as far as I go."

For the next few minutes, we discussed kids and family. Les had two girls in college, one at USC, the other at Berkeley—talk about tuition shock—and his wife had recently gone back to work as a teacher in Pasadena to help pay the cost. I talked about the kids, Abby's job, and said nothing about the dog or the hamster.

Then, before lunch arrived, I steered the conversation toward business.

"So what's shaking in the DA's office?"

Les shrugged. "Same shit, different toilet. People don't realize how much evidence they leave behind. Hard drives, cell phones. These days, nearly every crime involves a computer or phone, as if God came down amid the carnage and left a digital gift for cops. Last month, we had a group of Nigerians staging accidents on the 710. They'd target big rigs near the port, wait for a car to get between their vehicle and the truck, and then slam the brakes. Boom! Truck smashed car, car smashed Nigerians, and everyone sued the trucking company. Dumb shits coordinated the entire circus by email. Crooked doctors they visited, lawyers in on the scam…all of it."

"Never a dull day."

"You got that right, and the day never ends. For the past month, somebody's been knocking off gun dealers from Bakersfield to Oceanside. The bad guys take the store computers and grab the guns. Nothing else is touched, not even the money."

"Somebody's selling guns."

"Looks that way. Strange thing is, nothing shows up on the streets. You know these bangers. They get a new toy, they want to shoot somebody. Who knows? With this globalization thing, maybe they're exporting them to China."

"Doesn't sound like a job for the DA."

"Regional Cybercrimes Task Force. Five of the stores used DVR surveillance systems. The hard drives melted in the fires. The feds couldn't find anything, so we're taking a stab at the analysis."

"Let me know if I can help."

"Yeah, right. I told you the county budget sucks. We can't afford you. You're better off sticking with the FBI, painful as that is to say."

The sandwiches came then. For a few mouthfuls, neither of us talked. Then, after his third dip into the *jus*, Suarez narrowed his eyes.

"So how's your gig with the feds?"

"Not so good."

"Oh yeah." Suarez wiped his mouth and smiled. "I warned you, Boyd. So, what's up?"

"I can't be specific."

"You're holding out on me?"

"The most I can say is they're watching this guy, a neighbor of mine, but they're not doing a very good job. Last night, the guy beat the shit out of someone, and I watched it happen. I couldn't stop it."

"Jesus, the vic okay?"

"Maybe. I think so."

"Did you report it to the cops?"

"That's the thing. If the guy gets arrested, there goes the surveillance. I'm not sure what to do."

"Did you call the agent in charge? What's his name?"

"Fisk. Yeah, three times. He hasn't called back."

Suarez shook his head. "Typical fed. You'll hear from him when he needs you. One time, we worked this homicide in Echo Park. The vic was Salvadoran, used to be some military honcho down there. Feds let us narrow the shooter to one of two guys and then stomped in with both loafers and grabbed the case. I told you, Boyd, you gotta watch your back with these guys."

"I'm trying."

"No idea what it's about then?"

"Drug cartels. That's the extent of my knowledge. But I'm serious, Les, they beat the shit out this guy."

"They?"

"One of my other neighbors kind of initiated everything. You think the feds were watching? Would they just let that happen?"

"They might. It's happened before. Remember that SIS fiasco?"

"SIS?"

"Special unit inside LAPD, tasked with bringing down career criminals. Went after the kind of guys who start shooting if you pull them over for a busted tail light. Anyway, the unit got a rep for ignoring the crime prevention aspect of law enforcement and concentrating on aggressive apprehension, ex-post-facto, if you get my meaning."

"They let crimes occur and then made arrests?"

Les nodded. "Racked up big convictions that way. Sent guys off for long stretches. They also had the highest kill ratios of any unit in the department—caught in the act, most guys that bad don't go quietly. Anyway, the *Times* made a stink about the unfairness of it all, and things quieted down."

"So the feds might know what happened last night and do nothing?"

"That's what I'm telling you. But you could get lucky. You said the victim was okay, so maybe he'll go to the police himself. That way, things go tits up, but you're not at fault." Suarez shrugged, picked up his sandwich, took another bite and looked as if he were in love. "Good beef," he said, "but I still prefer Philippe's."

"We'll go there next time."

Beats passed as I tried to stop thinking about Walking Dead. After a mouthful of beer, I swallowed the images and felt ready to move on.

"Look, I have a question about cell phones."

"Forensically speaking?"

"Yeah."

"You're the expert."

"Not when it comes to phones. The technology changes too fast. I'd spend all day doing research in order to keep up. It's not worth my time."

Suarez brushed some crumbs from his hands. "Okay. Shoot."

"Why would somebody have dozens of phones, the exact same make and model?"

Suarez shrugged. "Could be they got a deal at Costco."

"I'm serious, Les."

"You mean for nefarious purposes?" He chugged some beer, glanced up at Mickey Cohen, and nodded. "I assume the phones are disposable. Low end?"

"They're smart phones. Web access, camera."

"So we're not talking about burners. And you're not sharing more details?"

"I don't have more to share."

"Then I'd guess the phones are stolen. Probably lifted from a truck somewhere."

"Would they work?"

"Sure, they might be cloned, but more likely a SIM card is being swapped in and out."

"Swapped?"

"You go to Target or wherever, buy a prepaid SIM card and put it in the stolen phone. The phone locks onto the network. You call your grandma or your girlfriend and have a nice chat."

"So what's the benefit? You're still paying the bill."

"This isn't about theft. It's a matter of security. If the subject had enough SIMs, they could swap cards all day long, effectively changing phone numbers at will. Tracking would be difficult. Even if you grabbed a number, the subject could switch to another SIM. Forensic analysis would be tough to impossible. Data would reside in so many places; unless you lucked out and got every phone and every SIM, you'd never recover all of it. I have to tell you, Boyd, if the feds have you working on this, they're getting ripped off. You seem a little behind the curve."

"Cell phone forensics was never my forte."

"I can tell. Even if he's swapping SIMs, you could pull data from the phone. Just like a computer, something's always left behind. Call logs. Contact lists. You might find out what he's up to. Depends on the phone."

"What if the phone is damaged?"

"You mean broken?"

"I mean smashed."

Suarez shrugged. "Like I said, there's always something."

I nodded. "Thanks for the info. How's your lunch?"

Suarez finished chewing, then wiped his mouth and frowned. "The sandwich was great. Your lunch debt is paid. Which brings us to our mutual problem."

"I didn't know we had one."

"These gun stores. The sheriffs are looking high and low, and needless to say this stays between us, but an interesting name popped up."

Something squirmed in my guts. "How is that our mutual problem?"

"A CI fingered Daniel Devlin as a possible go-between setting up gun buys. You know...as in Devlin Auto Body?" Suarez paused to let the implication settle. "Devlin's nephew Vince has been on our radar for years, with the drugs and his connections to La Eme, but this is the first we've heard of the old man being dirty."

Suarez was referring to Vincent Devlin's link to the Mexican Mafia. I had heard the rumors, met the kid a few times, and found them hard to choke down. Vince had an MBA from USC, drove a VW Beetle, and looked like a model. Hardly the vision of a dangerous gangster.

Suarez continued.

"Anyway, I thought you deserved a heads up. Your brother's hanging with the wrong crowd, Boyd."

After wiping crumbs from the table, I brushed my hands.

"Ran's a mechanic," I said.

"Yeah, I hope so. Anyway, with the firearms involved, the ATF might grab the case at some point. You should find your brother a new job, save us both a little embarrassment. I don't need his face popping up at Devlin's perp walk. You and me being associates, it would look bad come election time, and I doubt it would help your business."

I stared up at Mickey Cohen and the strippers and longed for a time when evil had a single source far beyond the family circle, when if you kept your guard up, the world's foulness never got close to home. With a brother like Ransom and a neighbor like Charlie Moreno, that time no longer existed.

"I'll talk to him. See what he knows."

"Good. Keep me posted."

Ten minutes later, lunch ended and we headed for the street and said goodbye.

Suarez shook hands and said, "You're an honorable man, Boyd. You pay your debts."

I appreciated the sentiment, but he was dead wrong.

*

Devlin Auto Body occupied a converted fire station in the City of Industry, not far from the Pomona Freeway, tucked into a neighborhood of flat-roofed commercial buildings and crumbling houses. Draped in wrought iron, most houses contained shrines to Our Lady of Guadalupe or some other patron saint of the poor, and featured large dogs attached to heavy chains patrolling yards as security. In my neighborhood, you bought alarm systems for protection. Here, for those of lesser means, God and man's best friend offered better odds.

Parking the Subaru, I avoided a tattooed kid pitching an oil change and walked into the service bay. I went no more than ten feet before Danny Devlin stepped out of his office and grinned as if he had spotted the Virgin Mary slipping into a pair of mechanic's coveralls.

"Well, I'll be damned," he said, twirling a set of keys. "Jack Boyd, standing in my very own shop."

Devlin closed the gap between us and extended a hand. I shook, felt the ropey muscle that ran the length of his arm and culminated in a shoulder the size of a hubcap, then let go. Close to sixty, he possessed sharp blue eyes that dug faster than any diamond-tipped drill and wore his long grey hair slicked back, held in place by what appeared to be thirty-weight motor oil. Whenever he stepped into the sun, a pair of Ray-Ban Baloromas shielded his eyes and made him look like Clint Eastwood in Dirty Harry—cool, lethal, and in control, all at once.

"How's it going, Danny?"

Devlin gave a quick shrug. "Look at this place," he said. "How do you think it's going?"

Surveying the mechanics, I noted a high proportion of tatted biceps and shaved heads. From the gutted state of the cars, most guys were better at tearing things apart than reassembling them, and some carried glares that had probably graced the walls of more than one bank or post office. Their presence didn't seem very conducive to luring customers, but the place looked busy.

"In a crap economy, people keep their cars longer," I said. "Must be good for business."

Devlin owned repair shops throughout Los Angeles County, in areas most people avoided—Compton, Watts, Boyle Heights, Westlake. Not just poor neighborhoods, but gang-ridden places where gunfire echoed hourly and people sank money into shitty cars because they had no choice. Devlin had always seemed like a decent guy, offering poor people a valuable service, but if Suarez was right about the guns, maybe some other motivation led him to such neighborhoods.

"Just opened a shop in Carson. Got another coming in Palmdale this spring. I could run this place twenty-four hours a day if I could find enough mechanics."

I wondered if there was some kind of drought at the local parole agency but kept the thought to myself. "Ran working out okay?"

"Damn right. He's one of my best."

Devlin spoke of my brother with affection in his eyes. Two years into a stint at Pelican Bay, Ran had transferred into a fresh pod and ended up cellmates with Devlin's half-Irish, half-Mexican son, Steven. One day, someone shanked the kid in a bathroom for being too white, or too brown, nobody ever knew which, and the boy bled out as Ran stuffed toilet paper into the holes. Weeks later, Devlin began monthly visits to my brother, and when Ran's parole ended, the old man took less than a minute to offer him a job.

"He around?"

"Out back." Devlin jerked a thumb toward a door. "But do me a favor. Ride with me first."

Five minutes later, heading north on the 57 Freeway, Devlin gripped the wheel of a 2005 Cadillac Escalade EXT and pressed the accelerator to the floor. The engine growled. Pushed back in my seat, I watched the San Gabriel Mountains expand in the windshield and held my breath as the speedometer ticked past ninety.

"Not bad for a truck," Devlin shouted over the engine noise. "Plenty of horses. Had a shift problem in the tranny, but your brother fixed it. Figured I'd use you as the test dummy."

He shot a grin and lifted off the gas. Weight seemed to leave my chest.

"What kind of car you drive, Jack?"

"Subaru. An Outback."

"Japanese, huh?"

"Yeah."

"Shit. My old man would have beat my ass if I'd ever bought Japanese. He fought on Okinawa. Marines. A real badass. Not the forgiving type, either. What's the matter—you don't like American cars?"

"Good financing deal."

"Yeah. Everyone likes a good deal." Devlin exited the freeway at Via Verde, crossed the overpass, and transitioned back on, this time heading south. Rejoining traffic, he tapped a palm against the wheel. "This is a fine American machine. Damn near a work of art. Know where it's made?"

"Nope."

"Mexico." He barked a laugh. "That's right, a sixty-thousand dollar vehicle made by people earning four bucks an hour. Doesn't sound right, does it?"

"Not really."

"Know where your Japanese car is made?"

"I'm thinking not in Japan."

"Lafayette, Indiana. Now you tell me, who's the real patriot? The guy buying a Japanese car made by Americans, or the one buying an American car made by Mexicans?" Devlin snorted. "Sometimes globalization is too screwy to comprehend. Not as simple as it looks, is it?"

"Not much is."

He glanced over and dipped his Ray-Bans. "I hear Jane Selig brought you two hard drives to examine."

"Yeah, I meant to thank you for the business."

Devlin waved a dismissive hand. "Ran explained to you that I'd like a heads-up if you found anything."

"He mentioned you were concerned about Jane, that she'd been depressed since her husband's death and you wanted to make sure nothing made that worse. But now, I'm guessing things aren't that simple."

"You catch on fast, Jack."

Devlin flipped his turn signal and adjusted his Ray-Bans, then transitioned into the right lane, prepping to exit the freeway. Glancing out the window, I spotted his shop amid the warehouses and thought I saw someone who looked like my brother working in the back.

"Don Selig did accounting work for me," Devlin said. "Sensitive work I'd rather stayed private."

"And you think the drives contain a record of that?"

Devlin managed a shrug. His shoulders pressed against his shirt like overinflated tires. "Don's insurance policy is being contested. With the question of suicide and all, if his insurance company finds out about those drives... Well, let's just say I'd rather not take the chance of them poking around."

"Then why send Mrs. Selig to me in the first place?"

"That was Janey's decision. If I had found the drives first, well, you and I wouldn't be having this conversation. I recommended you because we know each other."

We exited the freeway and stopped at a red light. I shifted in my seat and faced him directly. "Look, Mr. Devlin, I haven't examined those drives. Business is booming and we're swamped, so I'm not sure when I'll get to them. In fact, I might just call Mrs. Selig and tell her we can't take her business. I haven't cashed her check yet."

Devlin shook his head. "I'd rather you didn't. She's a strong-willed woman, and she'll take them somewhere else. At least with you looking, I have an avenue of communication. You're practically family, Jack. We're related by a common ancestor and have shared interests."

"You mean my brother, because he works for you?"

"Something like that."

"So what? I examine the drives or Ran loses his job?"

"Hell no, and it pisses me off you'd say such a thing. What I owe your brother can't be repaid. He can work for me for the rest of his life if he wants. That boy's more son to me than employee, but you have to realize, whatever hurts me eventually hurts those who work for me."

The light turned green, and Devlin punched the gas.

"Even if I knew what was on those drives, Mr. Devlin, without Jane Selig's okay, I could never tell you. That would breach privacy. She'd sue me, and she'd win. My business would fold. I couldn't show you the data unless Mrs. Selig gave permission in writing."

"Bringing Janey deeper into this would defeat the purpose."

"And what exactly is the purpose?"

"To protect her from the shit Don covered himself in. This isn't for me, Jack. I mean, I have an interest, sure, but I'm worried about that woman. If the wrong people sniff in the right places, her life will go from bad to fucking tragic. I can't allow that to happen."

"Can't?"

"That's right. *Can't.*"

"What sort of wrong people?"

"There's only one sort, Jack."

"Mr. Devlin, I *can't* tell you what's on those drives."

Devlin adjusted his Dirty Harry glasses and smiled. "Surely there's some way we can deal."

I thought of Suarez then. Of illegal gun sales and the ATF. Then I thought of Charlie Moreno, my useless dog, and the inadequacy of my home security system. Looking at Devlin, I seized the moment and opted for some fresh insurance.

"Maybe we can deal."

*

Back at Devlin's shop, I found Ransom in a service bay, gutting a Jaguar that someone should have euthanized ten years earlier. As I approached, he shot a questioning glare.

"What's the matter?"

"Nothing."

"Everything okay the other night?"

He was referring to my leaving the gentleman's club as if someone had just waved the flag at the Indy 500.

"It was just a misunderstanding. Sara's fine."

Ran grabbed a beefy wrench and ducked back under the hood. Grease stained his hands, giving them zebra stripes. He paused every thirty seconds to wipe them clean. After his arrest for chopping stolen cars, Ran had spent years in the prison auto pool learning to reassemble them. He had started his sentence at Chino but, after hitting a guard, found himself on the bus to Pelican Bay. Despite Abby's protests, I had always believed my brother was a talented mechanic with a shaded past, trying to walk in the sunlight. After lunch with Suarez and the ride with Devlin, I no longer knew what to believe. Once comfortable with darkness, maybe you stayed in the shadows for good.

He resurfaced, wiped his hands again, and said, "You okay?"

"I was downtown having lunch with a friend. You're on the way home, thought I'd stop by."

"One of your cop buddies?"

"Something like that."

"Must be nice having friends with juice."

"You know guys in Pelican Bay, right?"

"Of course."

"They have juice."

"Sure, if you want someone killed. Other than that, it mostly carries weight in prison."

"You need better friends. I can introduce you around."

"Most of your pals carry badges. Something tells me we wouldn't hit it off. Besides, I like my friends."

Turning his attention to the car, Ran adjusted something near the spark plugs, then wiped his hands and turned the key. The engine fired up and purred like a happy cat ready to eat. "Jags are a piece of shit," he said and cut the engine. "Thing took all morning, and I worked through lunch. You bring me a doggy bag at least?"

"I want to make you an offer."

"I don't need your money. I told you the other day."

"I want you to come and work for me."

"What?"

"At my office. I'd like you to work for me."

Ran waited a beat and then shrugged. "Why?"

"Why not? You'd be closer to home, a shorter commute, and you'd be helping me out."

"How would that help you? I know computers the way you know engines."

"That's not the point. And you'd be working the counter, taking care of the office, ordering, shipping, filing. Later, if you wanted to learn, I'd teach you the tech side. Point is you'd be freeing me up to focus on forensics…and you'd be away from here."

"What's wrong with here?"

"Just think about it, okay?"

"Does Abby know?"

"Abby?"

"Yeah, your wife. Does she know?"

"Abby runs her school. The business is my responsibility."

"I'll take that as a big fat no. From what I heard the other day, she's already pissed Carter can't go to that school. You spring this on her—the expense of hiring a fresh employee, especially when it's me—and you might need a divorce lawyer."

"She told you about The Phoenix Academy?"

"I overheard her talking to your neighbor. The one with plastic tits."

"Liz."

"Whatever." Ran shrugged and waved a hand. "Anyway, I don't know anything about running an office, so the answer is no." He grabbed a fresh wrench from the toolbox, picked up a rag, and started wiping. "You sure you're okay?"

"I'll train you."

"Why now?"

"I need the help."

He looked around the bay, took in the tools, the oil, and the hydraulic lifts as if they were home on a dark, storm-filled night, and shook his head.

"Nah," he said. "My friends are here."

"Look, get out of this place, away from these guys."

"I'm a grown man, Jack. My world isn't black and white, but I've learned to love the grey. You don't have to worry about me."

"I don't see it that way."

"Well, you're gonna have to." He closed his toolbox. "You sure you're good?"

Knowing it would go no further, I nodded. "I'm fine."

"If that changes for any reason, you know where to find me." He backed away, wiping his hands, and vanished amid the chaos of the bay.

I stood a moment, then felt eyes watching me as I returned to my car. Before I drove away, a skinny kid with a shaved head and a tattoo of an eagle on his left forearm approached the Subaru with a case of Pennzoil. I lowered the window, prepped to tell him the lube wasn't mine.

"Danny says to give you this." He circled around front, opened the passenger door, and put the case on the seat. Closing the door, he tapped the roof. "Pennzoil is shit, dawg. You need some high performance oil for this bitch."

Five minutes later, stopped in traffic on the I-10, I opened the box.

A sheet of paper lay atop the bottles of oil. Scrawled in black ink, a message read, *My end of the deal.*

Beneath the paper lay the gun.

Chapter Fifteen

Back at DRI, Fisher manned the front lobby, working one of the laptops from the college. Walking into my office, I set the Pennzoil on my desk and closed the door. Seconds later, gun in hand, I loaded the cylinder with bullets and felt the weight. The weapon was a six-gun, the kind old timers used in western movies, and from what little I knew about firearms, that was good. Revolvers never jammed the way semi-autos did. You pulled the trigger, the gun went off, and someone got hurt. I pictured Moreno at the end of the sights, lifted the weapon and stiffened my arm, trying to hold it steady.

The barrel danced like a snake's head.

Could I shoot a man?

When had I even last fired a gun?

Years back, a few of us from MicroLine had gone to an indoor range, thinking blue smoke and cordite would forge corporate bonding. It hadn't worked out that way. Most targets survived unscathed.

And before that?

Had to be when Ran and I were kids. Dad taught us to shoot one summer, deep in Lytle Creek Canyon, a boulder field littered with old cars, abandoned Barcaloungers, and rusted-out refrigerators. He had downed beer and offered up pointers reaped while changing bedpans in Nam. Squeeze gently. Don't close your eyes. Anticipate the kick. We'd stood near our truck, blasting away from sixty feet, perforating air. Ran had improved quickly, though, and driving home, wedged between my father's legs, steering the truck so Dad could sip a beer, was one of the few moments my brother basked in the old man's pride.

"Ransom's a better shooter than you, Jackson," he'd said. "Good hand-eye coordination. Give him time and he'll make a run at you in baseball."

Pushing the memory away, I opened a drawer and tucked the weapon into my desk. I wasn't ready to shoot anyone, not yet, but that didn't mean the gun was useless. Even if I never used it for self-defense, once Moreno left the neighborhood, I'd hand it over to Suarez. If Devlin was dirty, maybe the DA's office and the ATF could link it to the gun store robberies.

Glancing toward the frosted glass, I yelled into the lobby. "Fish, get in here."

The door creaked open. "What's up, boss?"

"Those hard drives I gave you last week?"

"Yo?"

"They getting close?"

"Better than close. They're done."

"Where's the report?"

"Probably under all the mail you haven't opened in the past two days."

The top of my desk resembled the dead letter department at the post office. I needed swim fins to wade the junk solicitations, catalogs, and two-for-one taqueria coupons that flooded our mailbox on a daily basis. Sorting through it ate man-hours and did nothing to bring in business, at least not for us, so I mostly let it pile up.

"You know, I pay you to run the office, Fish. Part of that means keeping my desk clear so I can find stuff."

Fisher curled a lip. "You pay me because I'm a better digital bloodhound than you. I'm a forensics god. You aren't even a demigod."

My mouth folded into a frown. Fisher got the hint, rummaged through the pile, and handed me a sheet of paper detailing the contents of Don Selig's hard drives. I glanced at the report and looked up.

"Well?"

"It's all right there. You can read, can't you?"

"It's been a long day. Give me the Cliffs Notes."

Part of me wanted to reestablish office pecking order, making Fisher spoon-feed me the report, but another part knew the truth. Fish was better. Reading the report was one thing, interpreting it was another.

"Mr. Selig encrypted the drives, but I blew through that like Hitler taking Poland. Tried wiping the sectors, too. Amateur hour, though. The guy didn't bother rewriting fresh data. He just deleted files. Easiest recovery I've done. There were only a few dozen files."

"Cliffs Notes, Fish. What kind of files?"

"Nothing much."

"Meaning?"

"Just a bunch of Excel files. Spreadsheets, number streams, financial statements of some kind. The data reveals nothing, but the encryption and deletion mean somebody didn't want it found, so I'd say it has value."

I glanced at the report and realized the drives provided no easy answer. Whatever Selig might or might not have been doing for Danny Devlin, the numbers told me nothing. I tucked the report and the drives into the jacket hanging on my chair, intending to go over them later at home, then looked at Fish standing in my office doorway like a loyal dog hoping for a Milk-Bone.

"Get back to work," I said.

Fisher left.

I began sorting mail.

Halfway through the pile, I spotted a certified letter from MicroLine. Tearing in, I found a missive from the company's legal department, informing me that working with the feds violated my severance contract. If I continued doing so, payments would cease and legal action would commence. My mood scurried further south then, prompting another call to Special Agent Fisk. On the fifth ring, he answered. The FBI man sounded tired, as if he'd woken from a ten-hour nap that wasn't long enough, but I didn't give a shit.

"Where the hell have you been?"

"This better be important," he drawled. "After twenty hours of surveillance, I need my sleep."

"Why haven't you returned my calls?"

"I just told you. Surveillance."

"You've been watching Moreno?"

"It's related to the case but someone else. And I'd like to get back to sleep, so what's up?"

"Where were you guys last night?"

The FBI man exhaled in a loud rush. "Don't worry, the old guy is okay. What the hell happened?"

Fisk knew about the incident in the park, which meant Suarez had been right. Fisk's agents had been there and done nothing. My chest tightened a notch, and for two minutes, I regurgitated most of what had happened, leaving out the part where I pinned Walking Dead to the ground while Dave beat the shit out of him. Fisk listened without interruption.

"Why didn't your men stop it?" I asked finally.

"The better question is why you didn't."

That had pinged through my head all day. Could I have stopped them? Both had weapons—a gun and torch—and more importantly, the will to use them. Should I have intervened? What could I have done? Then again, I hadn't just sat back and let things progress, had I? I held the old man down. Did Fisk know about that, too?

"Manker's a hothead," Fisk said.

"You know about Dave then?"

Fisk exhaled a long blast of irritation. "You weren't our only option for this operation, Boyd. We checked several possibilities."

"You talked to Dave? He knows about Moreno?"

"You're the only one who knows anything, and it needs to stay that way." Fisk spoke as if he had put something in his mouth, maybe a cigarette. "We looked at Mr. Manker and your other neighbors as possible contacts, but you were the best option."

"Why was I the best option?"

"Mr. Manker's obviously unpredictable, and your previous work with law enforcement was a plus; you have a dependable track record."

A few beats passed. I picked up the certified letter. My anger welled, and I fought to control it. "Have you contacted MicroLine yet?"

"About what?'

"The agent you sent digging into my background. I told you, he gave the impression I'm working for the FBI. I explained this to you, Fisk. Part of my severance agreement stipulates I go nowhere near MicroLine's clients, which more or less makes the entire federal government off limits."

A lighter clicked, and a sharp intake of breath confirmed Fisk was smoking. "What do you want me to do?"

"Inform them I'm not working for you."

Fisk exhaled long and slow. "I can't do that."

There was a drawn-out pause, and then I heard low voices. After a moment, I realized the agent was watching television. "Fisk?"

"I can't do that, not yet."

"Why the hell not?"

There was another pause. Then Al Bundy's voice roared in the background, and Fisk gave a soft chuckle. "We know Moreno's target," he said at last. "We've known since yesterday afternoon."

I went silent a beat.

"So you're going to arrest him?"

"Not yet.

"Why not?"

Fisk cleared his throat and his voice grew an edge. "This is a federal operation, Boyd. I'm steering the ship, not you. We informed you of Moreno's arrival as a courtesy. You let us use your property for surveillance, and we appreciate that, but this is an FBI investigation, and we move at our own pace. I don't have to tell you a damn thing."

The words hit like a slap. I nearly slapped back. Instead, I controlled my anger and asked, "How much longer?"

"Just stay patient."

Seconds ticked, filled by the drone of Fisk's TV. The agent sucked another drag from the cigarette, and I pictured the flickering television illuminating a blue swirl of smoke over his head. Then I thought of my mother, marooned in her bedroom, alone with her cigarettes and television, waiting to die. I pushed the thought away.

"How much longer, Fisk?"

"Days, probably. Maybe a week."

"Who's the target?"

"I can't tell you that."

"What do you want me to do?"

"Nothing."

"What do you mean nothing?"

"As in don't...do...a...thing." Special Agent Fisk heaved a sigh. "Look, I'm glad you're taking this seriously, Boyd, but not every piss the guy takes constitutes a threat to national security. You're not a federal agent. We have people watching him. I envisioned yours as a passive role. Like I said, be neighborly. But just the same, avoid more nighttime hikes with the guy. Know what I mean?"

"Yeah, I'll do that."

Fisk exhaled. "Feel better now with that off your chest?"

"I'll feel better when this is over."

"Just hang loose and stay out of his way. It'll be over soon."

"You no longer want his phone number, then."

"No. Things have changed. This close to his goal, Moreno will be jumpy. He's like a businessman about to close a deal. Anything unexpected pops up, he'll get nervous. I don't want him spooked. He gets spooked and he'll pull the plug and take off."

"Let's hope so."

*

When I got home, Sara was in the house alone. Walking into the kitchen, I saw her pick at a salad as she pretended to read a world history book while texting on her phone. We hadn't talked about what had happened on Tuesday night, partly because accusing Scott of theft was going to start a fight and partly because there was no way to explain how I had come about that information.

"I thought you had yearbook class."

"Canceled," she said. "Mom picked me up. Scott was going to bring me home, but Mom said no way." Sara barely looked up as she spoke. "I have homework. Tons."

"Scott's driving now? I thought he's only fifteen."

"His brother drives, Dad."

"Oh," I said. "Where's Mom?"

Sara didn't answer. I poured some water at the tap and looked out the window. Laughter bolted from the backyard. It sounded as if Abby and Carter were playing with the dog. Downing the water, I glanced at Sara and decided to use the private time for a father/daughter talk. Pulling a chair from the table, I sat.

"How's the ankle?"

"Better."

"What are you reading?"

"History."

"Something in particular, or are you trying to absorb the whole thing all at once?"

"Buddhism."

"Sounds heavy. Anything interesting?"

Sara fixed me with a glare. "Buddha claims life is a state of perpetual flux, and all things are forever changing. Fighting against that change only brings unhappiness."

"Sounds like the Buddha had kids."

"Funny, Dad."

She lifted the book and blocked her face. I reached out, lowered the book with a finger, and flashed a smile.

"You're growing up, Sara. I get that. Unbelievable as it may be, I even remember what that feels like. But you have to understand, a few years ago, you'd crawl into my lap and watch *Teletubbies*. Now you have boyfriends, and I'm a little nervous. Sometimes, I even get scared."

Her eyes left the book. "Scared about what?"

"Making a mistake that can't be fixed. I give too much freedom, you could make a bad choice and pay forever. I hold the leash too tight, you'll hate me. Neither option is good from where I sit."

"I'm not a dog on a leash, Dad."

"You're right. Bad metaphor."

"I think that was a simile."

"Whatever. It was a poor example, and this little exchange illustrates my point. You're a smart girl, and your future can be whatever you want. That said, you have to get to the future in one piece, and that's my job. Hopefully, we can remain friends during the process."

She looked at the book. Seconds lengthened into moments. "We're still friends," she said at last.

My blood warmed a little. "That's good," I said. "Now, about your boyfriend Scott."

"He's a friend, Dad."

"Okay, he's a friend. What I meant to say was, if he becomes something else—a real boyfriend or whatever—you could have him over to do stuff with the family. You know, dinner, watch a movie. I'd like to talk to him."

"About what?"

"I don't know. Maybe we'll talk baseball."

Sara wasn't smiling, but she wasn't frowning either. "Fine," she said at last.

"Okay. Good."

I sat for several minutes as she read. Outside, Carter laughed as Hondo barked. The kitchen felt hot. Autumn light spilled in through the windows, and Sara looked beautiful in the warm reflection, almost a woman, still a little girl. My soul nearly melted as I watched her read. After a few minutes, the light faded and the moment passed.

"Go back to your homework, kid." I stood, kissed her forehead, and headed for the back door. "I'll be in the backyard talking to Mom. Maybe we'll get pizza."

"Mom's not in the backyard," she said.

A few feet from the door, I stopped, not certain I wanted to ask the next question.

I did anyway.

"Where is she?"

Sara nodded toward the fence.

"Charlie invited them to swim."

MICHAEL HARBISON

Chapter Sixteen

Moreno opened the gate and smiled. "Welcome, neighbor. Hope you brought your suit."

Peering over the Mexican's shoulder into the backyard, I spotted Carter floating on the water in the middle of the pool. Abby sat nearby, shaded by a pergola, holding a drink in her left hand. Standing there, I felt my balls shrink down to hard, possessive stones, like a shepherd watching his flock play with a wolf. I looked back at Moreno and shook my head.

"Sorry, no suit."

He waved me into the yard. "Well, come in anyway. I hope you don't mind that I borrowed your family. A pool is for fun, and true fun requires a child."

Walking into the barren yard, I noted the pool's green tint, as if the Mexican had skimped on chlorine. He stayed behind and fiddled with the gate as I crossed the dead grass and nodded at Abby. She must have read my face, because her lips pinched into a frown. The drink in her hand smelled alcoholic, and more possessive tightness gripped my balls. She rarely drank booze. The few times I'd tried to get her drunk and take advantage, she had flatly refused, claiming the buzz and sex weren't worth the headache.

She shaded her eyes and looked up. "Hey."

"Hey yourself. You must have had a good day."

"Not really," she said, lifting the drink. "But this helps."

"Let's go home and get some dinner."

"Charlie invited us to swim."

Carter screamed in the pool, splashing up and down like a porpoise. Next door, Hondo stared through a crack in the fence and barked, excluded from all the fun. I yelled for him to shut up.

Abby frowned. "How was work?"

"Fine."

"Then why are you in a mood?"

"I'm not in a mood. What are you drinking?"

Abby looked at the glass. "Kahlua, I think."

Moreno came over and stood beside her, put his hands on his hips and grinned. He wore board shorts with a tank top, and his hairless chest looked buffed and hard, muscles swelling into a slow-building tidal wave of flesh.

"With a touch of tequila," he said, pointing at the glass. "They call it a Black Mexican. You want one? A beer, perhaps?"

"Actually, I came over to drag these guys home. I was about to order pizza."

"You sure? I purchased a barbecue yesterday and was about to fire up. Hot dogs for the boy, and I have this excellent *pollo* marinating in the kitchen. Lemon juice, cilantro. The juice helps the skin char."

Thinking of the old man last night, scurrying under the flames, I shook my head. "I promised Sara pizza. Delivery in thirty minutes."

Abby sipped from her glass and looked out at the water. "Order pizza tomorrow," she said.

Moreno touched her shoulder and grinned. "Your wife wants my chicken."

I wanted to rip out Moreno's windpipe but thought of Special Agent Fisk. This would be over in a week's time. I grabbed a chair and took a seat.

*

The chicken was good, with a citrus bite that kicked ass while I chewed and a soft jolt of earthy heat—red pepper flakes or chili powder—that punched my guts after I swallowed. Moreno was a consummate host, polite and doting, refilling empty wine glasses and offering more food whenever plates grew empty. By the time we finished, the sun had set and Carter was cold. After downing two hot dogs, he said goodnight to Moreno and followed Abby home for a hot bath. Like a good neighbor, I stayed behind to clean up.

Mounding greasy paper plates with chicken bones and scraps of hot dog bun, I stood looking for a trashcan as Moreno exited the kitchen, carrying two beers. Finally, I dumped the plates into an empty grocery bag hanging from the grill.

Moreno lifted a beer. "You want another?"

I wasn't drunk, but a faint buzz saw already cleaved my head "No thanks. I have to get going. Thanks for the meal. You're a good cook."

"Thanks for lending me your family."

I took a moment, not enjoying the implication. "Sure thing."

"You're lucky, Jack. You have a great home…and something of value to put there."

Killer or not, he was right about that. I glanced into his house, noted chintzy furniture, a humble TV—spartan decor one notch above prison cell chic, not much better than Marty Goodman's bed at Evergreen. Looking at how he lived, it wasn't difficult picturing Moreno drifting from place to place, existing alone and killing perfect strangers. What kind of life could that be?

"I am lucky."

"You recognize your good fortune, too," he said. "That's even more of a blessing. Most men have to lose something to know its value."

Once Abby had left the yard, I had expected him to bring up last night's violence in the park, to apologize as he had when the boys fought in my yard, but he never did. Maybe in his world, lighting a man on fire was no big deal. Or perhaps he considered me a willing participant. Whatever the reason, it made me hate him even more. Lifting the bag of plates and bones, I nodded toward the house.

"You want this in the kitchen trash?"

Moreno shrugged. "Dump it in the can by the garage."

"Okay." I nodded. "See you."

Carrying the trash along the side of the house, I looked up as the lights came on in my upstairs bathroom, and Carter yelled something about a missing Transformer. At the garbage bin, I stopped and lifted the lid. Illuminated by the light from my bathroom, the box of smashed phones rested atop the garbage. My pulse skipped beats as I considered grabbing one. Then Moreno came around the side of the house, moving like a dark shadow passing under a boat.

"You found the *basura*," the Mexican said, lifting his beer.

I dropped the bag and lowered the lid. "Yeah."

He followed me out front, saying nothing. Just as we cleared the gate, someone yelled, and we both glanced across the street as Dave Manker jogged toward us, still in his security uniform.

Dave looked upset. "We've got problems," he said. "The cops know about our little bonfire last night."

"What?" I said. "How?"

"You tell me, Boyd." Dave looked up at the light coming from my bathroom. "We need to get our stories straight, but not here. Meet at Talley's in thirty minutes."

Chapter Seventeen

"You're going out now?"

Abby had just finished pulling Carter from the bath. He was in his room playing, and she caught me in the downstairs hall slipping into a jacket, clutching my car keys. Her face wore that look of wide-eyed disbelief wives get when husbands do stupid things.

"Dave has some kind of problem. He needs to talk. We're meeting at Talley's"

I headed toward the door as her eyebrows arched.

"At a bar?"

I stopped. "Ab, I have to go."

I reached for the knob and twisted. A cold blast of wind seeped through the doorjamb and entered the house. The chill seemed to encircle me, then shifted around and came from behind.

"You've been drinking tonight. You shouldn't drive."

"I'll be fine."

I pulled the door open.

"You know, Dave's not the only one with problems," she said. "I'd like to talk myself."

"When I get back. I won't be long."

"I went to see the dean of admissions at The Phoenix Academy today."

I closed the door. "You did what?"

"Lenora Lopes. She was nice. I arranged a tour during lunch, and she showed me the classrooms and dorms. I got to sit in on a counseling session. Mrs. Lofton was right. I think Carter should go there."

"Ab, now isn't the time."

"Well, it feels like the time to me. Charlie said if we—"

"You talked to Moreno about this?"

My teeth clenched as I spoke, and the statement came out as a harsh snap.

Abby saw the anger but refused to back down. "His brother had autism. He went to a school in Mexico, and Charlie said it helped make—"

"His brother had autism? I don't believe this. You don't know what you're doing. I can't believe you talked to a stranger about our son. You have to stop."

"Stop what? He's our neighbor. I talk to Liz all the time about the kids. That never seemed to bother you."

"Abby, we don't even know the man."

"Well, I have to talk to someone. All I get from you are promises about future conversations we never seem to have." Abby lowered her voice. "Mrs. Lopes says if we intervene now, Carter has a good shot at—"

"Look, we can talk about this when I get back. I have to go."

"I'm not waiting. I mean it, Jack. If you don't want to talk now, I'll make my own decision."

Sucking a deep breath, I waited before saying anything more. What could I say? Moreno is a killer. Don't talk to him. That wasn't possible. Not without telling her about Fisk and explaining why I had lied for the past week, not to mention the cease and desist letter MicroLine had sent because I was helping the FBI, and by the way, Dave and Moreno lit an old man on fire last night. No matter how I spun things, I'd end up looking crazy. She might not even believe me. But thinking about Abby and Moreno discussing our son made blood rush to my fists, as if another man was encroaching on my territory, and I sensed a coming fight. Taking a deep breath, I exhaled in a slow, controlled stream of air, looked at Abby, and gave the only response that made any sense.

"We don't have the money for private school, Ab. We can't afford the tuition."

*

Hands balled into fists, I walked into Talley's and spotted Dave and Charlie in a booth near a plasma TV. On the big screen, the Lakers mounted a comeback against the Suns, and every time Kobe shot, Manker's pounding fists shook a forest of beer bottles resting on the table. As the pounding continued, some tipped over like felled trees. The Lakers were losing, and Dave wasn't happy. From what I knew, he gambled heavily but wasn't highly skilled. According to Kate Sawyer, one year he owed money to loan sharks and borrowed against his house to pay off the debt. With the real estate crash, that was no longer an option.

I pushed through the crowd and joined them. Talley's was in north Pomona on Route 66, the clientele a mix of college kids and blue-collar drunks, watching the game. A few serious drinkers—apparently not Lakers fans—sat at the bar and stared into deep glasses, lost in whatever dreams they sought beneath the ice.

"You want a beer?" Moreno raised his voice against the noise as the Lakers went down by six. He lifted his bottle and took a sip. The bottle was full, which meant Dave was doing most of the drinking. A bad sign.

"No thanks."

Dave shot me a look. "About damn time, Boyd." Manker glared across the table and lifted a bottle.

"What's this about the police, Dave?"

167

Manker didn't respond. Ignoring the question, he pounded the table as Kobe stole the ball, went the length of the court, and slammed for two. More beer bottles fell.

"Dave?"

Dave glanced over, kicked a chair toward me and frowned. "Keep your panties on and take a seat. The game's almost over."

I ignored the chair. "Did you call Danny and Ken? If the police are asking questions, they should be here."

Dave shot me a glare. "They don't know what happened, Boyd. We didn't tell them. At least, I didn't. Charlie didn't. What about you?"

After the beating in the park the previous night, we'd told Danny and Ken there had been a scuffle, but nothing more. Dave said the fewer people who knew, the better. Now I sensed a shift and decided the more people who knew, the better. With multiple stories, each one different, police interest was bound to grow. Moreno would feel heat. Maybe enough to leave the neighborhood. I glanced at the Mexican and felt a surge of power sweep down my arms and into my fists. Then I looked back at Dave.

"I didn't tell anyone."

Dave guzzled beer and slammed the bottle down onto the table. "Well someone did. Sergeant Mackay left a message, asked if we saw anything last night. Said there'd been an anonymous tip someone had been assaulted, maybe killed. They were up there today looking around."

"Killed?"

Dave clenched his teeth, keeping his voice low. "Don't give me that look, Boyd. We knocked the guy around a little, but he was breathing when we left. Anyway, I called the PD. They didn't find anything. I told Mackay we saw a homeless guy, asked him to leave the park, and that was that. If you get a phone call, that's our story."

The Lakers took a timeout.

Dave steamed and went to the bathroom.

I almost followed him, but Moreno reached out and stopped me. "Let it wait," he said. "Dave will be nicer when his bladder's empty."

I sat.

Moreno shot me a frown.

"You seem agitated, Jack."

On TV, the Laker girls danced. I lifted an empty bottle and signaled the hostess to bring me a beer. "I'd rather be home, resting on my couch."

Moreno nodded. "So go home. I can handle Dave."

The killer sat with his back to a wall, near a walkway with a clear view of the front door and the bathroom. His head moved on a constant swivel, clocking the room, stopping on me every now and then. Nobody would sneak up on him, that much was sure, and if he needed to make a quick exit, he had no doubt already chosen the way.

"It's not that easy," I said flatly. "That thing with the old man...it was wrong."

Moreno frowned. "Wrong enough for you to call the police?"

He's a businessman closing a deal. Anything spooks him, he'll leave.

"I didn't call anyone. But maybe we should."

Moreno lowered his bottle, kept one hand around the neck and smiled weakly. "Meaning what?"

"Meaning we should tell them what happened."

"You're serious?"

"The old guy attacked us. We need to explain our version of events before he does."

"And in that version, will you explain how you held the man down while Dave beat him?"

I glanced back at the TV as the hostess arrived with my beer. After paying, I drained half the bottle, looked across the table and washed hesitation from my throat. "I don't want you giving educational advice to my wife, Charlie."

"Excuse me?"

"Your brother having autism doesn't make you an expert any more than having bad ankles in the army makes you a doctor. When it comes to my family, I'll rely on experts, if you don't mind."

"Jack, I don't think you—"

"So what school did your brother go to? Where was it located? I wasn't aware Mexico sets the bar when it comes to treating autism."

Moreno looked at the TV and said nothing.

"That's what I thought. Do you even have a brother?"

On TV, the timeout was about to end. Dave Manker stepped from the bathroom and wobbled through the crowd. When he passed by a couple ladies, they spun suddenly, as if he'd touched them.

"Dave is different around you," I said.

"Meaning what?"

"Dave's always been an ass, but he was never violent. Now you show up, and he changes. The neighborhood changes. I hate change. People are going to notice changes like that. Yeah, they'll notice."

Moreno flashed a thin smile.

"Jack, I think you should go home."

"Maybe I should. Or maybe I should go to the police."

Choking down the last of my beer, I felt a sudden chill and decided not to push things further. A few beats passed before Moreno broke the silence.

"Everything changes, Jack."

"Whatever. I didn't come here to argue."

"Not an argument," he said. "A friendly disagreement."

I looked back at Moreno. "We're friends?"

Moreno nodded. "Of course."

"I'm glad to hear that. But you scare me."

For the first time, uncertainty creased the Mexican's face. His lips got that twitch. I ignored it and concentrated on Dave as he took a seat. "We need to talk, Dave. This thing that happened last night can't happen again. I haven't said anything to the cops yet, but I think we should. The patrols have to stop."

"Bullshit."

"I'll talk to the rest of the guys, tell them what happened. They won't be part of it. Things got out of hand. We need to pull the plug before somebody gets hurt bad."

Dave looked at the TV. "Keep your dress on, Boyd. We'll talk about it later. The game's almost finished."

"There's nothing to talk about. Stop the patrols, or I'll go to the police. They'll want to talk to us." I glanced at Moreno. "All of us."

"Don't be a pussy, Boyd."

"Dave, you're the one who beat the shit out of an old man. If anyone's manhood is in question, I'd say it's yours."

Dave's face morphed from irritation to rage. He fixed me with a glare and pointed toward the door. "Whatever your problem is, when we get outside, you'd better be prepared to settle it."

Dave got up and went outside.

Like an idiot, I followed.

*

Dark and wet, the alley ran between the bar and a dry cleaner, and Dave waited beside a Dumpster beneath Talley's neon sign, bobbing with his fists up. Moving from side to side, his shoes danced over pavement, squawking like sticky hinges on a warped door. Even with him drunk, there was no way I could win a fight.

"Let's go home," I said. "We'll talk about this tomorrow."

"You can't screw things up for me, Boyd."

I lifted my hands in surrender. "That's fine, Dave. Let's go home. We'll settle it later."

Dave stopped dancing. "Going to the cops? Think about what you're doing. The cops find out what happened last night and I'm losing my job. I did what needed done. Necessary force, Boyd. Keeping your family safe."

I tried to move past him.

Dave grabbed my shoulder and spun me around. His punch drove into my guts, nearly cracked my spine, and dropped me to the pavement, gasping for air. Curled into a ball, I sucked wind for several beats, smelled drenched garbage and glimpsed pink rats scuttling under the neon glow. When at last I grabbed a breath, I rolled onto my back while Dave pranced over me like a strutting rooster, shaking out his fists as if they had cramped.

"You happy, Boyd? You feel better? Don't even think about getting up, or the next one goes in your teeth."

I tried not to puke, pushed up on a knee and attempted to stand.

Dave grinned as if someone had just given him an early birthday present. "I told you to stay down." He darted forward, swung for my head, and missed. As I ducked, momentum carried him past me like a Matador overshooting a bull, and his face slammed into Talley's brick wall, cracking his nose.

"Shit!" he grunted.

Standing in the alley, ignoring my rolling guts, I held up my fists.

Dave touched his nose and saw blood. "Dammit, Boyd. What the hell?"

I took a swing and missed.

Dave spat blood and laughed. "You fight like a woman. Hey, did you see that swing? He fights like a fucking girl."

Someone had stepped into the alley. I turned to look.

Near the street, bathed in neon, Moreno leaned against the wall holding a cell phone. At first, I thought the Mexican was calling the cops, and then realized the chance of that was zero. Standing there, head shaking in a scolding fashion, his face registered amused boredom, as if watching two boys fight in a schoolyard.

"Boyd isn't man enough to protect his family," shouted Dave. "So when I step in and do his duty, he gets pissy."

Moreno shrugged. "The Lakers lost."

Dave threw up his hands. "There goes another two grand. Get out of my way, Boyd, or I'm kicking your ass." Dave pushed past, then stopped and smiled. "Oh yeah, one more thing. If Abby gets tired of your wilted dick, send her across the street. I'll take care of her."

My punch caught Dave on the point of his chin and drove him into the wall.

Stunned by the impact, his eyes grew wide. He lifted both hands, shielded his face, and began searching for an opening to retaliate.

I never gave him the chance.

Punching low, I caught him square in the guts and felt vomit spray as he tossed his dinner into the alley. As he dropped, I drove a knee toward his head, thinking of Abby and the kids, of Danny Devlin and Leland Reed, of Moreno and Fisk, of everything that had happened over the past week, and how badly I wanted Dave Manker to pay for it all.

Then everything went black.

MICHAEL HARBISON

Chapter Eighteen

Detective Vasquez sat across the table, holding a pen, tapping a beat on a yellow legal pad. Tired of talking, I paused and tried to swallow, felt a lump of sand in my throat, as if someone had fed me a bowl of Death Valley for breakfast. The empty water bottle offered no help, and from the impatient look on the detective's face, my thirst would only grow.

"What about MicroLine, Mr. Boyd?"

"I need to use the phone."

"Not yet."

"Am I under arrest?"

"We need to finish this interview. Tell me about MicroLine."

I could walk out, call Abby, and then come back in after making the call. Vasquez couldn't stop me without placing me under arrest. But that would strip the veneer of cooperation between us, and I'd find myself locked in a basement cell waiting for a lawyer. I still hoped to avoid that, planned to hold on for Fisk to arrive and dig me out of the hole. That said, I couldn't stop thinking about my family.

"My wife and kids, Detective. I need to know they're okay."

Vasquez clicked his pen. "Give me that number again. I'll have someone call."

He took down our voicemail number and code again and nodded toward the mirrored glass wall. Seconds later, the door opened and the same cop took the number, slipping Vasquez a note before he disappeared. Glancing at the camera, my gaze locked onto the flashing red light.

What had I said?

What had I left out?

The truth had been my goal, but the truth was now a distant land, and I had lost my map.

"Mr. Boyd?"

"Yeah, MicroLine. I'm getting there, Detective."

"You need to get there faster." Vasquez glanced at the paper the cop had handed him. "Here's some news. Patrol officers checked the house next door to yours. Except for old furniture and some boxes in the garage, it's abandoned. According to bank records, the place hasn't been occupied for months."

Moreno was gone.

"Talk to my neighbors. He was there. They saw him."

"Where is he now?"

"I have no idea. He dropped me at the airport last night and headed into one of the parking garages. I haven't seen him since."

"So, what? He finished his job and left?"

"I guess."

"Caught a plane back to Mexico?"

"Maybe."

"What happened last night at MicroLine?"

"You already know that."

"I know how the night ended. Now I'm interested in what came before."

I grabbed the water bottle, lifting it until a single filament of liquid dewed my tongue.

"Any word on Fisk?"

Detective Vasquez shot me a peeved expression. "Special Agent Fisk is on his way, but fed or no fed, you're in trouble, Mr. Boyd. What about MicroLine? Help me with the progression. How does Moreno moving next door end with you attempting murder?"

"I didn't hurt Roger."

"Who's Roger?"

"The guard."

"Oh, right. Moreno did it?"

"Yes."

"But he was smart enough to wear a mask and gloves, and except for an hour or two at your barbecue, none of your neighbors spent much time around the guy, so they can't really describe him beyond tall, dark, and good looking."

"Dave was around him the most," I said.

Detective Vasquez tapped the pad. "Dave Manker is not answering his phone, and no one is at his house. His car was found yesterday morning, abandoned. Could you tell me anything about that? Is it possible he's paired up with Moreno?"

I stared up at the blinking red light. "No, it isn't possible."

Vasquez clicked his pen. "Why so certain?"

"I'm pretty sure Dave is dead."

MICHAEL HARBISON

Chapter Nineteen

Despite the sunlight in the bedroom, Abby's face wore darkness. She leaned over the bed, placed a hand on my shoulder, and rubbed tight circles on worn skin until I came to life. Every cell in my body ached. Nerves fired overtime, thumping in rapid heartbeats of pain, adding to a deep sense of confusion.

"You awake?"

"Barely alive."

I rolled over. The room burned, sun high, sheets soaked with sweat. I craved sleep like a junkie chasing a boost and smelled really bad. Around midnight, I had woken in the front seat of my Subaru outside Talley's, head pounding, clothes and body drenched in piss, unsure whether the urine was mine, or if it belonged to the steady stream of barflies swarming the tavern. Driving home in a fog, I watched the rearview mirror for cops, careful to stay within the lines and keep a few miles per hour below the speed limit. Once there, I'd killed the engine, stood on the grass staring at Dave's house, then at Moreno's, trying to remember. The images came in disconnected bursts, a reality fractured into a thousand jagged pieces by a hand grenade exploding in my head. After a shower in the downstairs bathroom, I had gone up to bed.

Rolling onto my back, I stretched until my stomach muscles seized, and I spotted a salt trail glinting on Abby's face, marking the last faint scar of a tear.

"What's wrong?"

She looked away. "Kate called."

"What now?"

"Dave's missing."

My eyes drifted to the sheets, where a fleck of blood stood out on the wrinkled plane of fabric. Bunched fists and coiled muscles. Flesh and bone flying through air, crushing flesh and bone. My fingers ached. I flexed them, listened to tendons pop, and then noticed the cuts.

Abby wiped fresh tears.

I swallowed hard. "Missing?"

"They found his car in Pomona. Blood was inside. Kate said he owed loan sharks again. My god, Jack, this happened to someone from our street. Is that what you guys talked about last night?"

I closed my eyes, trying to avoid the images, still just fragments but coming together now. A dark alley a few miles away. Voices flying. Fists landing. A crushing knee. Then what? It was as if a curtain had fallen before the third act of a play. The story was over. You could guess at what happened, but the ending remained unknown.

"When did they find the car?" I asked.

"Jesus, you were with him."

"Abby, when did they find the car?"

"This morning."

Just like that, she was in my arms, pressed hard against my chest, touching fresh bruises, sending nerves into a riot. I held her anyway. She smelled good—long, dark hair tinted with faint strawberry, clean face pressed against mine like a sheet of thin silk.

"I'm sorry," she wept. "The thing with Carter, your brother... None of it matters. None of it matters. Oh, God. Poor Dave."

My fingers ran through her hair, pulled her close. I held on for a long time, saying nothing. Months had passed since we'd rested on the bed in the sunlight. Despite its genesis, I wanted the moment to last, because once she learned the truth, it might never come again.

"Dave and I fought last night," I said at last.

Abby lifted her head from my chest. "Why?"

"He was drinking. We had an argument."

"About what?"

"Just…stuff."

Sensing evasion, she pulled hair from her eyes and fixed me with a glare. "What kind of stuff?"

I counted slow breaths, tried to decide what to tell her.

"What kind of stuff?" she repeated, tone shifting up a gear.

I took a deep breath and hewed close to the truth. "Dave beat up someone in the park on Thursday night."

She looked bewildered. "Why on earth would Dave beat someone? Who?"

"A homeless guy. I think he did it to impress Charlie."

"Charlie?" She looked even more confused. "And where were you?"

"Standing there, watching."

Abby stared in silence. Her jaw flexed, and when she spoke, the words came slowly, as if she had to force them from her mouth. "Do you know how crazy that sounds?"

"I know it sounds bad."

"And you two fought about this last night?"

"We argued. Charlie was around and, well, Dave was drinking. You know how that goes."

For a long time, Abby said nothing. I sat on the bed, looking at her, waiting for something to fill the silence. Then a rhythmic strike echoed from outside.

Thump.

Thump.

Thump.

I went to the window and looked down.

Tanned and sweating, Moreno stood astride a fresh trench in his front yard, driving a pickaxe into the ground. Walking away from him, as if they had just finished a conversation, a heavy man in a dark suit moved toward Dave's house. Glancing up at the apex of a swing, Moreno spotted me and grinned.

"Your hands are cut," Abby said.

I glanced down at my knuckles. "From working in Charlie's yard."

"I didn't notice them earlier."

"They're fine, Ab."

"Tell me one thing,"

I turned and faced her. "Anything."

"When you argued with Dave, did you hit him?"

Like the other times, I fixed her with a steady gaze, took a calming breath, and lied.

*

Three minutes later, I was getting dressed. Abby had gone downstairs as some kind of drama shaped up in the kitchen. Voices rose, then fell. Carter was whining. Then a furious scamper climbed the stairs. Seconds later, my son entered the bedroom, carrying my cell phone.

"Shouldn't you be watching cartoons?"

He climbed onto the bed. "Mom says no. The phone's for you."

He gave me the handset and dropped his voice to a whisper. "Dad, I want to go, too."

"Who's on the phone?"

"A man."

My guts twitched as if a parasite had crawled inside and squeezed out babies. I lifted the handset.

Carter kept whining. "Sara's going. I want to."

"Hello," I said.

"Jack, it's me."

Moreno.

"What do you want?"

"Go to the computer in the corner of your bedroom."

My eyes slid left of the window and focused on the desk. Was the workstation visible from outside? Had I mentioned it to Moreno, or had the Mexican been inside our house? A chill crystallized my blood.

"Don't panic," Moreno said. "Your actions in the next few minutes could save your family."

Something in the killer's voice had changed. The foreign cadence was gone, and the syntax had shifted from Old Mexico to pure Made in the USA.

I glanced at my son. "Go downstairs, buddy."

Carter frowned. "I'm going with Sara," he said, then rolled off the bed and left the room.

Rising on shaky legs, I went to the computer and turned on the monitor. "What's going on, Charlie?"

"You'll see. Go to this website." Moreno read out an internet address.

I waited for the page to load as laughter burst from beyond the window. I went to the glass and looked down. Outside, my kids held beach towels and walked into Moreno's backyard, headed for the pool. I covered the phone, was about to yell for Abby when the webpage loaded and an image appeared on the screen.

Me throwing a punch at Dave Manker's head.

"Do you see it?"

I took a moment to uncork my tongue.

"Yes."

"One frame, but the entire fight is on video. They found Dave's car this morning with blood inside. From what I see in that picture, you're hitting him. I'm sure you know how that looks."

My lungs seized. I glanced out the window and searched for my kids.

"I didn't hurt Dave."

"Really? Do you remember? Anyway, it doesn't matter. Once the police see the video they'll pull you in for questioning. Your family will be alone."

"What do you want?"

"You're going to do something for me."

"What?"

"I'll tell you tonight. Until then, everything stays cool. Don't do anything stupid, and the video disappears. Fuck with me, and your family disappears."

The hardwood floor collapsed beneath me then, the chair and desk sucked into a black hole, my body tumbling toward its center. Somehow, I knew the fall would end in hell. The electric pain, the sickening numbness, the barely remembered crunch of flesh on bone all caught up with me, and bile rushed into my throat. Then I stared out the window and listened to my kids play in the killer's pool.

"You're about to have a visitor," Moreno said. "A cop asking about Dave."

I glanced toward the driveway, spotted the man in the suit crossing the street and heading toward my house.

"Be smart, Boyd. Make him happy. Send him on his way, and this will end tonight. Get stupid, and your kids will drown in my pool."

Chapter Twenty

Vons parking lot, Saturday night at a quarter past nine. Thirty minutes earlier, I'd told Abby I needed to go to work. Moreno's call had come after dinner, instructing me to meet him in the parking lot at nine-thirty. I wanted to get there early, give myself time to prepare. Devlin's revolver had been in my desk, and no matter what Moreno had in mind, I didn't plan to arrive empty-handed, so DRI had been my first stop.

For most of the day, I'd sat at the computer in my bedroom, pretending to work. The cop had asked common questions. When did you last see Dave Manker? Do you know anyone who would harm him? What happened to your hands? Afterward, I'd gone into Moreno's backyard and ordered the kids out of the pool. Unimpressed, Moreno had shrugged and told me to wait for his call. Once the kids were home, I called Special Agent Fisk half a dozen times, got nothing but his voicemail, and left a string of abusive messages.

He never called back.

At DRI, I'd retrieved the gun from my office, snapped up some bullets, and pulled the hammer back a few times. Again, the barrel quaked. I probably couldn't hit an elephant. All the same, I put on my jacket and tucked the gun into a pocket, then opened my cell and dialed Ran's number.

He answered on the third ring.

"What's up?"

"That thing you said about needing you?"

"Yeah?"

"Well, I do. An hour from now, I want you to go to my house, pick up Abby and the kids, and take them somewhere."

"What's going on? Take them where?"

"Out of the city. Somewhere crowded where you won't stand out. Call when you get there, but not my cell. I won't be able to talk. Leave a message on the home voicemail. Let me know you're okay, but don't say where you are. No matter where you stay tonight, in the morning, I want you to move. Keep doing that until you hear from me."

"What the hell is going on?"

"They're in danger, Ran, and I can't go to the police. You have to do this for me."

"Okay, but—"

I hung up and went to my car.

Two minutes later, heading north, I called Abby.

"There's a problem," I said.

"What?"

"This thing with Dave...the police called. They need to talk. You might have been right. They think Dave was gambling again. He owed money."

"Oh my god."

"There's something else, Ab."

"What?"

The lies came easily now.

"Whoever hurt Dave was probably following him last night. They saw me. Maybe I saw them. That makes me a potential witness, and the police aren't sure we're safe. I've called Ran. He's coming to get you and the kids to take you somewhere secure."

"But—"

"No arguments this time. I want you to do what I say."

A long pause, then she swallowed my lie. "What about you?"

"Me?" I pressed the gas, ran a red light, and felt the gun press my ribs. "I'll be fine."

*

At Vons, a crow skipped under the orange lights illuminating the parking lot, carrying a dead rat in its beak. The rat weighed too much, and every time the crow lifted off, it rose a few yards and sank back to the ground. After a while, the bird got tired of waiting and pecked the rat among the cars and empty shopping carts. Before the feast concluded, Moreno pulled up and the crow flew away.

The Mexican walked to my car and tapped the glass.

I lowered my window. He peered over my shoulder, past the back seat.

"No trunk?"

"Just a hatch," I said.

"We'll take my car."

I got out and followed him. His vehicle had changed. No longer a dented Ford Taurus, it had morphed into a Red Mazda 6. As I thought back, the change had occurred a few days ago. I settled into the passenger seat and he started the engine. Then he looked at me for several beats.

"Cell phone?"

"In my jacket."

"Take it out, strip the battery, and throw the battery out the window."

When I leaned forward to toss the battery, his hands pushed into my back, frisking my jacket.

"What's this?" He reached into my pocket and pulled out Mrs. Selig's hard drives. I had forgotten about them. "These are disks," he said.

"They're from work. They have nothing to do with you."

"Then you shouldn't have brought them." He tossed the drives into the back seat and finished his search. When his fingers touched Devlin's gun, relief and dread ran though me in a single rush. Moreno lifted the weapon.

"I have to tell you, Boyd, I'm impressed."

I said nothing. He opened the cylinder and checked the bullets.

".357 hollow points. Enough to remove a head. You know how to use this?"

"What happened to Dave?"

He closed the cylinder, lifted the weapon, and sighted down the barrel. "You tell me. Last I saw, he was unconscious and you were kicking him in the face."

"Is he alive?"

"Far as I know." Moreno pointed the gun at a woman leaving the store. Took in the trigger slack. "Do you know how to use this?"

"You squeeze the trigger. People die."

Moreno pulled a face and shook his head. "It should be that simple, really, but it's not. Here, I'll show you."

He flipped open the cylinder and shook the rounds into his lap. Then he chose one, reloaded, gave the cylinder a whirl, and snapped it closed. He proffered the weapon to me with one hand, then produced his own gun with the other and placed it on his lap.

"I'll make you a deal. Take your gun, aim at my head, and pull the trigger. That's a one-in-six chance of ending things here and now. Decent bet, Boyd. One in six. Everything ends. All you need is enough luck to find the bullet and enough balls to pull the trigger."

I looked at Devlin's gun. My hand rose to grab it.

Moreno's mouth got that twitch.

"Of course, you can't bet without putting up something to lose." The twitch became a grin. "If the hammer falls on an empty chamber, I'll leave here, go back to your house, and kill your family. Maybe, if I'm feeling generous, I'll spare one of your kids and take them with me. When they grow tiresome, I'll send you pieces in the mail from time to time."

My hand fell to my lap. I stared out the window.

"Good choice, neighbor." He stashed the .357 beside the driver's seat and tucked his own weapon between his legs. "It's going to be a long night. We need to get started."

"Where are we going?"

Moreno considered his response, and the twitch returned.

"Into the past."

MICHAEL HARBISON

Chapter Twenty-One

Forty minutes later, we crested Cajon Summit, and the high desert communities glowed in the darkness like glitter in a pool of motor oil. Victorville, Hesperia, Apple Valley. Epicenters of the housing boom, places where half-million dollar homes in a landscape from hell once seemed like a good idea. That night, moving north along the freeway, every third or fourth house bore vacant windows, and half the streets looked deserted. As Marty Goodman always said, you may sow the wind, but some day, the whirlwind comes to collect.

Five miles from the summit, past the junction for Highway 395, Moreno flicked his signal and got off at Main Street, then turned east. We stopped at a red light, and cold air seeped through the glass.

"Hungry, Jack?" He smiled at his joke and pointed across the road at a dusty In-N-Out Burger joint and a half-empty Denny's. "My treat, but we'll need to use the drive-thru."

I said nothing.

"Have you spent much time in the desert?" he asked.

I glanced at the clock. Almost ten-thirty. An hour had passed. Ran should have collected Abby and the kids. They would be heading out of the city. All I had to do was go along for Moreno's ride, keep him in sight, and they would get away. That's what I told myself—whatever happened, my family would get away.

Moreno waited on an answer.

"I hate the desert," I said.

The light turned green. Moreno pressed the gas. I tilted my chin and looked into the sideview mirror, noting a dark van getting off the freeway, shadowing four or five lengths back. Were the feds trailing us? My heart rate kicked up as the headlights grew intense. Then the van blasted past, turned down a dirt road leading into the desert, and became a pair of receding taillights.

Ten minutes later, housing tracts ended and Main Street became Rock Springs Road. Soon after, we came to a bridge over a dry scar torn into the desert's skin. An optimistic sign declared the scar a river. The Mojave. Turning off asphalt, Moreno drove onto a dirt strip, made a hard left onto river sand and pulled under the bridge. Killing the engine, he removed the gun from between his legs and looked over at me.

"This is it, Boyd. Time to go."

Out in the dark, a thin, black strip oozed along the river bottom. Nothing grew down there. No trees. No shrubs. Just dirt. An open killing ground providing nowhere to run. Moreno waved his gun, urging me out. I opened the door, trying to control my breathing, noting the air's damp chill, which seemed odd for the desert, like the dark corner of a basement.

Moreno walked over to my side and tapped his gun against his thigh.

"You don't have to do this," I said.

"You have a better option?"

"Whatever your job is, I won't interfere."

"You're not making sense, Boyd."

"I can help you."

"Okay. So help me."

I sucked a deep breath, pushed panic from my voice, and bet my last chip.

"The FBI has you under surveillance. They've been following you. They know you're here. The lead agent's name is Fisk. He came to my house before you arrived. They're probably following us right now."

"Really?"

"They'll arrest you."

Moreno glanced up at the bridge as a car moved across. I prayed for brake lights. The vehicle traversed the span and kept moving.

Moreno lifted the gun. "Really, the FBI?"

"You can leave. There's time. You don't have to do this."

"That's a good story, Boyd. And I do need your help. That's why you're here." He lifted his car keys, popped the trunk, and then nudged me forward. "You can't see where we're going, though. Get inside the trunk and relax. I'm not going to hurt you. Tonight, we're partners."

*

Miles later, asphalt turned to dirt and dirt became washboard. The trunk was a cave, opacity receding only when Moreno tapped the brakes, turning the interior into a dusty red fog. I sucked air and told myself every mile we drove took us farther from Abby and the kids, carving a buffer of safety around them. Time ceased. Minutes turned to hours, hours became seconds. I held on until a final set of bumps knocked air from my lungs, and we stopped. Minutes later the trunk popped open. From the night sky, stars looked down, and the wind blew hard from the west carrying the sound of a distant swarm of bees.

Moreno pulled me out and offered a water bottle. A gym bag sat at his feet.

"Sorry, Jack. You're a mess."

I washed my mouth and spat three geysers of dirt before I could swallow any water. We'd driven to the edge of the world. To the east, an abyss populated by the Milky Way's streaky brush filled the sky. City glow dominated the west. No other sound except the wind and that whine of bees, growing strong and then dying, as if the swarm raced in circles, half the time moving toward us and half moving away.

Clutching the gym bag, Moreno pointed up the road and told me to follow. A hundred yards later, we crested a small rise that looked down on a boulder-filled valley. Planted in the middle of the depression, a doublewide trailer encircled by high fencing and floodlights sat amid a sea of cars. Near the edge of the fence, an Airstream RV, sporting a handicap access ramp, gleamed under the lights.

Moreno reached out, gave me the bag. "Go down and hand that over."

Something inside the bag gave it weight.

"You know about biker gangs, Jack?" He nodded toward the doublewide. "Aryan Outlaws. Inside prison, my skin would be too brown for them, but out here, they like the green of my money. The old man calls himself Keller. Give him the bag. He'll give you what we need."

My eyes drifted toward the cars. Something moved within their shadows.

Moreno tapped my shoulder and grinned. "If things go wrong, try not to look scared, and hit fast and hard…You'll need to make an impression."

*

No one dodges a bullet. Just the same, heading toward the fence, I wanted to run. I did a quick calculation and decided the odds of Moreno nailing a moving target at distance with a handgun at night were long. Most cops said anything past a hundred yards took an exceptional shooter. Considering his profession, Moreno could probably shoot, but at night, with a little luck, I might get away.

But what then?

Judging by the city glow, help was miles off, and without a phone, I'd wander the desert for hours. How would that help Abby and the kids? If things hadn't gone just right at home, Moreno would drive back to College Heights and—

Cutting the thought mid-stream, ignoring the pull of the desert, I continued downhill.

Near the fence, a washboard road carved a half-circle around the property, climbed a rocky hillside, and then disappeared beyond range of the floodlights. Within the chain-link compound, cars sat neatly aligned as if riding a dealer's lot.

New.

Used.

Scrap.

Keller had them all.

At the fence line, a chain-link tunnel capped by razor wire ran to the doublewide trailer's front door. A wrought-iron gate blocked entry, and an intercom sat beside the gate. Glancing back, unsure of what to do, I looked to Moreno for guidance. He was gone. I tapped the intercom as a yappy dog barked from inside the trailer. Seconds later, the intercom sparked to life and the barking amplified.

"You're late."

The voice sounded old and pissed off.

My eyes fell to the bag. "I'm here to see Keller. Moreno sent me. I have the bag."

Seconds ticked by.

"Bastard wrecked my car. Put a gouge down the side. Going to need a new quarter panel. Leave the bag at the fence and get the hell out. We'll call it square."

A sound came from near the cars then, wind dragging sand over concrete, a creeping tick, tick, tick. Refocusing on the intercom, I leveled my voice, ironing out the fear.

"He didn't mention your car. You're supposed to have something for me. I'm to give you the bag."

"What am I supposed to have?"

"He didn't say."

Seconds ticked. "You're an errand boy?"

"I guess so."

"Then you'd better come inside. We'll talk. But don't think I'm forgetting the car."

The gate buzzed.

I was about to step in when the voice came back.

"Here's the best piece of advice you'll get all night, errand boy. Enter that tunnel, walk a straight line, and keep that bag away from the goddamn fence. I don't want to lose my money, and you probably want to keep your hands."

Two paces inside the tunnel, the dog hit the fence at full throttle, jaws snapping, a metallic river of sound trailing in its wake. Jumping back, pressed against the far side of the chain-link, I tried melting away but sensed another charge coming from behind. That dog was bigger, trailed another long chain, and hit with enough power to bow the fence. Unable to reach me, both snapped mouthfuls of air, but their jaws moved silently, and in the floodlight's glare, I spotted notched scars above their furless throats.

Someone had removed the voice boxes.

Silent killers.

A perfect security system.

An old man in a wheelchair with a Chihuahua on his lap frowned up at me when I reached the trailer. "You met the children, I see. Told you to stay away from the fence."

He grinned and waved me inside.

Hillbilly chic, the trailer's furnishings matched the lonely desert locale—sandblasted carpet, sun-rotted furniture—but Keller didn't live alone. Two bikers rode a sofa in the living room and watched a porn flick on an RCA console TV that probably still used tubes. They shot twin glares in my direction. One held a sawed-off shotgun, looked on a few seconds as I entered the room, and then resumed watching the show. The other followed each step of my entry, chin pointed at my head like the hot barrel of a gun.

I had seen the type when visiting my brother in Pelican Bay.

Aryans.

Biker trash.

Keller pointed at the watcher and nodded. "Get off your lazy ass."

The biker stood, moved close, ordered me to lift my hands.

"Lose the bag," he commanded.

Falling to the carpet, the bag made a loud thump.

He picked some kind of wand off the coffee table and ran it over me. The wand squeaked. The biker seemed unconcerned. Not wanting to seem weak, I puffed my chest.

"I just need Moreno's stuff. Then I'll leave. I don't want any trouble."

The guy's brown eyes grew black. "That's not how it works."

Biker two fingered the shotgun.

Keller stroked the Chihuahua and laughed. "Take off your clothes, errand boy, so we can look at your balls. Whenever cops are wired, it's always under their balls."

"I'm no cop."

"Yeah, I can tell. You look ready to piss yourself. All the same, I wanna see your nuts."

Biker two pointed both barrels at my neck.

I unbuttoned my pants. Thirty seconds later, I stood naked in front of them.

Keller had me lift my scrotum and spread my ass. All of them laughed. Keller allowed me to dress.

"Stop watching that filth," he ordered the men. "Bring the stuff to the kitchen."

Biker two got up, hefted the shotgun, and vanished into a back room.

Keller looked up at me and shrugged. "What can I say? They're grown men, but I don't approve of their addiction. It's not godly, watching people screw. Most nights I stay in the Airstream. That grunting makes sleeping damned hard."

He led me down a hall.

Biker one followed, holding the bag. A semi-automatic poked from his waistband.

In the kitchen, something acidic and chemical deflowered the air. Trying not to breathe, I surveyed the décor. It was different from the living room, as if Martha Stewart had gone to Corcoran State Prison and decorated Charles Manson's cell. Plush drapes covered a sliding-glass door that led to the yard, and a warped table, wood so dry it looked like bone, sat beneath a flickering fluorescent light. Food containers littered the countertops and a minefield of dog turds smeared the linoleum, adding to the ambiance. Judging by the smell, the place needed a scrubdown from a nuclear decontamination team.

Keller wheeled around the table and parked his chair. The Chihuahua yapped.

Biker two stepped into the kitchen, carrying a backpack. He placed it at my feet and took the gym bag from Biker one. When he opened it, bundles of cash spilled out.

"Count it," Keller ordered.

Resting the shotgun on his shoulder, the man took the bag to another room.

Keller looked at me, then at the backpack. "You should check the product."

My heart skipped. "I'm not part of this," I said.

"That's right. An errand boy. Not curious what you're picking up?"

"Not really."

Keller nodded toward the bag. "Guy I know down south contracts with the government to destroy shells on a gunnery range."

"I don't care."

Keller grinned. "Money's money, right? I'm with you. Don't give a shit who pays me. Jews, niggers, spics. Sometimes it's better the buyer isn't white. You know, mud people using the stuff against each other. But nigger, spic, or Jew, I never met anyone who handed over cash without checking merchandise, unless he planned on ripping me off."

My mouth filled with sand. I opened the bag and looked inside.

Paper-wrapped bricks and a couple of things that looked like grenades.

"Military thermite," Keller said. "Melt to China if you're not careful."

Zipping the backpack, I nodded toward the door. "Can I go?"

Keller shook his head. Then the guy with the shotgun came back into the room and dropped Moreno's gym bag onto the table. "It's light," he said. "By at least three grand."

Keller frowned.

Biker two continued with the bad news. "And this was below the cash." He flashed Devlin's .357, and then moved toward me, raising the sawed-off.

I took a step back, lifted my hands. "That's not min—"

The shotgun punched my guts, drove air from my lungs, and dropped me to the linoleum. Before I could inhale, the Chihuahua had my pant leg in its teeth, working toward skin.

Keller wheeled close and swatted the dog away.

The room went quiet.

My lungs tapped out a rhythm as I tried to breathe.

IN.

OUT.

IN.

OUT.

When the pain died, I looked at Keller. "You don't understand."

"I know," he smiled. "You're the errand boy."

"That's right."

Keller nodded toward the shotgun. Biker two stepped forward and pressed the barrels against my left knee. His trigger finger twitched.

Then the lights went out.

Biker two wavered in the half-dark, first pointing his weapon at me, then into the living room. He moved toward the sliding glass door then, and biker one followed. They never made it.

A shadow darkened the night beyond the glass, and two bright explosions blasted through and dropped both men to the floor. Seconds later, Moreno stepped through the shattered door, picked up the bikers' weapons, and pointed the shotgun at Keller.

"You okay, Boyd?"

He pulled me to my feet.

On the floor, the bikers groaned as the Chihuahua orbited, barking and snapping.

Looking down at them, I felt nothing but rage.

Moreno retrieved his gym bag and picked up the backpack. He switched the money to the backpack, put something inside the gym bag, and flashed a grin. "They were going to shoot you." He nodded at the shotgun and offered it to me. "Time for payback, if you want."

"What the fuck are we doing here?"

Moreno smiled. "Invigorating, isn't it?"

"They were about to kill me."

The Mexican shook his head. "That was never part of the plan. I'd have been here sooner, but cutting through the fence took time, and the dog was hard to kill. Your diversion worked, though, so well done."

Glancing at his hands, I noticed something dark with the consistency of blood.

"Spic!" Keller shouted. "You're dead."

Moreno frowned. "Technically, a spic is a Puerto Rican. I'm Mexican. That makes you ignorant, racist, and handicapped. A poor combination to be issuing threats."

One of the moaning bikers tried to get up. Moreno kicked both men until their moaning stopped. Each had a gunshot wound to the upper leg, and bleeding looked profuse. Within minutes, Moreno had bound them with duct tape, tipped Keller out of his wheelchair, and led me outside. He went back into the kitchen then, and an audible hiss filled the air, as if he were pissing on the bikers. I smelled gas soon after. Seconds later, he dragged Keller through the dirt and dumped the old man behind one of the cars. Then he pushed me away from the compound, up the hill. When we reached the Mazda, I started to shake. Picturing dark blood pooled on linoleum, I imagined my family drowning in a red sea.

When I looked down at the trailer, Keller squirmed in the dirt like a worm.

"They'll bleed to death."

"No, they won't." Moreno put the backpack in the car and opened the trunk. "Anyway, what do you care? They were going to kill you."

"You set me up."

"I saved your life. A little gratitude seems appropriate."

"You knew there wasn't enough money in that bag."

Moreno shrugged. "I was short on cash. You kept them busy while I got close. I'm serious, Boyd, you make a good partner."

"They almost shot me."

"I offered you the shotgun. You had your chance for revenge."

I sucked a few breaths. The air had gone frigid. No longer autumn, but sharp and biting, like deep winter. "I'm not a killer."

He patted my shoulder as if consoling me. "Give yourself time, Boyd."

Below us, the extinguished floodlights left the valley black. Looking down, I felt like a depressed man on a high bridge, contemplating a leap into a river, wanting the black water to swallow me and end the nightmare. Then I pictured Abby and the kids.

They needed me.

Survive the night.

By any means, survive the night.

That became my mantra.

I was about to get into the trunk when Moreno stopped me. He reached into his jacket and pulled out a cell phone. Flipping it over, he inserted the battery and handed the phone to me.

"Dial a number for me."

I took the phone, looked at the doublewide, and hesitated.

Moreno lifted his gun and uttered a string of digits.

My fingers moved automatically.

My thumb hovered over the send button as I stared at the keypad.

"Don't make me do this."

"You've done so well, Jack."

"Is it over after this?"

Moreno smiled and shook his head. "Over, no, but it's a good start."

Reaching out, he cradled my palm as if cupping the hand of a child, then pressed my thumb. The call went through. The ground shook. Keller's doublewide became a ball of white flame.

Chapter Twenty-Two

Moreno pulled me from the trunk outside Phelen, then we headed south on the I-15, watching the Inland Empire grow into a pink corona of intersecting light and gloom. Dust choked my throat, so I said nothing as we drove through the Cajon pass, just thought of Abby and the kids, imagining them safe and far away. The Mexican remained silent, and I tried not to look at him. Thirty minutes later, after transitioning onto the I-10, we exited the freeway at Haven in Ontario, and MicroLine headquarters came into view.

A bomb detonated in my belly then, the blast illuminating an obvious conclusion that had somehow eluded me until that moment. Moreno's arrival next door, his integration into the neighborhood, the reason behind my involvement—none of it had been random. How could I have missed the signs? MicroLine held some kind of evidence damaging to the cartel. Moreno was here to destroy it, and I was his ticket inside.

Then I started to laugh.

Moreno looked at me as if I had snapped.

"You've been misinformed," I said. "I no longer work for them."

He gave a sharp frown. "Cheer up, Boyd. This will be over soon."

"You don't understand. Whoever provided your intelligence, you should consider shooting them. I don't work for MicroLine anymore. I can't help you."

"Don't sell yourself short, Boyd. You can help."

"What do you want from me?"

"We have work." He pointed at the building. "In there."

Glancing in the sideview mirror, I checked for anyone behind us. Traffic streamed past on the freeway, but we sat on the off ramp alone. Fisk claimed the FBI knew Moreno's target. So why weren't feds surrounding us? Why hadn't they pulled us over on the freeway? Why had those men died in the desert? Suarez's story about the SIS came to mind. Waiting until crimes occurred before taking down bad guys. Did the feds use the same field manual? Was that Fisk's plan? Follow until Moreno completed his task. Then what, open fire? Or had Fisk's priorities changed?

We need to follow Moreno and see where he leads. Then we can pressure the Mexican government to go after Aldama.

From the start, breaking the cartel had been Fisk's goal, Moreno a stepping-stone, Aldama the prime target. If so, then the feds might not be watching, which meant I might be alone. The night really had become a matter of survival.

I looked at Moreno.

"I'll help get you inside, but no killing."

Moreno reached under the seat and flashed his gun. At some point, he had attached a suppressor. "Too late for that, Jack. You pressed that button, remember?"

A truck blew through the intersection then. Lights flashed, and I saw Keller's trailer exploding in the night, a bright flare illuminating the old man as he lay in the dirt. He may have survived, but the bikers in the trailer were surely dead.

"I had no choice."

"What makes you think you have one now?" Moreno pointed the gun at MicroLine. "Our businesses are similar. In there, you've crushed competitors. Used associates for personal gain. Those are acts of violence, right? Stopping short of bloodshed, perhaps, but acts of violence nonetheless. Business is war. Damage is done. Lives ruined. Careers destroyed. Our worlds aren't so different."

The light turned green. Moreno hit his blinker and resumed driving.

"I won't hurt anyone else," I repeated.

Moreno's face grew stony. "I understand. My first killing was also difficult," he said. "I was fourteen. My father worked as a runner in Chihuahua, delivering marijuana and cocaine. Fast money, easy work, two qualities he admired most in a job. Regardless of how that sounds, I was happy he ran drugs. Before that time, his work involved pornography—sales, distribution, production—much of it sordid. Believe me, drug running was an improvement."

Through the windshield, MicroLine grew closer.

Moreno continued. "He worked for a man named Soto, a *narcotraficante* with the face of a pig. One night, at a police roadblock, my father panicked and lost a sizable amount of Soto's product. His solution was to get drunk and hide. One morning, on my way to school, Soto's men pulled me into their car. Soto thought my old man would come for me. He was wrong. For two months, I lived at Soto's ranch in the Sierra Madre. He fed me, gave me a room, taught me to shoot, even provided me with a tutor so I could continue my studies. My father never showed. He had tried abandoning me before, begged my mother to take me, even left me with nuns once. In truth, I was happier away from him. Then, one night after dinner, Soto said I was free, but that I must repay his hospitality with a favor. He had an old mule to put down. Soto pointed to a barn, handed me a gun loaded with a single bullet, and said once the mule was dead I could leave. I walked to the barn, went inside, and found my father chained to a post."

"I don't want to hear this."

"He was a drunk. An abuser of children and women. But he was *familia* and deserved a better death. So I killed Soto and fled, then listened to the screams as Soto's men hacked my father to pieces with machetes. They hunted me for months, but in Mexico, notoriety brings protection. Everyone wanted a piece of Soto's young assassin— competing traffickers, the police. You know, once you've killed a powerful man, anything seems possible."

"I'm not a killer."

"What if I had handed you the gun at Keller's trailer and told you the only way to save your family was by killing those men? Would you have done it?"

"I'm not like you."

"We're not that different, Boyd. Killing Soto wasn't easy, but in the process, I discovered a gift. Who knows? Had your life gone a different path, you might have been like me."

We pulled to a stop in front of MicroLine.

Moreno killed the engine and gazed up at the building. "Do what I tell you in there, and after tonight, you'll never see me again." He reached under the driver's seat, pulled out a mask—a clown with stiletto teeth— and put it over his head. Then he slipped on a pair of latex gloves.

I glanced inside the building at the radiant lobby.

A guard was behind the desk.

Saturday near midnight, Roger Saldana was hard at work, and death had just pulled to the curb.

*

Three years after my mom died, Bergeson Medical Instruments fired my dad for drinking on the job. By then, entrepreneurs could have bottled the old man's sweat as high-grade hooch, so finding new employment had proven tough. After months, he ended up pulling nighttime security work at a thoroughbred stud ranch in Saugus, selling hi-tech medical equipment one day, guarding horses that lived better than he did the next. It was a long fall, and he never really stuck the landing. Something about working late hours aged him at warp speed, and the despair turned him brutal. When Ran started getting in trouble at school, and then with the cops, Dad's solution was to beat him, sometimes until the kid could barely walk. At the time, my baseball skills were peaking, and with Marty Goodman's tutelage, I stood a decent chance at earning a scholarship from a good school. Preferably, one far away— Michigan, maybe Florida State. One night after dinner, when my dad was at work, Ran found my applications and confronted me, begging me not to leave, and I never forgot that look: pure panic capped by disbelief and betrayal. The same look I saw in Roger Saldana's eyes as we stepped into MicroLine's lobby and Moreno lifted his gun.

My impulse was to push Saldana into the building, tell him to lock the door, then dial 911 and wait for the cavalry. Before the impulse became action, Moreno ordered us inside and stripped Saldana's weapon.

"You have a panic button at your desk," he said to the guard. "Once pushed, the elevators shut down. It also sends a 911 signal to the police."

Eyes bouncing between us, Saldana nodded.

"If you go near the desk, I'll kill you," Moreno said.

Saldana lifted his hands. "I'm not moving."

"Put your hands down," Moreno commanded. "You have a cell phone?"

Saldana nodded.

"Throw it on the floor and crush it."

Saldana followed orders, sending a spray of plastic across the tile.

"Where's your master access card?" Moreno asked. "You're going to need it."

Eyes on the gun, Saldana plucked a card key from his shirt pocket and held it up.

"Good," Moreno said. "Now the keys to the lobby door."

Saldana pointed. "They're in the lock."

Moreno shifted his mask toward me. "Boyd, get the backpack from the car." He pointed the gun at Saldana's head. "Come right back and lock the door behind you, or I'll kill him."

*

We rode the elevator in silence. Saldana and I stood close, joined by handcuffs. Moreno held the gun and backpack, watching the numbers tick upward. The cuff was tight and bit my skin.

"What's this about, Mr. Boyd?" Saldana asked.

"I have no idea. Just do what he says."

Moreno looked away from the numbers and eyed Saldana through the mask. "The building is empty?"

"Yes." The guard waited a few seconds before adding, "But my replacement comes soon."

Moreno grunted. "Your replacement arrives at eight in the morning. Once an hour you patrol the building and then outside along the perimeter. Twice a night you go to the roof. There you have a smoke. Not cigarettes, a cigar, I think. You spend the rest of your shift in the lobby watching a TV you hide under the desk. As a precaution, the alarm feeds directly into the police computer system, and any interruption in power supply causes two basement generators to kick on. There are twelve security cameras throughout the building which record to DVRs and automatically write to external hard drives. Anything else I should know?"

Saldana looked at the floor.

"I thought not."

The elevator began to slow. When the doors opened, Moreno shouldered the backpack and looked at me.

"Lead me to the bunker."

*

Moreno stopped in front of the bunker elevator and lowered the pack. He stood for several beats, said nothing as he studied the access control unit. Standing there, Roger Saldana's eyes probed

208

mine, looking hard, triangulating my role in his nightmare. I shook my head and tried to send a message.

I'm not part of this.

Moreno turned and spoke. "I'm going to need your help, Boyd." He tossed me the handcuff key. "Cuff his hands together and come here."

I released my wrist, cuffed Saldana's hands, and stepped forward.

Moreno looked at the guard and lifted the card key. "This master access key will get me into the bunker?"

The guard looked at me for guidance.

"Tell him," I said. "You have no choice."

"Part way." Saldana nodded at the access control unit. "There's a retinal scanner. You need the card and a scan. I don't have biometric access. It's a secure facility. Only certain people get inside."

"Which people?"

"Mr. Reed, Mr. Singh, our security chief, Rezko. I'm not sure who else."

"And getting back up here from the bunker?" Moreno lifted his weapon. The silencer protruded from the end like a bayonet. "Does that also require a bio scan?"

Saldana shook his head. "The elevator stays down there; it's programmed that way. You don't need a card for the trip up. Just hit the button. The idea is to keep people out, not trap them in."

Moreno nodded. "Once inside the bunker, what security measures can I expect?"

"Two doors. One leading to the mantrap. That one opens with the card key. The lock into the bunker is biometric as well. It takes a thumb scan to get inside, not a retinal scan."

Moreno nodded. "You're doing great. What's inside the mantrap?"

"Monitoring station, computer, a desk. The computer monitors temperature, humidity, fire sensors and suppression equipment."

"Does the bunker alarm tie in to police and fire?"

Saldana hesitated again. Six months ago, I could have provided the answer. The bunker had been my baby. I presented the idea to Reed but left before its construction. My knowledge of its functionality was theoretical. Which prompted a question. Why in the hell was I there?

"The bunker's on a separate alarm," the guard admitted. "The walls withstand temperatures up to two thousand degrees and an internal suppression system kicks on if a fire starts. The system uses a gas-extinguishing agent. The last thing we'd want is the fire department in there with hoses."

"Anything else?"

"No."

"What about surveillance cameras?"

"There's a camera in the mantrap and another in the bunker."

Moreno ran a hand along the elevator door. Then his eyes narrowed within the mask and he faced the guard. "Once I'm in the mantrap, will the doors stay open, or will they close behind me?"

Saldana hesitated.

The question made sense. Some facilities required one code to get inside a secure area and a separate code to leave. Security in layers, a system of redundancies. If the bunker had such precautions, they hadn't been part of my pitch to Reed.

"You enter a code on the computer in the mantrap," Saldana said. "The doors stay open after that."

"What's the code?"

Saldana told him.

"I hope you're telling the truth."

Moreno's silenced automatic coughed and a wet slap echoed from the guard's left side. His cuffed hands moved to the wound and clutched at the red blossom spreading on his shirt as he slid to his knees.

"If we get locked in, you're going to bleed to death."

Hurrying to Saldana, I pushed his shirt aside and stared at a scorched knot of flesh. The guard writhed on the floor. Serious blood flowed along his side.

"Keep your hands over it," I said. "Apply pressure."

He tried but the cuffs interfered.

"He can't press down."

Moreno shrugged as he approached the elevator. "You have the key. Cuff him to a door. That'll leave one hand free."

I unhooked Saldana's left hand and cuffed his right to an office doorknob. Moreno watched to make sure I did it right. Glancing at the plaque, I saw the office belonged to Singh. Months ago, it had been mine.

Saldana pushed me away. "Why are you helping him?"

"I'm not. Keep pressure on the wound. You'll be okay."

Moreno barked. "Boyd, get the pack and come with me."

I left Saldana hanging by one arm.

Moreno swiped the access card, and I joined him at the elevator door. "Put your eye against the scanner," he ordered.

I hesitated. "They built this after I left. I don't have access. Whoever told you I could get you inside that room, they screwed up."

Moreno slammed my face into the wall. The hot press of his gun against my throat induced a cringe as the silencer burned into my skin.

"Question me again, and I'll put a bullet in his head."

Retinal scanners work by reading the eye's vascular structure, and each signature is fingerprint unique. MicroLine's upper management had retinal mapping done as part of yearly physicals, but I was a former employee, scanning my eyes would produce a negative result.

I pressed my right eye against the scanner.

Nothing.

"Your left eye."

This time, a red light traveled down my field of vision, and the lock cycled. Twenty seconds later, the elevator doors opened.

"You first," Moreno said, handing me the pack.

*

Two minutes later, we stood in the mantrap. Moreno unloaded the bricks of thermite in stacks of two. Even in the climate-controlled atmosphere, the chemical odor was overpowering, like rotten fish and sulfur wrapped in wax paper and left to ferment in the sun.

Bricks stacked, Moreno pulled out three grenades.

"You're going to blow it up," I said.

Moreno smiled.

"M-36 white phosphorus. It doesn't blow up; it burns. The fuses work on a delay. Burns at nearly five-thousand degrees. The bricks contain thermite. No explosion, no bang, just enough heat to melt a car."

Standing next to the monitoring computer, Moreno placed the grenades and bundled thermite on the desk, then glanced at the screen. Number strings indicated the bunker's temperature and humidity. Deviation from an acceptable range would trip an alarm and trigger the fire suppression system. Watching the numbers dance, I saw the flaw in his plan and shook my head.

"There's a suppression system. It'll kill the oxygen. Fire won't burn in there."

Moreno shrugged. "Thermite carries its own oxygen supply. Plus, your bunker has a weakness. The manufacturer provides the manual free of charge on their website. Even the best machines in the world require upkeep. The suppression agent needs maintenance twice a month. Sometimes the chemicals go inert. There's a service mode in the software that sets the entire system to standby for ten minutes. More than enough time."

"You're going to destroy the drives."

"Well observed, Boyd."

"You're wiping out evidence for the cartel," I said.

"Cartel?"

"You're working for them."

"I told you, Boyd, I sell concrete."

"Bullshit. You work for Aldama."

"Who's Aldama?"

"Your drug boss."

Moreno's eyes slid from the monitor and froze on me. "You think I work for such people? After what I told you about my father?"

"That story was bullshit. You're one of them."

"Don't make things complex, Boyd. Most crimes have simple motivation—money, power, revenge is good. Sometimes motive is intricate, but more often than not, it's uncomplicated."

"Where do you fit in?"

"I'm a businessman."

"You're a killer."

He shrugged. "How much money did you make working here?"

"What?"

"Your salary. How much?"

"A hundred and twenty thousand a year."

"Good money."

"What's your point?"

"You had a talent. You used it to make a living. I'm no different. Only I don't carry a briefcase, and I hate long meetings. Give me a target, a deadline, and my natural gifts shine, but I'm still a businessman, and I'll make more in this one night than you made in an entire year."

"Your plan won't work. You can melt the drives, but whatever evidence you're destroying exists somewhere else."

Even without entering the bunker, I knew that was true. Digital forensics was about preservation. Every time a memory device booted, the operating system made changes to files. For the investigator, the goal was to collect the evidence without changing the source. You accomplished that by imaging the suspect device, making virtual copies, and examining them in depth. That meant creating backups, and lots of them, following the forensic investigator's maxim: access the original once, the forensic copy twice, and the working copy as often as necessary. Whatever Moreno's target, it probably existed in several iterations, scattered among multiple agencies, and he would never get them all.

"Destroying evidence is like breaking glass. Pieces fragment, but they hang around. You might clean up, but you never get everything."

"Who says I'm destroying evidence?"

"Nothing else is down here."

"There soon will be." Moreno lifted a grenade and grinned. "A little destruction."

He glanced at the bunker door. The barrier looked submarine strong, no way to blow through it with a grenade. You'd need a torpedo or a missile. There was an access panel on the wall beside the door—a keypad, card reader, and fingerprint scanner.

"If the thumb scanner reads an error, the outer door will close," I said. "We'll be locked inside."

"You mean the guard lied?"

"He was scared."

"Why are you telling me?"

"I don't want him to bleed to death."

"Why haven't you tried to get away, Boyd?"

"You have a gun. Where could I go?"

"Put your thumb on the scanner."

Despite my warning, Moreno showed no hesitation.

I followed his order.

The scanner moved over my thumb. Like the retinal scan, nothing should have followed. Instead, a loud thunk shook the door and a bolt shifted. The door slid open.

Moreno held out a hand.

"You never gave back the handcuff key."

I reached into my pocket and handed over the key.

Moreno threw it into a floor vent, listened to it rattle, and then tossed the card key onto the desk.

"Get the thermite." He pointed to the camera high on the wall. "And don't forget to smile for your close-up."

The bunker was a disappointment. Just a clean room with a storage locker and six workstations fanned around racks of hard drives. Lights flashed on the drives, cooling fans hummed, but most of the workstation computers were unplugged, the mice and keyboards in boxes. The place looked as if Singh, halfway done setting things up, had lost interest.

"Drop the thermite on the floor and get the rest. Don't worry, it won't blow up."

I dropped the thermite and went back for more.

Moreno followed me, dug into the pack, and retrieved a roll of duct tape. He tore three long strips and wrapped each one around a grenade and four blocks of thermite. From what I knew, thermite needed high heat to burn and required close contact with an ignition source. Strapping a phosphorus grenade on top would probably do the job. It might also melt through the floor, drill a hole through the foundation, and bring the building down.

"Spread the bundles around. Anywhere near the drives." He glanced at the cameras. "Save one for the DVRs. People see the recording—you carrying grenades—and you'll have some explaining to do."

The implication I had a future gave a brief flash of hope. I let it die.

"You're going to kill me," I said without thinking.

Moreno frowned. "We're almost finished, Boyd. To be honest, it's gone well. Once the thermite is planted, we pull the pins, take care of the guard, and you can go home."

Home.

I tried to picture it.

I saw my family in the backyard, eating lunch on a warm day in June.

Sara and Carter chasing the dog.

Abby watching from across the table, soft wind pushing hair into her eyes, sweat beading on the slope of her breasts.

Perfection.

Then the other half of Moreno's statement registered like a hard slap.

Take care of the guard.

"No more violence," I said.

Moreno shrugged. "He saw everything. Imagine what he'll say about you."

"You can't—"

"I don't intend to. You'll do it for me."

"No."

"In my business, comebacks are a liability. No loose ends."

"I'm a loose end."

Moreno thought about that and shook his head. "I told you, Boyd. We're partners."

*

Three minutes later, we stood in the mantrap, and as Moreno typed a code into the computer, I saw my chance and ran. The master key opened the mantrap's outer door, swiping it again might seal that door shut. Or I might end up dead. Either way, Roger Saldana wasn't going to die by my hand. When Moreno bent over the computer, I grabbed the key and bolted for the door.

Card swiped, a mechanical whir filled the air. The door began to close.

Moreno turned and lifted his gun. For a moment, the silencer locked onto my chest, and then he pointed at the biometric lock and pulled the trigger. The slugs thumped steel as the mantrap slammed shut.

I was already in the elevator punching buttons.

The ride up took ten seconds.

In the hall, clutching his bleeding side, Roger Saldana remained cuffed to the office door and winced as I lifted him. "Unlock me," he croaked, rattling the cuffs.

Blood covered the floor, and his face had paled into an over-bleached sheet.

"No key," I said.

The guard's cheeks colored with a bolt of red. He tugged at his chained hand. "Get me off this door."

There was a loud pop from down in the bunker.

Then another.

Followed by a third.

Moreno had detonated the grenades. His focus would soon turn to us.

I tried ripping the cuff from the doorknob.

Saldana nodded down the hall. "What about that?"

My eyes landed on a fire axe encased in glass.

I broke the glass with my elbow and grabbed the axe.

Three blows and the knob flew. The guard was free. I helped him stand and then moved toward the elevators, holding the axe, gripping the handle until my fingers grew white.

The bunker had gone quiet.

I strained to hear anything.

Then I did.

Metal sliding on metal.

The sound of an elevator motor kicking in.

"Shit, he's coming," I said. "We have to take the stairs."

Kicking the stairwell door open, I helped Saldana stagger onto the landing. Then I hesitated. Down led to city streets, an open kill zone. Up led to cubical farms with places to hide, and phones and computers we could use to summon help. More than anything, I wanted to get out of the building. Instead, looking at the guard, I said, "We're going up."

Saldana's eyes locked onto mine. "You're helping him."

"No."

"You're part of this. I saw you."

"He threatened my family."

"I don't believe you."

"You better." Glancing down, I grabbed the open handcuff dangling from his wrist, slid it around mine, and then clicked it shut. "We're in this together."

*

We stepped onto the sixth floor as a door opened below us and feet pounded up the stairs. Moreno was coming, and he wouldn't take long to catch up. Taking our chances on the street now seemed a lot smarter. Up here, survival meant hiding, and Saldana's blood made that difficult. The guard leaked a steady trail of red, smeared with shoe prints, marking our path.

I pushed him toward an open office.

"In there."

The climb had drained him, and he moved in low gear. Blood brushed his side, a falling scarlet stream, and each lurching step brought a wince. He pulled me toward a desk and grabbed a phone.

"Call the cops."

"He's too close."

"My hands are cold. I need water."

"Shut up and move. What else is on this floor?"

Saldana's panicked face became total confusion. "I don't…just HR…and Rezko's office."

"Shit."

"Rezko's gun," Saldana said. "It's in his desk."

I tightened my grip around his waist and moved toward Rezko's office. "We'll be all right," I lied.

The guard nodded as if he believed me.

*

Two axe swings cleaved the door. Wood splintered and sparks flew as the lock sheared and the interior of Rezko's office came into view. Behind the desk, an American flag hung alongside the

Republic of Vietnam's, as if for Rezko, decades after the war, one could not exist without the other.

Saldana knelt behind the desk, yanking on a drawer. "It's locked."

"Get back."

Leaning to swing the axe, I heard the stairwell door bang open in the hallway and froze.

Saldana tugged me behind the desk.

I got on the floor beside him and clutched the axe. The guard breathed heavily and shivered. Maybe from blood loss. Maybe fear. His wound left a puddle on the floor.

Moreno's footsteps echoed in the hall. Then his voice. "Boyd, I know you're here. Come out. This is stupid."

Saldana's breathing grew labored.

Then Moreno stepped through the door, pointing his automatic. He took a slow look around and chuckled.

"Boyd, what a mess," he scolded. "What have you been doing?"

I took a deep breath and prayed to a god I no longer believed in. Then, behind the mask, Moreno's eyes locked onto the handcuffs linking me to the guard and he gave a sharp laugh.

"No key, Boyd. Very smart. Very resourceful."

"No one else dies."

Moreno glanced at Roger Saldana and then looked back at me. He stepped close, pointed his gun at my head and tugged the fire axe from my hands. My guts did a slow roll as he hefted its weight.

Roger Saldana groaned.

Moreno lifted the axe. "Okay, Boyd, no one dies, but someone loses a hand. Will it be him or you?"

I opened my mouth but nothing came out.

Moreno laughed. "You're no hero, Boyd, but I guess we already knew that."

The axe fell. For thirty seconds, I closed my eyes and listened as Roger Saldana screamed.

Chapter Twenty-Three

Detective Vasquez drummed the table with both hands as the look of permanent suspicion that had creased his forehead for so long began to ease. Several beats later, the drumming stopped.

"That's it?" he asked.

"Yeah."

"So Moreno just let you go?"

"He gave me an envelope and dropped me at a shuttle booth at the airport. Then he drove into a parking structure. That's the last I saw of him. A handcuff key was in the envelope."

"And you have no idea what he was after at MicroLine?"

"He never said."

"What do you think it was?"

"Obviously something on the drives that threatened the cartel. MicroLine doesn't just handle criminal evidence. Could be discovery for a lawsuit. Something regarding a business the cartel owns. Money laundering. Who knows?"

"But he failed, right? The evidence on the drives. It exists somewhere else?"

"Probably."

"Meaning what?"

"Detective, I no longer work for MicroLine, and I have no idea what evidence those drives held. Whatever it was probably exists in many locations. Companies keep multiple copies of almost everything: email, invoices, business-continuity files. Law enforcement does the same thing. Whatever Moreno was targeting, the odds that he got the only copy are slim."

"Then why do it?"

"You'll have to ask him."

Someone tapped the mirrored glass then. Detective Vasquez walked out, spoke with somebody in the hall, then came back. When he sat down, he flipped through his note pad. The look on his face said he had some news.

"What?" I asked, still thinking of Abby and the kids.

Vasquez flipped his notebook closed. "The guard left surgery two hours ago. He more or less confirms your version of events. Says you probably saved his life."

Leaving MicroLine, I had punched the panic button on Saldana's desk, sending the 911 call. Moreno had just laughed and shaken his head, then pushed me toward his car.

"Thank Christ for that," I said and stood up.

"Please sit down, Mr. Boyd."

"Am I under arrest or not?"

"Not at the moment. We'll forward a report to the district attorney's office. They'll determine what charges you face, if any."

"Then I can go?"

"Not just yet. We're not done."

"Sorry Detective, I need to make sure my family's safe."

"Your family is fine Mr. Boyd. I had someone call your voicemail service and retrieve your messages like you asked. Your wife called. She said they were safe and that someone was guarding them."

Two tons of fear melted from my shoulders. Fisk had kept his word. He had abandoned me, but he'd looked after Abby and the kids, and I owed him for that.

"A few more questions," Detective Vasquez said and tapped his pen. "Back to Moreno's target. Harvey Rezko, MicroLine's security chief, says the drives in the bunker were zeroed out. No data was on them yet, no evidence, a blank slate. The bunker wasn't even operational. Does that surprise you?"

"I guess not. Singh told me they were ramping up, just getting started."

"Then why did Moreno target the drives if they were empty?"

"No idea."

"Is it possible Moreno wasn't targeting the drives?"

"I don't see how. That's what he went after."

"What I'm asking is, could the company itself have been the target?"

That thought hadn't occurred to me and made no sense. Monday at nine, MicroLine would open for business, damaged maybe, but far from broken.

"If so, then he failed. The fire, the cleanup, rebuilding the bunker...it'll cost MicroLine money. But Moreno didn't shut them down. The company's reputation might take a hit. Competitors' stock will rise. But you're talking about a hundred-million-dollar organization. They're not out of business."

"Moreno didn't achieve much, then. Except to screw up your life."

I said nothing.

Detective Vasquez stood, put away his pen, and then looked up at the camera. The red light no longer flashed. "I appreciate your cooperation. Before you leave, someone else would like to talk to you. Won't take more than a few minutes."

"All right, Detective."

He stepped outside.

I glanced up at the camera, wondering once more how much I had said and what I had left out. Two things had been intentionally omitted—the fight with Dave Manker and the explosion at Keller's. Both were crimes, and with Dave's fate unknown and the police unaware of the Keller incident, avoiding details seemed prudent for the time being. Better to wait for the feds to back me up, then I'd talk.

The door opened then.

A fresh detective walked in.

He was tall, well dressed in a church-going suit, with cropped gray hair and a deep frown that creased the edges of his mouth into dark slots. He nodded in my direction.

"Hear you have quite a story to tell, Mr. Boyd."

I buried my aggravation. "Not at the moment, I don't. I've talked enough. Detective Vasquez can tell you everything. I'm going home."

"Not just yet. You're gonna talk to me."

"Yeah? Who the hell are you?"

"Special Agent Dennis Fisk."

My breath left me then, forced out in a single, heaving rush, as if a fist dug into my stomach. When it returned, I breathed a single word.

"Abby."

Chapter Twenty-Four

By the time we reached the Surfrider Motel in north Laguna, the sun had cannonballed into the Pacific and splattered red light against the clouds. In the motel's parking lot, the body lay covered with yellow plastic that matched the crime scene tape encircling the waving palm trees. Despite the sheet, fluids seeped onto the asphalt, and the first glimpse I caught of Abby, she was wiping some of it from her shoe.

"You stay in the car for now," Agent Fisk said. "Locals get nervous when feds arrive. We don't need a turf battle."

Back at the station, within twenty minutes, the real Agent Fisk had used bank records to track Abby to the motel in Laguna, and then informed me there was a problem. Not providing details, except to say Abby was okay, he'd offered to drive me there. On the way, I had eased my fear by patiently recounting to him all that had transpired over the past ten days. Now my patience was exhausted.

"Fuck that, Fisk. I want to see my wife."

Pushing the door, I stepped onto the lot and passed the corpse. Abby sat talking to a cop, looking at her shoe, dabbing blood with a tissue. Seeing me, her eyes sagged with shock and fear, as if she'd woken from one nightmare and found herself stuck in another. Around the lot, activity revolved in a series of concentric circles, the yellow body sheet serving as a point of locus. Closest to the blood, men in plainclothes took notes and photographs. Beyond the crime scene, officers conducted field interviews and gathered statements from my wife and people who looked to be motel staff. Beyond them all, held back by another line of yellow tape, onlookers gawked, unable to resist the carnage. A patrol cop defending the crime scene spotted me and lifted a hand, ready to eject me from the area. Fisk intervened, flashed an ID, and then pushed me forward.

Abby grabbed me then, and her trembling lips broke into an uncontrolled spasm.

I struggled to breathe.

She started to cry.

"Ab...Jesus. Are you... Where—"

Ran stepped from the motel office, drying his hands with a towel. Until that moment, I'd feared my brother's body might have been under the yellow plastic. Relief grew into hope as I waited to see my kids.

Abby stopped crying then and took a step back.

"They're gone, Jack. Someone took our babies."

*

Fisk wrote down our phone numbers—cell, home, and work— prepping for a trace if Moreno called. Over the next thirty minutes, the agent made three calls of his own, then tossed interagency diplomacy to the curb and demanded to see the motel's surveillance tapes. Laguna was a small P.D. and lacked the stomach to fight the federal government, so the locals folded. The motel had six cameras, most trained on the parking lot, and this time there was no black and white to shield the ugliness. The horror show came in gouts of color.

On the computer monitor, a man sat in a plastic chair in the middle of the motel breezeway, watching the crowded parking lot.

Cars and SUVs occupied most spots. Heavy vegetation, tropical and green with broad leaves, dominated the landscape. Painted in Miami pastels, the motel looked one part Art Deco and two parts circus tent. Gazing at the screen, I half expected to see monkeys and parrots, maybe someone dancing the limbo. Instead, I watched a man die.

"Who is he?"

Ran's voice came from behind me, shaky and weak.

"Bodie Katz. He works with me at Devlin's...or did."

"What the hell was he doing here?"

Ran took a moment to answer. When he spoke, his voice had an edge. "You said Abby and the kids were in danger. I wanted backup."

"I never told you to involve other people."

"You didn't tell me much of anything."

"Where were you?"

"I went to get food. Abby was in the shower. Carter was in my room, and Bodie was watching him. You know, if you were so goddamned worried—"

Fisk lifted a hand. "Let's take a time out, gentlemen."

Refocusing on the screen, I watched someone move into the breezeway. Sunlight fell in dappled pools, creating deep reservoirs of shade in the gaps, and the person wore a hoodie and moved fast, appearing to be little more than a darting shadow. Before Ran's coworker could react, a knife plunged into his chest.

"That's Moreno, I take it?" Fisk asked.

"I can't tell. The body shape looks right."

Fisk advanced the tape.

Carter appeared in the breezeway then, led toward the parking lot as he clutched the man's hand. As they passed Bodie, the wounded man tried crawling out of the way, painting a red smear on the concrete. The attacker let go of my son and bent down with his back to the camera, then stabbed Bodie in the neck. As Bodie died, my son wore a blank expression and calmly retook the killer's hand.

"What about Sara?"

"The tape doesn't show anything."

"But she's gone?"

"Yes."

"She was at the pool," Ran said.

"You let her go swimming?"

"She didn't have a suit. There were chairs by the water. It was sunny. You know how she is. She kept talking on that damn phone."

"I asked you to watch them."

Fisk shut off the monitor. "That's a brave son you have. He barely flinched."

"Carter has an empathy condition. He might not even believe what he saw was real. Like it was something on TV."

"Let's hope so."

"That had to be Moreno."

Fisk pulled a frown and his eyes pinched. "Not necessarily. Someone came to your office impersonating a federal agent, so we know Moreno isn't working alone."

"The guy who came to my office was fat and slow and didn't look capable of killing a man with a knife."

Fisk looked at Ran and nodded toward the parking lot. "You mind leaving us a moment?"

Ran left, and Fisk shot me a look doctors gave when about to impart bad news. "I'm going to be honest, Mr. Boyd. We're not in a strong position here. We can issue an Amber Alert and send BOLOs to every agency in the Southland. We can forward that information to the National Crime Information Center. But without a vehicle ID or a name for this guy, I'm not optimistic."

"His name is Carlos Moreno."

"I'm going to let you in on something. One of those calls I made was to a contact with the DEA. From what he tells me, there is no cartel named Asesinos de La Sierra. No drug boss named Javier Aldama. Whoever this guy is, I doubt his name is even Moreno. This was bullshit from day one, Mr. Boyd, some kind of setup. That empty house next door to you? The bank still owns it. They're so backed up with foreclosures, they haven't checked it in three months. Anyone living there was squatting. You've been played, Mr. Boyd."

"Played?"

"That's right. What do you have that this guy wants? Because, whatever it is, the fact he took your kids suggests he isn't through with you."

"I don't have anything."

"Money? Information? Someone who bears a grudge?"

"A grudge?"

"Business? Personal?"

"I spent years helping put people in jail. Probably all of them hold grudges. But I worked in the background and searched computers. How could they know who I am?"

"Information is easy to buy, Mr. Boyd. And then, of course, there's your brother."

The room seemed to compress. Glancing at the monitor, I focused on the body under the yellow sheet, the way the form suggested a human being who might, despite the carnage, get up and walk away at any moment. Daylight had faded, but the cops brought in floodlights that pushed away the shadows, and beneath their glow, ponds of blood gleamed in perfect black circles.

"My brother?"

"A stretch at Pelican Bay, working in a garbage can full of ex-cons... Maybe he's brought bad habits to your doorstep. Think about it; why ask someone to back him up? Maybe he knew what he was up against. Did you tell him about Moreno?"

"No."

"Then why'd he ask his buddy for help?"

"I told him Abby and the kids were in danger. I didn't get specific. Ran wouldn't put my family at risk. He was here to help."

"These are your children we're talking about, Mr. Boyd. You want to find them, you'd better not rule anyone out, including your brother."

Lunch with Suarez came to mind then. Devlin and the illegal guns. Jane Selig and her hard drives. Was Moreno part of that mess? If so, was Ran involved? Could my brother have stood by while this storm swept in a sucked my family out to sea?

"The Los Angeles DA's office thinks Devlin is running guns."

"Devlin?"

"My brother's boss. I have a contact in the DA's office. They're looking at Devlin."

"That sounds like a decent place to start."

"But it doesn't make sense." I nodded toward the parking lot. "Ran wasn't armed. Neither was his friend. The guy was an extra pair of eyes with muscle. Like a bouncer at a club. If this was about guns, and they knew, they'd have had weapons."

"People do stupid things all the time, Mr. Boyd."

That was true. But it still made no sense.

"Fisk, ask whatever questions you need to in order to find my kids, but I'm telling you, my brother's not involved."

The agent managed a nod. "Here's a question, then. When I called the DEA, I put your name through a records search. L.A. County says you have a sheet. Now, in my experience, most of the time, shit both good and bad happens for a reason. People wreck cars because they drive too fast, and get robbed because they let down their guard. Someone kidnaps their children because they have something of value. Point is, one way or another, people bring hurt down on themselves. Convince me you're the exception to the rule. Tell me your criminal record has nothing to do with your situation."

The room compressed more. Glancing at the monitor, I saw Abby and Ran head toward his car. Both moved in slow motion, lost souls in an earthquake, trying to find balance on shifting ground.

"That record is sealed."

"Why?"

"I was a juvenile. I assaulted someone when I was seventeen."

"Assault doesn't really qualify for notorious-criminal status, Mr. Boyd. Why the mystery?"

"The guy was a cop."

Fisk pointed his chin and nodded. "Go on."

"I was in high school. The couple next door got into a fight, and the wife beat the husband with a baseball bat. He went into a coma. A detective came to interview my brother. Ran was a kid. The cop was aggressive, going after him, asking what he saw, trying to establish motive for what happened next door."

"Your brother was a witness?"

"We both were. For some reason, the cop said Marty was having…well…inappropriate contact with kids in the neighborhood. It was bullshit. The cop was fishing, but he wouldn't let go. He kept insinuating Ran was holding back, clamming up because he liked what Marty did. I got sick of listening, so I pushed the guy out of our house."

"You were arrested?"

"I pled guilty to a misdemeanor and got probation."

"You were a minor. Why wasn't the record expunged?"

"By the time I got around to trying, I was already working for MicroLine. I figured business might suffer if cops knew I had assaulted a fellow cop. You guys tend to stick together that way. It was so far in the past, I felt safer letting it rest."

Fisk thought it over and nodded. "Okay, Mr. Boyd. I'll accept that, for now. Like I said, assault is hardly a crime of the century. Just like to know who I'm dealing with."

"Now you know. So what about my kids?"

"As I said, we'll issue an Amber Alert and an interagency be-on-the-lookout. We'll interview your neighbors and your work associates. We can tap your phones in case the guy calls, hope for a trace. College Heights PD is going over Moreno's house as we speak. Hopefully they come up with something that gives us an ID. Don't count on it, though. From what I've heard, the place is well scrubbed."

"What do I do, Fisk?"

"You go home and wait."

"I'm not sure I can do that."

"You don't have a choice."

His phone rang then. Holding up a finger, Fisk answered. "Where's the ping?" he asked seconds later. He wrote something down and closed the phone.

"What is it?"

"You need to wait here."

"What is it, Fisk?"

"Stay here, Mr. Boyd. I'll be back."

Fisk stepped into the parking lot and spoke with one of the cops. Whatever he said jolted the crime scene like a power surge. Two uniformed cops ran to cruisers, fired up engines, and pulled away. No lights or sirens, but moving fast.

Where's the ping?

Then somebody turned up the floodlights, and I understood. They had a signal from Sara's cell phone. How could I have forgotten? How much time had I wasted through my stupidity? What price had my kids paid?

Opening my phone, I tapped the *Locate* icon on the screen. When the program booted, I touched the icon that read Sara, and almost at once, a throbbing red dot showed up on the map.

Beating like a heartbeat.

Less than a mile away.

I ran to my brother.

"Stay with Abby," I said. "I need your keys."

*

Parked at the top of a canyon overlooking the black Pacific, a Toyota Corolla pulsed with incandescent blasts of blue and red. Three Laguna P.D. cruisers and Fisk's Crown Victoria blocked the road, two cops were pulling away from the Toyota's windows, holstering their weapons. Dual sirens clawed the damp air, piercing the night like tsunami warnings as I ran toward the car, hoping to outrun the wave.

Fisk spotted me and moved to block my way. He yelled above the sirens' wail. "Stay back, Mr. Boyd."

"Are my kids in there?"

"Go back to your car and wait."

"Fisk! Are my kid's in there?"

Two of the cops grabbed me, wrapped my arms back. Then something animal kicked in and I pushed past.

"My kids…"

Fisk held up his hands. "The car is empty. It's empty. No one is inside."

The cops grabbed me as someone killed the sirens. This time I allowed them to hold on, propping me up, to keep from falling to my knees on the asphalt and withering into a seething ball of pain. Without the siren's wail, silence descended, disrupted only by the wind and the intermingled sound of traffic and crashing surf near the beach.

Then a scream came from the trunk.

Weapons drew on the Toyota.

Fisk held up his hands and edged forward.

The scream grew louder.

The cops gripped hard, keeping me in place.

Then someone popped the trunk, and I saw blood covering two bodies in the cramped compartment.

One of the bodies moved, and Sara rolled onto her back and kicked her legs, trying to get out.

The other body remained motionless.

A cop moved forward, gun extended, and yanked Sara up. She ran to me then, screaming, as we all gazed down at Dave Manker's lifeless eyes and at the wide, fleshy half-smile carved into his throat.

Chapter Twenty-Five

Back home, upstairs in our bedroom, I told Abby everything. As I talked, her face drained of color, and as the story unfolded, whatever trust she had regained since the incident with Leila Krebs crumbled. When I finished talking, she took several deep breaths, looked down at her open hands, and slapped me. The blow came fast and sharp and left a deep bite. In nearly two decades of marriage, we had fought our wars, but never had one of us laid hands on the other.

"You put the kids in danger," she said. "And you lied to me."

I let the sting die slowly. "I wanted to tell you," I said. "I've been living in two worlds since Fisk showed up."

"I don't give a damn what you've been living through. You put us in danger—all of us—and you should have told me."

"What would you have done, Ab?"

"That's not the point. We're family, Jack. We share things. We don't go it alone. I'm not sure what I would have done, but that son of a bitch wouldn't have gotten near my kids."

"Fisk—the guy I thought was Fisk—ordered me to keep quiet. I never meant to lie to you. I should have told you. I thought I could handle things."

Her eyes grew sharp and she wiped away tears.

"Did Charlie kill Dave?"

"I think so."

"Did you see him do it?"

"No."

"But he videoed the two of you fighting?"

"Yes."

"He wanted the police to suspect you?"

"He wanted leverage so he could force me to help him at MicroLine. But we're long past that now."

"Now he has our son. This can't be real, Jack. It can't be."

"For ten days I've been telling myself the same thing."

She glanced out the bedroom window, toward Moreno's roof. Since we'd arrived home, a tide of cars had pulled next door. People cycled in an out—maybe cops, maybe feds. If they found anything, no one bothered sharing that information with us. Fisk told us to wait at home by the phone, either for his call, or for Moreno's.

My cell phone was in my pocket, the ringer at full volume.

"I want my son back," Abby said.

"We'll get him. I promise we will."

Heading downstairs, I detoured into Sara's room. My daughter sat in the dark on her bed, staring at her phone screen as the faint glow sparked tears on her cheeks. Flicking on the lights, I took a seat next to her.

"What are you doing?"

"Texting Scott," she said.

"For now, the details stay private, Sara. Until we know what's happening, for your brother's safety, we have to watch what we say."

"You talked to reporters, Dad. Our privacy is pretty much dead."

Before leaving Laguna, Fisk had me give a statement to the press, asking for the return of my son. Emotion-wracked parents tended to motivate the public, and the footage had aired several times already, along with the Amber Alert.

"That was to help find your brother, and it was just a statement."

Her fingers continued to move. "Dad?"

"What?"

"I'm sorry."

Reaching out, I pulled the phone from her hands and held her. She cried for a long time, and when she finished I wiped tears and kissed her cheek.

"This wasn't your fault, Sara."

Sucking a mouthful of air, she asked the million-dollar question.

"Then whose fault was it?"

*

In the kitchen, Ran had brewed a pot of coffee, grilled some cheese sandwiches, and sat at the table chewing. After every bite, he wiped his mouth and hands with a napkin. Biting into a sandwich, the first thing I'd eaten since the police arrived at my doorstep that morning, I approved of how my brother had slathered butter on both sides of the bread—the way our mother always had—and decided we needed to talk.

"I have to know something."

Ran swallowed coffee and nodded. Even at the table, his shoulders slumped with a forward tilt.

"Shoot," he said.

"Is Devlin selling guns?"

"Not that I know."

"Would you tell me?"

"What do you think?" Ran chewed more of his sandwich. "How's Abby?"

"She's pissed and she's scared. We have no idea what's going on. Two hours ago, I was living a nightmare, but a nightmare I understood. Now this guy has Carter, I have no clue who he is, or what he wants, and it scares the shit out of me. If you know anything, you have to tell me."

"What could I know?"

"Devlin wants Selig's hard drives. Why?"

Ran chewed his sandwich, grinding slow to draw out the pause, and then seemed to reach a decision.

"Danny's cheating on taxes. In a big way."

"That's it?"

"Far as I know."

"No weapons sales?"

"Weapons?"

"Selling guns."

Ran shook his head and pulled a face. "Why do you keep asking that?"

"Never mind...and don't look at me like I'm crazy. With his nephew's connections, anything is possible."

Ran took another bite and chewed. He didn't bother swallowing before he resumed talking.

"You know, people always talk shit about Danny. Mostly because of Vince and Stevie, but also because he gives guys like me a second chance. A man offers convicts a hand up and he's suspect, you know. But selling guns, that's not Danny's style."

I told him about the gun Devlin gave me in exchange for passing along information about Selig's hard drives. Ran shrugged it off.

"You've seen the neighborhood. Half the mechanics in the garage come to work strapped. Probably got it off one of them. Look, from what I know, and this is rumor, Selig maintained two sets of financial records for the garages, one official for tax returns, and one not so official. Our customers aren't exactly credit worthy. They pay in cash, and that makes skimming easy. Danny's been nuts since Don's accident. He's worried Jane's fight with the insurance company could get nasty. With those records loose, he's exposed, so he asked me to hit you up to see what's on the drives, and I did." Ran bit into his sandwich and chewed, but this time, he seemed to have trouble swallowing it down. Then he wiped his hands. "You're looking for some way to make this my fault, aren't you?"

"What?"

"I understand."

"What are you talking about?"

"Hell, after what happened with Marty and Janis, our shit heel dad, if I'd built all this security to fill that hole—the house, the family, the job—only to find myself as neck deep as everyone else, I'd be looking for someone to blame, too. But this isn't my fault, Jack, and far as I know, Danny Devlin's got no part in it."

My cell phone rang then.

The screen flashed *unknown caller.*

Before I answered, Ran gave me a look. "You know, if you need help finding Carter, Danny can raise an army. That guy killed Bodie, and Bodie had plenty of friends—the kind of guys who like payback."

I answered the call. "Hello?"

"Jack?"

Hoping to hear Moreno, I couldn't peg the voice right away. Then I did.

"Leland?"

"Were you planning to call me and explain?"

"Look, we need to talk, but not now. Carter is—"

"I saw the news. I'm sorry, but we need to meet."

"I can't. Things are—"

"Shut up and listen to me. You led that bastard through my front door, and you need to make things right."

Taken aback, I fell silent.

Ran shot me a questioning look.

I shook my head.

"What do you want, Leland?"

"The same thing you want, Jack. The son of a bitch who took your son."

Chapter Twenty-Six

Destroying computer evidence is akin to crushing diamonds. You make smaller pieces, but unless you're highly skilled, the jewels never go away. When the space shuttle *Columbia* burned up during reentry, a commercial Seagate hard drive secreted in its hold flamed down to earth and slammed into a dry lakebed in Texas. Five years later, a team of recovery engineers pulled data from the drive's platters. Talk about hardware. Staring through the bunker door, I took in the damage Moreno had wrought, and knew Reed faced a far easier task.

"What do you think?" he asked.

"At first glance, you'll be okay."

"We can recover?"

"In terms of hardware, sure, but your reputation's going to take a hit. A security company that can't protect itself doesn't exactly inspire confidence."

"Thanks for grasping the obvious. I was talking about data,"

"What exactly are you trying to recover? From what I heard, the drives were empty."

Reed made a face and looked at his watch. "We need to be up and running before word gets around. I can't use my own people. I need your help. Make an initial assessment and determine how much data he compromised. Decide what's recoverable and what isn't."

"Leland, I can't do this. Carter is—"

"The fire burned hot and flamed out. A coat of paint will fix the cosmetic damage, but I need you to recover the drives. The fewer employees who know, the better. I don't want anyone down here until you finish, not even Singh. You report to me." Reed pointed to the burn marks on the floor. "Your friend was in a hurry. Either that, or he was incompetent. Most of the thermite didn't ignite. Should have pried open the drive cases, used acid or some other corrosive."

Beyond the scorch marks, the room had sustained negligible damage. Two racks of hard drives had melted, but two more sat untouched, and the black, sooty ring in the middle of the floor looked innocuous, as if a band of girl scouts had started a campfire. Other than that, and a chemical tint to the air, harm to the bunker seemed minimal. Not much payoff, certainly not worth hacking off a man's arm and abducting a young boy. Thinking of Carter, my feet began to burn, urging me back home. Abby hadn't been speaking to me when I'd left, so I'd told Ran where I was going and instructed him to call if anything changed.

"I can't be here, Leland."

"Bomb squad hung around until noon." Reed ignored my statement. "Most of the thermite was old, they said, practically inert. Accelerant caused the damage."

"Phosphorus grenades."

"What?"

"He used grenades to ignite the thermite."

"Well, like I said, he was no expert. But until we assess the damage, who knows? Approach it as you would any recovery. Mount the drives, image everything—"

"I know how to execute a recovery, Leland. But why bother? Rezko and Singh said the drives were empty."

Reed shook his head. "Over the past week, I shipped discovery for the Hartmann-Rydell lawsuit up here. Singh was sorting through it. Problem is Hartmann thinks I'm doing all the imaging down there. That's what they paid for. We have back-up copies of everything, but if word gets out before I know what that asshole compromised, or if it starts showing up on the Internet, the contract is gone, and our reputation follows."

"Have you notified the Board?"

"Not yet."

"You own the company, but you have investors. You think that's wise?"

"For now. I lose Hartmann for mishandling evidence, and the feds will find out. That happens and our chance at SCIF approval evaporates into lost paperwork and bureaucratic run around. First step to navigating this is keeping Hartmann's lawyers happy. That means knowing what this guy damaged. If nothing was lost, Hartmann doesn't need to know the details, neither do our investors, I'll spin it as a run of the mill burglary. You led the bastard in here, Boyd, I need your help making it right."

"I can't."

"Do this and I'll make your no-compete clause go away. Or don't…"

Despite the bravado, Leland's eyes held flat desperation, a guy inside a narrow tunnel staring at an onrushing train. The opening was a long way off, but the only option was to turn, hope for the best, and run toward the sunlight. I recognized the look, had seen it in my reflection over the past ten days, and felt guilt. But I had troubles of my own.

"Once Carter is safe, I can help. But for now, I need to be home. You have hours of work here. Probably days. Sorry." After a few beats, I suggested an alternative. "I know someone, though. He works for me, and he's good. He can help."

Reed gave a disgusted grunt and shrugged. "If he can keep his mouth shut, get him down here."

Placing a call to Fisher, I told him MicroLine needed his services and discretion and would pay well for both. He was on the way before hanging up. When I rejoined Leland, he stood in the mantrap and stared into the bunker like a man home from a long war, only to find his wife in love with someone else.

"You spend that severance yet? Maybe you should buy some Vector shares. Once the Street hears about this, that stock will tick north. Who did this, Boyd? What do you know about him?"

"Nothing real."

"The guy grabs your son, and you have no ideas?"

"He took aim at your company. Maybe you know him?"

"Yeah, maybe."

"Who wants to hurt you?"

"You mean competitors, or personally?"

"At this point, I mean anyone. Why would someone target your company? Who profits when you bleed?"

"You're kidding, right? With the volume of evidence that runs through this place on a weekly basis, it could be anyone."

"Whatever the reason, he has my son. That's all I care about."

Reed's mouth pinched into a frown. "I get that."

"I need to go home."

We left the bunker and moved toward the elevator.

"What do you hear about Roger?" I asked.

"Considering someone cut off his hand, he's doing okay. They can't reattach the limb, but he'll recover. Going to need a prosthetic. Probably sue me the moment he gets out."

"The man could have died."

"Yeah, what can I say? I'm a selfish prick." At the mantrap entrance, Reed pulled a face and tapped the keypad. "All this damn security, and it means nothing. You spend a few hundred grand, guy just waltzes past your defenses and lights you on fire."

True enough. Security protected from external threats, but even high technology faced vulnerability from within. Once the enemy breached the castle walls or moved next door to you, anything was possible. As I thought that over, a question returned from the previous night.

"There's something I meant to ask you. Why was my data coded into the locks?"

"What data?"

"The retinal scanner and the thumb scanner both recognized my bio data. That's how he got inside the bunker. Why was I authorized for entry?"

"You weren't."

"I'm telling you, my thumb went against that scanner, and the door opened."

Reed paused for a long time and then gave a shrug. "Had to be some kind of screw up."

I thought it over and shook my head. "Moreno knew ahead of time the scan would work. That's why he brought me. How could he have known?"

"He couldn't have."

"The more I think about it, only one explanation makes sense. Someone in your shop helped him."

Reed said nothing for a few beats, then shook his head. "Bullshit."

"Think about it, Leland. Nothing else fits."

"Yeah, well, I have bigger problems, Boyd. The guy got in, end of story. I have a business to run. All I care about is getting this place operational before tomorrow. The how and why, I'll leave for the cops. And anyway, like you said, you should be worrying about your son."

"This is about my son. If Moreno had someone inside here, that person provides a link. We can squeeze them to find Carter. Who set up bunker security? Rezko?"

"You're flailing, Boyd."

Reed approached the elevator.

"Tell me, Leland. The cops are going to ask soon enough. Maybe even the feds. What do you want me telling them? That my data was supposed to be keyed into those locks, or that one of your employees entered it when they had no reason?"

Reed stopped but didn't turn. "Rezko handled set up."

I thought it over and spotted a problem. "Rez doesn't have access to bio data. You keep those records in medical histories, which are part of employee cumulative files. That's human resources. Who had access to my fingerprints and retinal scan in HR? Can't be a long list."

The way it worked, HR sent retinal and print data to security and security entered the data into the locks, pairing it with an employee number coded into the mag stripe on the back of every employee's card key. Names and personal information were not part of that package, just the biodata and employee numbers linked through a hash code.

"Who sent the files from HR?"

Reed kept staring at the elevator doors, as if they might allow him to escape. "You're wasting time, Boyd."

"Who had access to my bio data?"

When the doors remained closed, he looked cornered and shot a frown. "Leila was in charge."

For several beats, I said nothing. "Leila was a temp."

Reed seemed to withdraw into a shell. "I know."

"Why put her in charge of something that important?"

"She wanted responsibility. I was thinking about offering her a permanent position. She's smart, Boyd. Jesus, you know what she's like…she—"

"You were banging her."

Reed was unable to meet my eyes.

"Give me her address, Leland."

*

Leila Krebs lived ten miles south in Chino, a suburban enclave once home to cattle ranches and dairy farms, but now, like most of Southern California, offering houses, strip malls, and overcrowded schools. I pulled off the Pomona Freeway at Euclid Avenue, lowered my window and caught a residual whiff of cows, then headed south.

According to Reed, Leila had a three-bedroom condominium in a complex named Portofino, not far from Chino State Prison. Once inside the complex, I found a visitor space and parked, then followed a winding path along a flat, blue swimming pool before turning down a walkway that led to Leila's second-story unit.

My heart tapped a staccato as I climbed the stairs. Standing in the office at the Surfrider Motel, watching the surveillance monitor as Moreno led my son away, disbelief had crashed over me, as if ordered into battle holding a broomstick. Whatever might be coming, I felt unprepared. Moreno held the high ground, had all the advantages. Everything I knew about the man was a lie. There was no way to track him. The Fisk who came into my office was an untraceable impostor. Moreno, a fiction. How can you find a boy taken by a man who doesn't exist? Now, for the first time since leaving the motel, I grasped a thin thread of hope that might lead to some answers.

I tapped Leila's door.

No response.

Glancing across the foliage to the neighboring condominium, I spotted a young couple on a sofa, watching TV. Out in the parking lot, a car pulled into an empty spot. I stepped closer to the door and tried the knob.

It turned.

Pushing the door open, I peered inside. Darkness peered back, but the air had a tinge, like a garbage can full of meat left in the sun for too long. Barbs dug into my stomach, deep down, and I reached for my cell phone.

Then someone came up the stairs behind me.

"Jack?"

Leila Krebs stopped a few steps below holding a laundry basket. She frowned, not quite scared, but concerned enough not to move any closer.

"What are you doing here? What's going on?"

"The door was open. I thought you were gone."

"So you were just going to walk in?"

"No. I mean…" I trailed off, suddenly feeling defensive. "You always go out and leave your door open?"

Leila frowned. "Not that it's your business, but I was doing laundry. And you never answered me." She shifted the laundry basket as if prepping to run. "Why are you here?"

I walked down the stairs and took the basket from her. "My son has been abducted, and you're in trouble," I said. "We need to talk, and if I don't get some answers, I'm calling the police."

*

Leila sipped from a water bottle as she carried a lit candle from the kitchen. I stood at the window, peering out at the lights of the Inland Empire, and followed her reflection in the glass. For someone guilty of a crime, she displayed little fear. Turning from the window, I noted her frown—a sort of bored contempt iced with anticipation—and felt my confidence waver.

"What's this about?"

"MicroLine was hit last night. The guy who did it took my son."

I sat down in a chair across from the sofa. Despite the candle, the room smelled of death. Leila had left town for the weekend, and by the time she'd returned, a clump of chicken skin in the garbage had fouled. Smelling the rot, I thought of Dave in the Corolla's trunk, of the body in the motel parking lot, of Keller and the burned bikers in the desert, and tried to take shallow breaths.

"I'm sorry, but what does that have to do with me?"

I explained my theory about her coding my bio data into the locks. It seemed to amuse her.

"You can't be serious."

"Reed put you in charge, Leila. It would have been easy for you to slip my data into the records you sent to security."

"A lot of people had access to those records, Jack."

"But only HR had everything, and you were in charge."

"I had nothing to do with it."

"You're lying. I don't believe you."

She sipped more water and shrugged. "Well, you don't have a choice."

Beating a confession out of her wasn't my style, but there were options. I opened my phone.

"What are you doing?" she asked.

"Last week, you sent an email to my wife."

"No, I didn't."

"An empty draft. Almost like you were trying to work up the courage to send a message and couldn't make yourself do it. What were you trying to send, Leila? A warning? Did you get cold feet and try to back out of the plan?"

"I have no idea what you're talking about."

"At first I couldn't figure out why you sent it to Abby. Now I know. The only email address you had for me was at MicroLine. Obviously, thanks to you, I no longer use that one. I've changed cell phones since then, and my home phone is unlisted, so you had no way to reach me. My HR file listed Abby's email address, though. A good second option, but you chickened out."

"You're nuts, Jack."

I lifted the phone. "At the moment, this is between us," I said. "Leland and I know of your involvement, no one else. All I want is my son back. Leland wants to pretend none of this happened and get back to work with his company intact. That means you have options. Help me find my son, and you can walk away."

"I can't help you."

"Can't or won't?"

Leila said nothing.

I tapped a few numbers on the keypad, dialing Fisk, then thought of Ran's offer, about Devlin sending an army, and hesitated. How would that look for Leila? Four or five tatted guys breaking down her door, taking turns until she pleaded for them to stop. Even now, with Carter taken, that wasn't in me.

I lifted the phone. "You can talk to the feds."

She snorted like a trapped animal. "We met twice at a Denny's along the 15. She called herself Vonda and said I could make some easy money. You have to believe me, Jack. They never mentioned grabbing your son."

"They?"

"There was a guy with her."

From the way Leila described him, the guy with Vonda wasn't Carlos Moreno. He sounded more like the man at my office who had pretended to be Special Agent Fisk.

"The guy have a name?"

"She called him Walt. He didn't speak much. Vonda talked, and he mostly sat at the counter drinking iced tea. She seemed to run the show. At least, that was the impression I got."

"Tell me about her."

"White. Middle-aged. Red hair and glasses. Said she tracked me down through TechTemp, the agency that sent me to MicroLine. She'd read about what happened between you and me—"

"Nothing happened between you and me, Leila."

"That's a matter of opinion, Jack. Anyway, we had lunch. She was nice and said I could make some money. Walt stayed quiet, just stared and mashed his teeth, like it was hard letting Vonda do all the talking. You could see he liked being in control."

"Do they have my son?"

"I don't know."

"They want some kind of ransom?"

"I don't know. They never said anything about your son."

"What did they say?"

"They offered me five thousand dollars to slip your biodata into the package I sent to security. They never said why. I didn't ask.

They seemed to know a lot about MicroLine's security setup, though."

"You told them."

"No."

"Then how did they know?"

Leila shrugged. It took me a while to finish the computation, but after a few beats, I figured things out. Fisk had been right. I had been played. But the game had started long before I realized I was a participant.

"Singh said an FBI agent came into MicroLine, asking questions about me."

Leila nodded. "Yes."

"But it wasn't this Walt guy?"

"No."

I shook my head. "Describe the guy who came in."

She did. The man's description sounded like Moreno. If so, then MicroLine's security cameras must have recorded him. Maybe the feds could use the image to nail down his identity and find him.

"He asked about MicroLine's security system?"

"Yes. He had credentials. I thought it had to do with the bunker. You know, that federal clearance thing, so I sent him to security."

"The guy wasn't an agent. He's the man who has my son, doing recon, figuring out how to get inside."

"He asked about you. He said it was standard background, and that you'd be working together."

"I was his way in."

"You have to believe me, Jack, I didn't know."

"But you took the five thousand dollars."

"They only paid me half. Three weeks ago, I was supposed to get the rest. They never showed up. That's when I started thinking about the possibilities, and none of them looked good. So I quit MicroLine."

"Why'd you send the email?"

"I spent one afternoon trying to come up with a way to warn you. Something that didn't sound nuts. Nothing came. I couldn't just contact you out of the blue. I deleted what I wrote, but somehow, my email cycled and sent the empty draft."

I lifted my phone.

"What are you doing?"

"Calling the FBI. You're going to tell them."

"I've told you everything."

"You can describe these people. Where you met. That restaurant might have security cameras. There could be pictures of the car they drove. A license plate. You have to tell them everything you know."

"I saw their car."

"Describe it."

"Well, that's the thing. Each time we met, they drove a different car. Both were really shitty."

"Whatever you remember, Leila. You have to tell the feds."

"Will I be arrested?"

"That's not my concern. I need to find my son."

She looked past my shoulder, out the window. "Vonda and Walt are going to kill me," she said.

"They said that?"

"Not in words, but last night, someone sent this to my phone. I took it as a warning."

She pulled her phone from the coffee table, called up a video, and pointed the screen in my direction. I grabbed the phone and held it close. For several beats, the display remained black, random pinpricks of light dotting the background. Then white heat blossomed, shapes took form, and I recognized the scene at once. A trailer blowing up in a dry desert valley. Two men standing on a hill, one holding a cell phone as the explosion lit the night. Either Leila hadn't noticed I was that man, or she was too damn scared to mention it. On the screen, the blast lasted no more than a second, and as the glow faded, whoever had done the filming shifted focus toward the obliterated trailer. Tracking along with the motion of the camera, I noted movement behind one of the cars, spotted an old man crawling in the dirt, and suppressed a grin.

Keller had survived the blast.

*

Back on the freeway, I headed home and dialed Fisk. The agent answered on the first ring. Weaving through traffic, I informed him about Vonda and Walt, then about Leila's role. Fisk listened and seemed to be taking notes. When he came back on the line, his voice carried an edge.

"I'll pass the information along, but you were supposed to stay home. The field office has a team of specialists taking over. I'll be involved, and you can contact me whenever you want, but these people have specific skill sets. They'll assign a family liaison to keep you in the loop, and they'll set up a trap and trace on all your phones. ERT will need to search your son's room. Will any of that be a problem?"

"ERT?"

"Evidence Response Team. Like CSI on TV, only smarter."

"No, that won't be a problem."

"You'll be in good hands, Mr. Boyd. Do what they say. It'll help get your son back."

"When can I speak to them?"

"The team is assembling now. Coordinating with local agencies will take some time. They need to set up a command center. I'll let you know. Should be sometime in the morning."

"Morning?"

"That doesn't mean nothing's happening now. I told you, the Amber Alert is active. Believe me, there are a lot of white hats out looking for your boy."

"What about the car Sara was in? The Toyota?"

"Plates were stolen in San Diego. Someone pulled the VIN tags. They're tearing the engine apart as we speak, looking for an etched number. From what I've heard, it's not going well. Just go

253

home and sit tight. I'll call when I have something. You were supposed to wait by the phone in case things came up, remember?"

"I am by the phone. Things came up. You had better get some men to Chino. Leila was there when I left, but she won't stick around long."

Fisk took down her address. I heard him relay the information to someone else.

"Get home, Mr. Boyd. I'm sure your wife needs you."

"She's not talking to me at the moment. I'd rather keep moving."

"You should go home."

He sounded ready to hang up.

"There's something else," I said. Then I explained the transaction that had transpired at Keller's compound, the different cars Moreno and the others had used, leaving out the explosion, the dead bikers, and the guilt I felt over my involvement. Lying to the feds wasn't smart, but acknowledging my role in a double murder would only result in a return trip to the interrogation room. That couldn't happen until I had my son back. "Keller must have been supplying them with cars."

"Changing cars makes tracing more difficult," Fisk said. "Could be a junk service or storage yard. This place in the desert—you have a location?"

"That's the problem. I was in the trunk for most of the ride. Somewhere near Victorville or Hesperia."

"That's a wide chunk of desert. I'm afraid it does us no good, Mr. Boyd."

Nearing the junction with the 60 Freeway, traffic bunched into tight knots of red. Two women to my right saw me holding my cell phone and shot dirty looks. I switched lanes and pulled behind a station wagon full of kids. Almost nine at night, and families streamed back into the city after a long weekend on the move. I longed to be among them, but at that moment found it difficult to believe I ever would be again. Darting into the carpool lane, I refocused on the phone.

"Keller is a link to these people. He provided them with cars and thermite, for Christ's sake, he has to know something. We have to go out there."

"But you don't know his location, and I don't have twenty agents to send combing the desert." Fisk paused, and when he resumed speaking his voice had lost some of its edge. "Listen, if I was in your position, sitting and waiting would be damn near impossible. But there's a way these things unfold. We have protocols. You need to be home with your wife and daughter, Mr. Boyd. Let us find your son."

Shifting into the fast lane, I pressed the gas.

"I can't sit around until morning, Fisk. I won't."

MICHAEL HARBISON

Chapter Twenty-Seven

At home, Ran met me in the driveway and held up his hands in the universal gesture of surrender, trying to hold off a fight. Behind him, standing on my front doorstep, taking up space like a big-block Chevy engine, Danny Devlin cracked his knuckles and nodded in my direction.

Slamming the Subaru's door, I glared at my brother. "What the hell is he doing here?"

Ran nodded toward Moreno's house. "The cops wrapped up about an hour ago. I felt a little exposed, so Danny came to help."

Empty and dark, Moreno's place looked the same except for a strip of yellow tape that sealed the front door. Whatever the police had found, collecting hadn't taken long. A single patrol car sat along the curb across the street in front of Dave's house, the bored cop staring at his computer screen.

"We have police protection. I want Devlin gone."

"Fine. You tell him."

Devlin left the house and walked toward us, closing the gap with three long strides. He held out a hand and touched my shoulder. "Jack, I'm sorry as hell about your son."

I barely looked at him.

"Took the liberty of placing two of my guys in your backyard. There's another down the street. Between them and the cop, you're locked up good and tight. You should get some sleep."

"We don't need you here."

"Get some sleep, Jack. Things will look better when you're rested."

"Really? Don't tell me what to do."

I pushed past him and went inside.

*

After I stopped talking, Abby took several long beats to respond. "What next?" she asked at last.

No demands, no conditions. Just a simple question, as if my next move wasn't a choice but an act of fate. Over the past ten minutes, I had explained the situation—Leila, Vonda, Walt. But naming our tormentors brought us no closer to finding Carter, and it did nothing to quiet the fire that burned in Abby's eyes, shooting heat in my direction. Extinguishing those flames would require action.

"Keller is our best option. He knew Moreno. They did business. Someone arranged that deal between them, and that person is another link in the chain. I have to find Keller and see what he knows."

"Then find him."

Standing up, I moved closer to her. "Ab, I want you to know..."

She rolled onto her side and faced away from me.

I turned to leave.

"Take Ran with you," she said. "I don't want you going alone."

"That leaves you alone. Ran should stay here."

"You saw the men in our backyard?"

"Yes."

"I'm not alone."

She pulled the blankets up around her shoulders.

I went downstairs.

Devlin and Ran sat at the kitchen table. Devlin promised to safeguard my family, and despite the lack of confidence that instilled, I thanked him. Describing Keller's compound, I detailed the sea of cars that sat within, the way Moreno and Walt seemed always to be driving something different, and the old man nodded.

"Sounds like a chop operation," Devlin said. "Probably VIN switching. Dude buys a salvaged car, gets a clean VIN and title, and then transfers the title to a stolen car. Boom, now the guy has a legit ride to sell and cuts the salvage for parts. If that's Keller's gig, a place in the desert makes sense. Cars in and out all the time. You don't want neighbors looking over fences and calling the cops."

"And what? He's renting them out?"

"Like I said, he'd have a lot of cars. Bad guys do creative things for money."

Devlin seemed to be an expert. Whatever the reason, I tried not to think about it, and then told Ran we should go. As I walked to the door, I decided to relay one more piece of news to Devlin before we left.

"Selig's hard drives," I said.

Danny shrugged. "Not at the top of my list right now, Jack. Just find your son."

"The drives are gone."

"Gone?"

"The man who took Carter has them."

Devlin's mouth creased into a flat line. "How the hell did that happen?"

"They were in my jacket after I left work. He searched me, found them, then threw them into the back seat of his car."

Devlin stood silent, calculating something. Then he and my brother exchanged glances, and I felt a cold breeze as Ran opened the front door and went out to the car.

Devlin nodded then. "Like I said, Jack. Find your son."

*

Around ten, we crossed Cajon Summit, and the desert unfolded in the night like a map leading nowhere. Before leaving home, I had checked satellite images on my phone for anything east of Victorville that resembled Keller's compound, and found countless possibilities. Somewhere, in all that darkness, an old man in a wheelchair might lead closer to my son, but from here, that darkness seemed to stretch forever. My cell phone was on. If anything changed at home, Abby would call. Until then, all I could do was keep moving.

In the passenger seat, Ran looked out the window. "Winter is coming," he noted. "Desert looks like hell in the summer, but it freezes come December."

"This is where we turned off," I said.

Ahead the Denny's and In-N-Out glowed yellow and white, and as we passed, both looked full of customers. Foreclosures had decimated the surrounding neighborhoods, so diners were probably travelers deviating from the interstate for a quick snack, munching burgers and sipping soup, blind to the suburban wasteland surrounding them. As we headed east, abandoned houses lined the road like shells on a beach where people no longer came to swim.

I hated the desert.

"Dead lawns. Empty driveways. Probably squatters, too," Ran noted. "They ought to give the deeds to families who could look after them. Mow the yards, pick weeds. Banks would rather watch them rot."

I kept driving.

"A burger sounds good," Ran observed. "Maybe some coffee."

I said nothing.

"Yeah, I'm not hungry," he said, then let it die.

As a kid, whenever my brother sensed disharmony, he soothed tension with excess conversation. Some nights, when our dad came home pissed off, Ran would talk endlessly about his day at school, the neighbor's cat, a glob of wax he'd plucked from his ear, or anything else that might postpone the old man's metamorphosis from drunken loser to full-blown abuser. Most of the time nothing worked, but Ran kept talking just the same. Tonight I wasn't in the mood to listen. After his failure to protect my family at the motel, something had broken between us. My accusations had cut deep, carving to bone, and no matter what came next, the wound had left a scar. Considering the information about Leila and the mystery couple, Vonda and Walt, the idea of my brother's complicity now seemed absurd, but I couldn't help feeling he had failed me. Then again, maybe I had failed him.

"I should never have called you," I said.

"What?"

"Should have gone to the police. It's not your fault Carter is gone."

Ran looked out the window. More gutted housing developments slid by to the south.

"You're right," he said. "You should not have called, because one way or another, I was bound to screw up. That's what you mean, isn't it Jack? But that's okay, because you're right. If you had called the police, Bodie would be alive, Carter would be home. I made bad decisions, but I wasn't the only one."

"I'm not blaming you. That's the point. I'm sorry."

"Yeah, well, that and twelve bucks will get me into a movie. Not everything can be helped, Jack. Sometimes shit just happens, and all you can do is endure."

"I know that, but that's the problem. I have no idea why any of this is happening. Is it MicroLine? Devlin? Something personal?"

"I can tell you it's not Devlin."

"But how can you be sure? The hard drives. Maybe there's more to it than you know."

"There's more to it, but not what you think. Danny's not selling guns. He's buying them. He cheats on taxes and uses the money to buy guns from bangers in the neighborhoods. Selig got wind of the DA looking into things and panicked. Dumb shit drove his car right into a tree."

Processing the information took a moment. Once the data aligned, an obvious question stood out. "You sure Selig had an accident? Maybe someone helped him off the road."

"Are you listening to anything I say? Danny's buying guns and crushing them in his salvage yard, trying to clean up bad neighborhoods. He's taking guns off the streets. He buys them with gift cards and food vouchers. He's helping families."

"Okay. Why?"

Ran shrugged. "It's his way of making amends for what happened with Stevie. Danny screwed up as a father. Stevie went down a bad path. That can't be undone, but he doesn't want other people making the same mistake and losing their kids."

"And Selig's hard drives?"

"Taxes and business records, Jack. That's all they are. You ever fudge a little on your taxes? Look, Danny has some rough edges, but he's no killer."

I waited a few beats as the information settled. Even if it were true, Devlin would be in trouble with the feds and not just for tax evasion. Unless the guns in question were antique, weapons transactions required notification to the ATF, no matter the intended outcome. Even more reason Devlin would want the hard drives under his control. Problem was I saw no logical link between what happened at MicroLine and Devlin, and thus, no logical link to Moreno.

"Last I saw them, Selig's hard drives were in Moreno's car," I said.

"That's not why Danny's at your house."

"Why is he at my house?"

Ran thought it over a moment, honing the answer, wanting to get things right. Then he took a deep breath and pushed the words out in one gasping rush.

"He's there for me. What Marty was for you, Danny is for me. He helps me walk a straight path. For him, it's as if he's getting a second chance at helping Stevie. I don't know, maybe that's weird, being a stand-in for a dead son, but I don't care. Danny knows how I feel about your family...and about you. That's why he's with Abby and Sara. I didn't have to ask, Jack. Once he heard, he just showed up, and it had nothing to do with hard drives. "

Once things soaked in, I nodded. "I'm glad you told me."

Tired of looking out the window, Ran nodded and met my eye. "Okay. Say we locate this Keller guy. What then?"

I shrugged. "Call Fisk, tell him."

Ran shook his head. "Do that, and Keller will swallow his tongue and lawyer up."

The road narrowed to one lane. The bridge loomed beyond, the place where Moreno had forced me into the trunk. From that point on, my compass was broken. All I knew was that Keller's compound lay east of the city lights and that beyond it nothing waited but the black deep of the desert.

"Then I guess we'll see," I said.

Ran nodded. "I guess we will."

"What would you do?"

"Me? I'd start asking questions."

"What if he won't answer?"

"Then I'd ask harder."

*

The highway broke into a Y ten miles east of the bridge. One fork headed toward Victorville, the other east to Lucerne Valley. No traffic came from behind us, so I sat at the stop sign and recalled what the ride in Moreno's trunk had felt like, hoping body memory could point the way.

Asphalt.

Jarring washboard and choking dust.

Other than that, nothing.

We were looking for a dirt road, which narrowed options down to a few thousand. Along the sandblasted highway, boulders rose in clots, mounding into low hills that blocked the surrounding desert from view. As I sat there, my stomach twisted, and I knew

Fisk had been right. Driving out here hoping to find Keller was an exercise in wasted motion, a way of fighting the awful truth that a killer had my son, but like a shark that couldn't stop swimming without drowning, all I could do was move.

"What's the problem?" Ran asked.

"We'll never find him. Even if we do, you're right. Keller's not going to talk."

"I hate being right. Pull over, so I can take a leak."

I pulled off the highway onto a one-lane gravel road, stopped once the highway receded, and then left the engine idling as Ran stepped behind a bush. Then my phone rang. I pulled it out and flipped it open. The screen flashed *unknown caller*.

"Hello?"

I heard a sniffle.

"Daddy?"

My heart stopped dead.

"Daddy, I'm tired."

"Carter. Hey, buddy. You okay?"

"Dad—"

His voice cut away. Someone else came on the line.

"Boyd, I'm disappointed you went to the police. We are officially no longer friends."

I cupped the phone hard against my ear. "I want my son, Moreno."

"I'm afraid I've permanently left the neighborhood."

"What do you want? Tell me. Whatever it is, I'll do it."

"I don't want anything. You should be happy I took pity and left you one child. Keeping both seemed rather cruel."

"Why are you doing this?"

"You'll have to figure that out. Oh, and by the way, remember that conversation we had about taking your kids? I mentioned something unpleasant you might receive in the mail. If that becomes necessary, would you like morning delivery, or do you prefer afternoon?"

Something hot jammed my throat. Fear. Rage. Whatever it was, I choked it down and begged.

"Please don't hurt him. He's just a kid."

"Pleading is unimpressive, Boyd. We're quite alike, your son and I. He's entertaining. Maybe I'll enjoy him a while longer. I haven't decided yet."

"Let him go."

"You sound weak. Try a little more anger."

Then Carter began to cry

"You fuck," I yelled. "I'll kill you, I swear. You hurt him, and I'll hunt you down and take your fucking head."

Moreno laughed. "Much better, Boyd. Almost convincing. Before you can kill me, though, you have to find me."

"Why are you doing this?"

Moreno said nothing for a few beats. I listened to him breathe, a slow give and take, barely audible above the silence. Then he gave a dark laugh. "Ask your brother."

He cut the call.

Ran came back to the car and read the look on my face.

"What's all the yelling? What happened?"

Ignoring the question, I dialed Fisk and spent five minutes recounting the conversation. Fisk relayed the information to a colleague and promised to trace the call. We both knew it would go nowhere.

"You ignored my advice. You're in the desert," Fisk said then. "You find anything?"

"Nothing but sand. I couldn't sit at home."

"Your son is alive, Mr. Boyd. That's good news. Actually, I was about to call you. We caught a break. They pulled a VIN from the Toyota. The registration kicked back a match. If it's our guy, his name isn't Moreno. Hell, he's not even Mexican. Toyota belonged to a man named Lewis Polk. Mean anything to you?"

"Why would it?"

"An old client? Somebody you once trained at MicroLine?"

Polk. A common-sounding name, but no instant recognition.

"I don't know. Why would I have trained him?"

"Polk's a cop."

"What?"

"He *was* a cop…in Calexico. Down on the border. He went through FLETC training a few years back—anti-terror, border security—so we had his prints. According to his watch commander in Calexico, Polk handled their computer stuff. The guy was trouble from day one, killed a citizen in an off-duty bar fight a year back. The DA ruled justifiable homicide, but his career ended just the same. Last the commander knew, Polk handled security for bars across the border in Mexicali."

"Drug cartels run bars?"

"I'd forget about drug cartels, Mr. Boyd. This seems to be going in a different direction."

"What direction? Polk had some kind of beef with MicroLine?"

"MicroLine seems to have been the target. And you, of course. You guys worked with different enforcement agencies. Maybe you trained him. Maybe you did a bad job, maybe he screwed up a case, maybe it cost him, and maybe that pissed him off and led him into that bar where he killed a guy. Could be he blames you for every shitty thing in his life. Who knows? At this point, it's all maybes and what ifs. What matters is we have a name. Come home, Mr. Boyd. We're getting closer."

"Thanks, Fisk."

I cut the call.

Ran looked at me

"What's up?"

I brought him up to speed and asked if he recognized Polk's name

"No."

Starting the car, I made several attempts at a three-point turn. Not enough room. Mounded rocks along the road made backing out dicey, so I continued down the dirt track, hoping it carved a loop back to the highway, unable to silence Moreno's parting words.

Ask your brother.

Another mind game. Fisk said Polk was a cop, and the investigation was moving toward MicroLine. Ran had nothing to do with MicroLine. Had never even set foot in the building.

Moreno was full of shit.

Despite the late hour, adrenaline leaked into my bloodstream. I wanted to call Reed, see if he could dig up any record of Polk going through MicroLine's training. Even if he could, that didn't answer all the questions. If the attack on the bunker had been an act of retribution, why involve Walt and Vonda, and why take my son after damaging MicroLine? Why not get out of town and make a clean getaway? Too many things didn't make sense.

Before an answer came, the dirt road morphed into asphalt, and we found ourselves in a parking lot. Ahead, some kind of stadium rose from the night.

"Strange place for football," Ran noted. "Kind of hot in the summer."

I shook my head. "Not football."

"What then?"

Pointing at a billboard, I recalled the sound of circling bees to the west as I climbed from the trunk of Moreno's Mazda and stared down the hillside at Keller's doublewide trailer. On the billboard, a biker pumped a triumphant fist, and I conjured the buzzing sound.

Not bees.

Motorcycles.

The compound was close.

*

The doublewide trailer had seen better days. Blasted debris swept the desert in a broad arc, and the subsequent fire had turned the trailer and several cars into harsh skeletal outlines resting on sand. Keller's homestead once existed. Now it was simply gone.

"Somebody's there," Ran said, pointing at the Airstream trailer near the back of the compound. "But if it's Keller, he's not alone."

The Airstream glowed with faint light. A pickup and two motorcycles sat close by, clinging to shadow. Two burly guys hung by the door, smoking and lifting bottles. Despite the destruction, numerous cars remained, and after a quick search, I locked eyes on a dark, partially burned Ford with a dented left side. Then one of the motorcycles fired up, pulled away from the Airstream, and headed east.

"Biker trash sucks," Ran grumbled. "Born white, all the advantage and none of the brains to use it. They're mean as hell, though. You'd better call the feds."

"Keller's our link to Moreno."

"I thought you said his name was Polk?"

"Whatever his name, Keller's our link."

"Then call the FBI. Get them out here. Feds love playing Daniel Boone. They'll pick those leather goons off one by one."

I shook my head. "The feds start tearing this place apart, even if Keller doesn't put up a fight, like you said, he's going to shut down and wait for a lawyer."

"We're two guys. Neither of us is armed. We don't really have a choice."

"I have a plan."

"You're going down there and ask nice? When I suggested we pump Keller for info, I was kind of assuming he'd be old and alone."

I tossed him my keys and handed over my cell phone. The Subaru sat a hundred yards back down the road. "Give me five minutes to get down there and ten more to make a deal. If things go south or I don't come back, call Fisk and tell him where to find us. You can get coordinates from the Subaru's nav system."

*

The explosion had knocked down large portions of chain-link fence and crumpled floodlights, so it was a simple matter of wending through clots of boulder and debris, sticking to shadows and moving toward the Airstream's dim glow. Halfway there, I remembered the dogs and stood at the compounds' perimeter for three long beats, listening as my existential clock ticked closer to midnight. Nothing moved toward me. No sound. No wind. Then I pictured my son wrapped in the grasp of a killer and decided whatever threats I faced—meth-hyped bikers or flesh tearing dogs—didn't matter.

"On your knees. Don't move."

The voice came from behind, sharp and cold, someone accustomed to barking orders. My eyes slid in that direction and landed on a shadow next to a large boulder. The shadow pointed something long and metallic at my head.

"I need to see Keller."

"Get down."

I dropped to my knees, felt gravel bite into skin, and then lifted my hands. The shadow stepped close and grew detail. Not a bearded loser like last night's bikers. This guy was clean-shaven, with short hair and intelligent eyes. Not the hired help. Management. He pushed my head down, pitched me into the sand, and dug a knee into my back.

"I want to see Keller."

His gun touched my face as he laced my wrists with plastic ties. Once patted down, he flipped me onto my back.

"Who's Keller?"

"We want the same thing."

"No shit. What's that?"

"The man who blew him up."

*

The old man sat at a chipped dining booth illuminated by a dim yellow light, wedged against the Airstream's side window, and squinted as I ducked through the doorway. His folded wheelchair rested next to a grease-blotted stove. The Chihuahua sat in the booth beside him, stubby tail thumping vinyl like a fast-beating heart. Beside the stove, a Rottweiler the size of a bull sprawled with its mouth open, ready for dinner.

"Remember me?" I asked.

The gunman pulled my wallet and tossed it to Keller.

"I'm old and forgetful, but last night is seared into memory. I'll be smelling smoke for weeks." The old man stared at my license, then looked past me to the guy holding the gun and moved his chin. "Cage, feed Mr. Boyd to the dogs, will you? Don't be in a hurry either."

The gunman grabbed my neck and yanked me toward the door. The Rottweiler snapped to its feet, jaws open, scratchy rasp coming from its throat.

"Wait," I said. "I can help you."

Keller held up a hand.

Cage stopped.

"Lewis Polk," I said.

Keller rolled his lower lip into a sausage and chewed. "Nice name. What's it mean?"

"The man from last night." I pointed to what remained of the doublewide. "You knew him as Moreno, but his name might be Polk. He abducted my son. I can find him for you."

Bored with sitting beside the old man, the Chihuahua climbed onto the table and stretched beneath the light as if absorbing the summer sun, mewing like a cat until Keller rubbed its belly. The Rottweiler turned a few circles and then collapsed by the fridge, shaking the trailer like an earthquake.

"Why help me?"

"He took my son."

"Why should I care?"

I waited a few beats, swallowing panic, allowing fear to morph into bravado. "You're a businessman, like me, and reputation is everything in business. Looking around, I see the wreckage from last night. Your place burned down. Cars torched. One thing I don't see is cops. Two men died last night. Just the same, no crime-scene tape, no arson investigator, no ATF. You didn't report what happened. Or if you did, you claimed it was an accident. You want things quiet. My guess is, in your line of work, on matters like this, justice is best handled alone."

Keller gave a sharp snort. "What line of work is that?"

I scanned the compound and then rolled my shoulders. "That's obvious. You rent cars."

"I rent cars?"

"Yeah...like Hertz. And in any business, when competitors sense weakness, they pounce. Word of what happened gets around, you stand to lose market share. Respect too. Any way you crunch the numbers, letting Moreno get away hurts business. But you can't exactly go to the police and file a complaint, can you?"

Keller snorted again. "I don't need the police."

"That's why I'm here."

"You can help me?"

"I have certain skills."

"You can find this man with your skills?"

"Maybe."

"How?"

"That Ford with the dent—the Taurus—Moreno was driving it, right?"

Keller's eyes slid toward Cage. Something passed between them, and whatever it was seemed to buy me credibility. Keller took another pull on his lip and shrugged. "I have no idea who was driving what. Rental agreements were the responsibility of the men you killed last night."

"Moreno blew your place up, not me."

"Either way, I can't answer your question, can I? Sorry, but your son isn't my problem. My problem is you said you can help me, but so far, I'm not seeing how."

"I assume you don't advertise your services. Probably have a limited clientele base. How do you set up deals?"

"Word gets around to the people who need to know. From what I recall, Moreno was a friend of a friend type of deal. As I said, my associates set it up. Difficult to trace. But I'm working on it."

"Could a guy named Walt or a woman named Vonda be involved? The guy middle-aged, balding? Ten days ago, he showed up at my office impersonating an FBI agent."

The old man drummed his fingers on the Chihuahua's belly, then lifted its lip and examined the dog's teeth.

I continued. "The other night, you told me Moreno damaged that Ford."

The old man shrugged.

"How long did he have your car?"

Another long bout of hesitation, then Keller said, "Two weeks."

"The GPS on that Taurus writes to a 10 gigabyte hard drive. Track logs, routes, waypoints. 10 gigabytes covers a lot of GPS data."

"Meaning what?"

"I can tell you where Moreno went during those two weeks. We'll see patterns."

"What kind of patterns?"

"Like footprints in sand. Footprints we can follow."

Keller stroked the Chihuahua and grinned.

"Cage, help Mr. Boyd get what he needs."

*

When the drive rested in my hands, Keller flipped through the family photos in my wallet, lips twisting into a half smile. Cage slipped me a piece of paper containing a scrawled phone number. After a while, Keller tossed my wallet back.

"You won't forget us, Mr. Boyd."

"I won't."

"When you have the information on our mutual friend, unless he's dead, I want everything."

"He might be in custody.

"That won't matter to us."

"You'll get it. After I have my son."

"Good luck finding your boy."

Ten minutes later, I climbed the hill and walked back to the Subaru. Beside it, Ran paced in the dark.

"Fifteen minutes," he grumbled. "You've been gone thirty."

"You called Fisk?"

"Hell no, I was watching. You seemed all right. So I let it play."

"Good."

His eyes fell to the hard drive from the Ford's navigation system. "What the hell is that?"

Without bothering to reply, I opened the hatch and retrieved my laptop.

"You drive," I said. "I have to work."

MICHAEL HARBISON

Chapter Twenty-Eight

By the time we reached asphalt, I had pulled waypoints, track logs, and data files from the GPS partition on the Ford's hard drive and begun sifting the information through one of MicroLine's analysis programs. Lack of statistics wasn't the problem; the Ford's navigation system recorded vehicle location and speed data at periodic intervals, merging that information with date and time stamps into track logs. The issue was lack of time. I stared at the screen and waited as the program plotted information on a graph.

"Shit," I muttered as the dots spread.

Ran glanced over and saw red points growing like a virus. "Doesn't exactly narrow it down, does it?"

My hope for a quick resolution carved slow circles down the drain. "Analysis will take hours."

"Those are places Moreno went in just two weeks?"

"Twenty-four hours," I said. "The last day he had the car. Track log starts at nine-fifteen in the morning and ends at eleven-thirty. First waypoint is in College Heights, the last at Keller's compound."

Ran shook his head. "Two hours and fifteen minutes to go from your place up to here. Traffic's a bitch, but that's a lot of time. He must have stopped along the way."

Studying the screen, I realized my brother was right. Moreno, or whoever had driven the car back to Keller, had stopped multiple times. Short intervals mostly, probably traffic lights and stop signs. Then I noticed a long time gap between two waypoints a short distance apart—twenty-five minutes to go less than a mile. Speed data indicated the Ford had been stationary at one waypoint.

Could have been a stop light.

Maybe he stopped for lunch or had problems with the car.

Or it could have been something else.

"What is it?" Ran asked.

"He stopped near here before he went to Keller's."

Typing the coordinates into the Subaru's navigation system, I selected the map's satellite view. Part of me feared what I would see. An intersection monitored by traffic lights, a railroad crossing, explaining the Ford's lack of motion, putting one more notch of distance between Carter and me.

Then the map loaded.

"Well?" Ran demanded.

"It's a house."

*

We found it near midnight in a neighborhood of flat-roofed houses with lawns of rock, and I called Fisk and told him where to meet us. While I talked, Ran positioned the Subaru fifty yards down the street, facing the house. A white pickup sat in the driveway, and kid's toys—bikes, big wheels, a turtle-shaped sandbox—lined the walkway near the garage. I tried reading the truck's plate numbers as I talked, but the dim streetlights turned them into a dark smudge. Fisk listened without interrupting and then sighed, drawing out the sound into one long, disapproving groan.

"Under no circumstances are you to approach that house. I'll alert San Bernardino County. They can send deputies. When they arrive, I want you gone."

"No way, Fisk. My son could be in there."

"And it could be some innocent family bedded down for the night. Even if Carter is there, you can't go in. Leave this to the pros, Mr. Boyd. You go pounding on doors at midnight, one way or another, this will end badly. I'm on my way, but I want you out of there."

"Fisk—"

"I'll make things simple for you. If you're in the area when deputies arrive, I'll have you arrested."

Fisk cut the call.

I tossed my phone to the floor.

Staring at the house, images flashed in my head, black things I had seen on computer screens hundreds of times—kids abused, pimped-out, mutilated—things that infected my sleep, kept at bay only by the hope my own children would never face such monsters.

Hope was gone now.

A monster had my son.

Possibly inside that house.

I opened the door and stepped outside.

Before I went two paces, the front door opened and a paunchy man wearing a hat and a security uniform walked into the porch light's yellow glow. He carried a lunch box and thermos, and a blonde woman stood at the door and extended on her toes to kiss him goodbye. The woman looked very pregnant. Definitely not Vonda. My heart sank. They looked normal, a husband and wife, saying goodbye as the man started a midnight shift at some factory or warehouse. Then light fell on the man's face as he walked to the truck and recognition dawned.

Fisk, the imposter.

Walt.

Before they spotted me, I returned to the Subaru.

"That's Walt," I said.

Ran clutched the wheel and gritted his teeth. "What now?"

The choices weren't good. Stick around, hope Carter was in that house and risk arrest, or follow Walt's truck.

"Fisk is on the way. We know about the house. I want this guy."

*

Walt drove east into the desert—past the turn-off that led to Keller's compound, onto a stretch of highway without artificial lighting—and the road meandered like a conduit to oblivion.

"Stay back," I said. "There's not much traffic. He'll spot us."

A quarter mile ahead, Walt's taillights glowed.

"We'll lose him," Ran said.

A road sign flashed, indicating Lucerne Valley five miles ahead. From behind us, bright light flooded the Subaru's cab, and seconds later, a van blasted by on the left. I noted the initials RJI on the rear door panels as it passed, then caught the glint of wire mesh on the windows. Something about the initials tapped my head, linking the van to a memory, and then went away. For a while, the van blocked Walt's truck from view. Then it passed him as well. Walt's high beams flashed multiple times before his taillights swept in a hard left arc and disappeared.

A mile later, a flat glow climbed from the darkness. Lucerne Valley.

By the time we reached town, Walt's truck was no longer on the road.

I choked down panic.

"Told you we'd lose him," Ran said.

"Keep driving."

Lucerne Valley was a shithole, as if the charred pieces of Keller's trailer had blown into the desert and taken root in the barren soil. Everywhere I looked, destruction ruled, spitting up crumbling businesses, burned-out homes, and gutted cars. Thirty seconds later, a more prosperous section of hell appeared and the highway forked, an offshoot leading up to Big Bear, the ski resort in the mountains. At the junction, a Circle K and a Vons, surrounded by two gas stations, gave off a civilized veneer of light.

"There," Ran said.

His finger drew a bead on a pickup in the Circle K parking lot as Walt exited the minimart, tapping a cigarette box against the blade of his hand, the way my father once had. Halfway to his truck, he exchanged words with a woman in a Chevy Blazer. The woman shared Walt's uniform. In the Circle K's fluorescent glow, her hair looked red, and as she spoke, she kept adjusting her glasses.

Vonda.

Walt leaned into the Blazer and they talked for several minutes. Not quite fighting, but tense. Then Walt headed to his pick-up as the woman pulled back onto the highway and drove east. Once in the pickup, Walt lit a cigarette and rejoined the highway in the same direction, out of town, back into the dark.

"Where the hell is he going?" Ran asked.

A road sign loomed. Walt hit his blinker, indicating a left turn. The sign came into view, sporting the initials RJI. This time, a string of words ran beneath, giving the acronym meaning.

My heart rate picked up, tapping a staccato against my ribs as I read the words.

Restorative Justice Institute.

Walt was no rent-a-cop. He was a prison guard.

Then the drill working in my head since glimpsing the van completed the shaft, and memory surged up in a gush that made me physically ill.

"She did time here," I said.

Ran was already turning, heading toward the prison.

"Who?"

"Janis Goodman."

*

Thirty seconds later, prison lights crawled out of the desert and sprinkled the horizon. In less than a mile, Walt's truck would pull inside the compound and we would lose him.

Polk.

MicroLine.

Janis Goodman.

It made no sense.

"How can Janis be involved in this?"

"She can't," Ran insisted. "She's dead."

"She served the last years of her sentence here. We're driving toward the prison, following a man linked to Carter's abduction. You're telling me it's coincidence."

"I'm saying Janis is dead. You saw the newspaper. She can't be involved."

"Yeah, I saw the paper."

"Then stop thinking about it. If that asshole gets inside the prison..." Ran stomped the accelerator. The Subaru's underpowered engine coughed up more speed. The gap to Walt's truck began to narrow.

"What are you doing?"

"Whatever I have to."

If he saw the headlights come from behind, Walt never panicked. His speed remained constant, and as we got close, he edged the truck to the road's sandy berm, making room for us to pass.

Ran didn't hesitate. He pulled the Subaru alongside the pickup and tapped the horn.

Walt looked out the window, face creased in a bemused grin, lit by the glow of his dash, probably thinking coworkers from the prison were having some fun. Then, in a flash of dual headlights, he spotted me.

The grin vanished.

He sped up.

Ran cranked the wheel hard right and forced Walt off the road.

*

Marty Goodman breathed air, but for the past twenty-two years, I had considered him a dead man. The night Janis killed him, a hurricane spun off the coast of northern Baja, pumping a wet fist against the Southland—thunderheads, long sheets of rain, lightning. Hell was breaking loose, and if I had bothered to notice, I would have known something bad was coming. But I was seventeen, my mother was dead, my father a drunk, my life so dark I had nearly lost my vision.

That night I had cooked dinner for my father—a steak and potato he doused with vodka—and made a sandwich for myself. Ran was at Marty's. By the time I'd cleaned up the dishes, my father had passed out watching *Family Ties*. Turning off the TV, I went upstairs and studied. My SATs were coming, and thanks to Marty, my pitching arm had turned hot over the spring. Scholarship visions entranced me—Florida State, Michigan, anywhere a thousand miles away. When Ran hadn't come home by nine, I'd decided to call Janis.

Somewhere between dial tone and ring, the screams began.

*

Ran punched Walt twice in the face and then pushed him into the passenger seat. The pickup had drifted off the road and slammed into a Joshua tree. Dazed, the prison guard offered no resistance. Ran hit him once more, shoving Walt into the foot well, then jumped behind the wheel of the pickup.

"What are you doing?"

"We can't stay here." Ran put the truck in gear and backed up. Tires thumped boulders. The suspension bounced hard, scraping stone, filling the night with sparks.

"Follow me," he yelled out the window.

My eyes darted to the prison lights, then into the surrounding darkness.

"Follow you where?"

Walt began to stir.

Ran hit him again.

"Someplace we can talk to this piece of shit."

*

Marty and Janis argued in an office directly across from my second-floor bedroom. Due to the heat, both houses were open, and profanity laced the air, crackling like embers in search of fuel. I watched from my window, unable to move, guts rolling as the last stable piece of my world crumbled. After my mother's death, I had imbued Marty and Janis with qualities they probably never deserved and certainly never claimed. Counterpoints to my dead mother and useless father—a shadow family, perfect because they never faced the burden of reality. Too much idealism for anyone to live up to, and that night, when the fantasy burned, it ignited like a mountain of dead grass.

"You're...sick!" Janis screamed.

Her volume climbed, syllables cracking like bullets hitting glass, and Marty flinched at each one. Her voice had always been warm and soft, matching the swell of her body when she wrapped you in a hug. By any measure, Janis was obese, but as she screamed, muscles tensed in her neck, and her hands shrank to stone fists. Then she spat on Marty's face. He took a step back and dropped out of sight. When he came up, something was in his hand. Some kind of paper he waved in front of her like a threat.

"This is my fault!" he screamed.

Janis spat again.

Marty hit her.

Seconds later, Janis lifted the bat.

Chapter Twenty-Nine

Behind Walt's truck, I steered with one hand, trying to see through the kicked-up dust as I reached out and answered my ringing phone.

It was Fisk.

"Tell me you found my son," I said.

"Carter wasn't there. The deputies searched the house and the property. Three kids, but they belong to the woman. She's being interviewed, but it's going nowhere. Where are you?"

"Following a guy who's probably her husband."

"Boyd, that's a bad idea. Whatever you're planning, you need to stop."

"It's the guy who came to my office pretending to be you, Fisk. He's a prison guard in Lucerne Valley."

"Prison guard?"

"Restorative Justice Institute. It's a private prison."

"Okay, Boyd. That means we know where this guy works. You need to stand down. This is federal now. This guy assumed the identity of an FBI agent, and that place will be occupied territory within an hour, I promise you. You go in first and you're obstructing."

Ran tapped the truck's brakes. Red lights flashed. He began slowing down.

"I'm not waiting. This guy knows something. He can tell us how to find Polk."

There was a pause, and then Fisk broke the news. "Lewis Polk is dead."

My head swam hard for a moment, going down in a riptide, and I almost drove off the road.

"Someone killed Polk in a Mexicali bar three months ago. Beat him to death with a baseball bat, then cut up the body and left pieces along the highway to San Diego. Guy running the bar says Polk hung with bad people. Cartel people. Polk's car was never found."

"Meaning?"

"We have no idea who has your son. For all we know, his name might be Moreno. He could be Polk's killer; maybe he just stole Polk's car. We don't know."

I clutched the phone and said nothing.

"You need to come home, Mr. Boyd."

Ran had pulled off the road near a cluster of buildings.

I pressed the brakes and followed. "Not yet," I said.

*

A dry-bone crunch echoed from the tires as I pulled into some kind of abandoned ranch shielded from the highway by a copse of dead trees. A semi-circle of crushed white stone carved an arc through the property, forming a driveway leading past two gutted homes, one mud brick, the other a shack of warped boards and tarpaper. Behind the houses, some type of outbuilding with a collapsed roof sat atop a mound. Timbers jutted from the sides, white and hard in the headlights, like protrusions of bone. The painted outline of an oversized chicken on the wall suggesting some type of hatchery. The building seemed freshly burned, the air heavy and scented with charcoal.

Dousing the Subaru's lights, I watched darkness creep in like a tide, senses twitching and electric, as if plugged into the night. My brother dragged Walt from the truck, carrying a set of jumper cables, heading toward the wooden house. Walt limped, clutching around his liver, barely resisting. I got out and followed. Behind us, cars drove the highway and headlamps filtered through tree branches, landing on Ran and Walt, casting them with pulsing bursts of black and white.

By the time I reached the house, Walt rode a gutted recliner inside near the front door, and gouts of stuffing mushroomed around him like an explosion of tumors. Ran used the jumper cables to tie the guard down, pinning his arms back. Walt's chest heaved. The house was so dark I barely saw his face. Then another car drove past, sending a flash of light. Walt's eyes looked wet.

I stepped close. "Remember me, Special Agent?"

My hands dug into his flabby neck and moved over his windpipe.

He started to gasp.

Then the headlights moved away.

I let go of Walt's throat. He sucked air. Tried working his hands loose.

Ran turned his cell phone into a flashlight and placed it on the floor—two-by-fours and some buckled plywood—igniting the room in a blue-gray shine. Walt's eyes bounced, not landing in one place for long, a man caught in a forest fire, certain he was about to burn.

"Where's my son?"

Walt looked at the floor and shook his head.

"I don't know."

Ran slapped him with an open hand.

Walt's body lurched hard, and the chair nearly tipped over. Beneath the chair, floorboards groaned and then splintered from the shifting load.

I grabbed Walt's throat and squeezed, digging my thumbs deep, feeling the notched ridge of his windpipe as it threatened to buckle. Bulging and fat, his eyes swelled as if they might explode.

"Ease back," Ran said.

I let go.

Walt sucked deep, wet gasps.

"What's his name?"

"What? Who?"

"Moreno...What's his real name?"

"I don't know. He called himself Moreno."

"Bullshit."

On the chair, Walt squirmed as if the springs were snakebites striking his skin.

"Man, I don't know nothing else. He said his name was Moreno."

"Where's my son? He wasn't at your house. Where is he?"

"What? You went to my house?" His eyes grew hot. "Leticia and the kids got nothing to do with this. You hear me, they got nothing—"

"The FBI is there. If you're lying and she knows something, your wife is going to federal prison."

"She doesn't know shit."

"Where's my son?"

Walt moaned and shook his head. "It wasn't supposed to work this way."

"What wasn't? Why are you doing this?"

Walt's mouth formed a big oval, sucking oxygen like a sprinter running from a lion.

Ran slapped him hard, and Walt's eyes ran tears.

"Stop hitting me. Christ, you broke a tooth." He corkscrewed his tongue, running over incisors and molars, a trail of bloody spit leaking from his mouth. "That bridgework cost two grand."

"It'll get worse," Ran said.

Walt drew air and spit. "He screwed me."

"Who?"

"Moreno. That's who we're talking about, right?"

I lifted my hand. "What's his real name?"

"I don't know." Walt sank back into the stuffing. "I don't know his name."

"Where's my son?"

"That's what I'm telling you. He never said anything about taking your kid. He paid me to be an FBI agent. I was acting. I'm an actor. It was a gig. He never said nothing about the rest. Nothing about your kid."

"An actor?"

"Yeah, man."

"Pretending to be a prison guard?"

"No, man, I am a prison guard. I act on the side. The prison has an acting group."

"How do we find him?"

"I have no idea."

"What about Vonda?"

Walt's eyes narrowed and he shook his head. "Don't know her."

"The red-haired woman you were just talking to?"

Walt said nothing.

Ran hit hard.

Walt's lips ruptured into mashed grapes. Blood squirted. He screamed loud and long, and the way sound carried in the desert, I began to worry about company. All we needed was someone calling the sheriff, Ran and me going to jail, giving the man who had my son time to disappear from the face of the earth.

Walt sucked a long streamer of bloody spit. "You broke another tooth, goddamnit."

Ran bent near the chair, dug a fleshy nail from the floorboards, forced Walt's mouth open, and shoved the nail inside. He picked up a board. When Ran swung, the board smashed Walt's jaw and the nail ruptured from his cheek. Ran pulled it out, tugging it through Walt's skin as Walt screamed.

My stomach churned, and I stared at my brother for several beats.

"Jesus, Ran."

Ran's eyes were cold, almost dead, working on autopilot. I looked back at Walt.

"The woman you were talking to in the Circle K parking lot," I said.

Walt sucked air and spit blood. "Vonda's not her name. Shit man, you cut my tongue."

"How do we find her?"

He coughed more blood.

Ran forced Walt's mouth open and shoved the nail back inside.

Walt shook his head and spit the nail out.

"Jenny Pierce. Her name's Jenny Pierce. She works at the prison. She didn't know, either...about your son. I'm telling you, it wasn't supposed to...go down this way. Moreno screwed us. He's a fucking wild card. Whatever his name is. Jenny knows more than I do. She found him. She set it up. Jenny knows."

"Jenny hired Leila Krebs to put my information into MicroLine's security system. You went with her. She must have told you why."

Walt shook his head and cocked his eyes, trying to glimpse his damaged face. "I don't know. My head's swimming to the moon, man. I'm bleeding all over the place, damn it."

Walt's tongue worked over his teeth, and he frowned.

"Jenny knows more than me. Hell, maybe she screwed me, too. Maybe they're in it together. They took your son, not me. She's the one who found Moreno for her. She can tell you. She just started her shift at the prison; go ask her."

Found Moreno.

"Jenny found Moreno? What do you mean?"

"Whatever his name is, Jenny found him."

"For who?"

Walt spat blood and smacked his lips.

"Janis."

"Why would Janis Goodman want Moreno found?"

Walt shook his head, as if I were the dumbest man he had ever met in the world.

"He's her son."

MICHAEL HARBISON

Chapter Thirty

Without our testimony, Janis would have avoided jail time. A simple matter of he-said, she-said, only Marty wasn't in position to say anything. But I had seen the fight from my bedroom window, and Ran had watched Janis swing the bat from downstairs in the Goodman's house, crushing Marty's skull like the brittle shell of an egg, sending him into two decades of oblivion. Marty took the blows, careened a few times, and then pushed Janis hard, trying to drive her away. Already dropping, he caught her flush in the chest with a fist and drove her toward the stairwell. As I ran from my bedroom, I caught one last shadow—the bat lifting high and arcing down on Marty repeatedly. Sixty seconds later, inside the Goodman house, I found Ran at the bottom of the stairs, crouched next to Janis, near the crimson bat. She was unconscious, and Ran kept nudging her head.

"Wake up! Wake up!"

I grabbed my brother and pushed him toward the front door.

"Go home and call the paramedics," I ordered.

He stood a moment, eyes stained with disbelief, fat tears running hard. Then he ran. Glancing at Janis, I saw a deep cut on her forehead. She was alive, but my brother's pleading had brought her no closer to consciousness. I ran upstairs to check Marty. He was on his back, sucking shallow breaths, wet gasps coming through broken teeth as his chest rose and fell. Blood ran from his shattered mouth into his throat.

I rolled him onto his side to let the blood drain.

Then I saw the pictures.

Not all of the boys were naked. Most wore underwear or tee shirts, some were fully dressed, but their posing was unnatural, and even at seventeen, I knew enough to realize a bent mind had taken the pictures. Some were strangers, kids with deep eyes and hollow chests; others I knew. Jack Weiss. Steve Volker. The Valle twins. Janis's nephew, too, a pitiful kid with crutches, standing half-naked in the hot sun. Ran's picture was near the bottom of the pile—pants down, wearing underwear, grinning as if caught in the middle of a prank. Even unconscious, Marty reached a hand toward the Polaroids, as if grasping for the source of his pain, and I kept replaying what he had yelled at Janis.

THIS IS MY FAULT!

THIS IS MY FAULT.

This is my fault?

Not a statement, but a question filled with disbelief.

He groaned, head turning from side to side as if trying to flee a bad dream. I left him and went downstairs. Standing over Janis, I thought about going back home, waiting on the sirens, trying to forget what I had found. But I kept seeing Ran's picture and hearing my mother's brittle voice telling me to keep him safe. Then I kicked the bat into the hallway and went back upstairs.

Grabbing the pictures, I shoved them into my pockets.

Marty groaned, dull-eyed from blood loss, fading out. He seemed to notice me then. His eyes locked onto mine and gave one last flare. Then, before slipping into the black, a final assertion escaped his lips.

"Not her," he said.

Later that night, I burned the pictures in our garage.

Chapter Thirty-One

We left Walt in the desert, bleeding and tied to the chair. Going to the prison was out of the question. We'd never make it through the gates, and the feds would be there soon. Fisk had promised to have us arrested if we showed up at Walt's, so we headed south, back toward home. Ran drove. Fatigue reached down my throat and raked my guts. I didn't trust myself behind the wheel. Within twenty miles, I became a hollowed out shell, a shadow man waiting for the sun to rise and dissolve me in a blast of bright, heated light. My exercise in perpetual motion had failed. Keller. Walt. Vonda. So far, despite the new information, nothing had brought me closer to Carter or to Carlos Moreno.

On the Subaru's nav screen, declining numbers indicated we would arrive home in exactly forty minutes. A final countdown before facing Abby. I had no idea what to tell her. MicroLine. Carter's abduction. Moreno. Janis.

Fisk had been right. This was very personal.

Unable to sleep, I pulled my laptop out and powered up. Within minutes, I was looking at Moreno's GPS data. The screen showed the waypoint plot from the last day he'd had the Taurus. I closed that window, scrolled to a different date, and the computer coughed up fresh coordinates. Staring at the numbers, I fought to see a pattern. Random digits in random places. Speed. Time. Location. So much data, all but meaningless, like looking into the sky on a dark night, trying to decipher planet from star. I scrolled to the date Moreno moved next door to us. Again, a series of numbers, but much shorter. Maybe twenty waypoints.

I tapped the car's navigation screen.

"What is it?" Ran asked.

"Not sure."

I entered the last set of coordinates. The Subaru's nav screen displayed a satellite view of our street in College Heights. Moreno's final destination that day. I already knew his endpoint. But where had he started? Entering the coordinates, I could tell by the slight number change the location wasn't far away. Certainly not in Mexico.

The screen shifted east and settled over a point on the map.

Close to the freeway.

In Fontana.

A street near the Kaiser steel mill where my mother had planted flowers that my father let die and where Marty Goodman's wife had knocked him into permanent twilight.

Camino de Huesos.

Road of Bones.

I pulled out my phone to call Fisk.

My battery was dead.

"Give me your cell."

"Why?"

"I know where Moreno is. I need to call Fisk."

Ran shook his head. "I drained the battery. You know...with Walt."

"Get off at the next exit and find a payphone."

*

We pulled into the Shell station. Ran stopped next to the phone booth, face aglow with fluorescent light from the station. Near two in the morning, the place looked deserted.

"Don't send the feds," Ran said. "We should go alone."

"No way."

"They go in heavy, Carter will get hurt. This guy's whacked. He's not about to roll over and quit. Not only that, but…"

"But what?"

Ran shook his head. "Some of the things we've done. I mean. We fucked that Walt guy up pretty bad. I did. You have connections. People will look out for you. I'm a con. They'll send me back inside."

"We'll be okay."

"There's another way. A way to get him without the feds or the police knowing what I did."

"Goddamnit, this isn't about you. We're here for Carter."

Ran looked at the floor, suddenly ashamed. "Yeah, I know."

Making sure I had change, I opened the door. Depending on Fisk's location, getting to Fontana might take some time. Then what? The feds would assemble a team, a negotiator. Was that the process? How long would it take? Looking southeast, down the alluvial slope, I spotted Fontana's lights a few miles away, sparking like shorting wires, illuminating all the possible ways things could go wrong.

One scenario, the most likely of all, I couldn't even consider.

Moreno and Carter might not be there.

Once at the phone, I saw it had no handset, and the coin slot had been welded shut.

Then an electronic click near the Subaru broke my chain of thought.

Ran had just locked the doors.

My car backed out then, whipped around, and headed toward the freeway as my brother dug into his jacket, pulled out his cell phone, and made a call.

MICHAEL HARBISON

Chapter Thirty-Two

When I was a kid, long before housing tracts carved into the foothills, we ran the dead vineyards near the steel mill and felt the twisted arms of brittle vines reaching up from the rocky soil, catching our shoelaces like fingers escaping a grave. Beneath our feet, boulders that had washed down from the mountains crowned the surface, becoming skulls of the dead, prompting us to run even faster. My brother was always behind me in those days—slow, frightened, a burden—and I prodded him to speed up, hinting the boney hands reaching out to grab him might belong to our mother. Now the vineyards were gone, but running toward our old house, trying to catch my brother, I still felt bones underneath my feet.

*

Thirty minutes later, Marty's house sat lightless and dead, rising two stories above a brown yard, looking abandoned except for the Mazda in the driveway and the *For Sale* sign jutting up from the dirt.

My Subaru was nowhere in sight, and I breathed a thankful blast, glad my brother had been too afraid to follow through with his plan or too incompetent to find our old house.

I would confront Moreno alone.

When I was halfway across the lawn, the front door cracked open. Moreno stood, lit by street lamps and the strange pink glow the city gave off at night. Dressed in a white cotton shirt, more summer than winter, he gave a half smile as I approached the door.

"Boyd, you're not a disappointment after all."

"You wanted me to find you."

"I hoped, but I wasn't going to make it easy."

"Where's my son?" I asked.

Moreno looked past me. A gun jutted from his waistband.

"No police?"

"Where's my son?"

"He's fine. This is between us," he said. "Always has been."

"Twenty-two years is a long time."

"Might as well finish." Moreno opened the door wider. "Come in. We'll work something out."

Inside, the house wasn't much different from when Marty and Janis had lived there. Living room to the left, dining room to the right. Carpeted entryway leading to stairs, and at the top, the landing where Marty had collapsed.

"You're the boy with crutches. Her son, though. Not her nephew."

Moreno gave a weak grin.

"I saw your picture that night. With the other boys."

Moreno frowned. "Believe it or not, most of what I told you was true. My father was a pornographer who catered to lovers of children. Nothing graphic, more suggestive than sexual, but often, I was his only subject. He was Janis's first husband."

Moreno continued walking, his back to me, leading us into the kitchen. A Formica table sat against one wall. The filthy surface, crusted with dirty dishes and forks and spoons, gave the air a rotten tint. I reached out and grabbed a fork, then slipped it into my jacket pocket.

"My father brought me north that summer to live with Janis and her new husband. He had grown tired of dragging me around. You have no idea how badly I wanted to be here. There were negotiations and money, and in the end, Martin Goodman agreed. But my father started taking pictures of your brother and his friends, paying them to pose. My mother found the pictures one day. My father panicked and was afraid I might talk, so we left. Janis blamed Marty for the pictures, and you know the rest."

I hesitated before I spoke. "Your mother knew about the pictures. Marty had nothing to do with them."

Moreno shook his head. "She knew my father was an animal. Nothing more. Before we left, he grew fearful the boys might talk, so he put photos in Marty's drawer. When she found them, my mother assumed the obvious...that her second husband was exactly like her first."

"Ran said she knew."

"Your brother lied. She would have killed to protect your brother and the other boys. That's why she confronted Marty. Then you put Marty in a coma and blamed her for the crime."

"I never touched Marty."

"Neither did Janis."

"I saw her swing the bat."

"You saw nothing."

A few beats passed. A bead of water dripped from the kitchen faucet onto a flooded plate. The drop hit the surface and rippled to the edge.

"Ran saw her," I said.

Moreno turned his back to me and walked toward the sink. I followed, slipping my hands into my jacket, gripping the fork as he kept talking.

"We moved from city to city until we settled in Chihuahua. What I told you about Soto was true. One day my father stopped at a police roadblock. Soto's marijuana was lost, and when my father was unable to pay, Soto took me until my father came up with the money. Soto was a *narcotraficante*. He was also a policeman."

I pulled out the fork.

"I'm sorry about your mother, Charlie, but I want my son back."

I rushed forward.

Moreno turned, gun in hand, silencer protruding like black bone.

I froze.

"Your son is outside, Boyd. I told you, I won't hurt him."

"I want to see him."

Moreno shot my right arm. The room spun. I hit the floor and fought to breathe as the world shrank to a slow disconnect of diminishing heartbeats. Adrenaline flooded my veins, vision blurred, the combination tugging me toward a dark cave. No tunnel of light. No choir of angels. Just tall, lanky death standing over me, wearing white pants and a gauzy cotton shirt flecked with blood.

I tried to look death in the eye.

Failed.

"You're not a man, Boyd. I knew the moment we met," Moreno taunted. "Here we are. I've taken everything you have, or nearly everything. The best you can do is hold a fork."

Moreno lifted his gun, pointed, and pulled the trigger.

Death never came.

The bullet did not enter my brain.

It drilled into the linoleum beside me, and as the smoke cleared, Moreno pulled me to my feet.

"Dead men don't suffer, Boyd, so I'm offering you a deal."

He opened a drawer, pulled out a dishtowel and tore it into long strips, then wrapped my arm, stanching the blood. A few seconds later, he smiled and patted my shoulder.

"Soto was like a father. I wanted to live with him forever. My health was better, the food perfect. When he came that day and pointed to the barn, saying I was free after I killed the mule, I knew what he meant. My father was inside that barn, and I knew. It was a test, an ordeal to measure how much I would sacrifice in order to keep my new life."

Clutching my arm, I glanced out the window, searching for any sign of hope. Heavy foliage shielded the neighboring houses from view. Nothing moved. Our old house was a black hole next door. Only Marty's detached garage was visible, a faint shape in the darkness, beyond reach of the lights.

Moreno continued. "What future did I have, pulled from city to city, posing for photographs whenever my father needed money? Children have no obligation to love their parents. My father was blood, but Soto was the family I craved, the safe place I once hoped to find with my mother and Marty. The place you and your brother stole from me. So I took the gun Soto offered, went into the barn, and killed that mule."

I stood bleeding on the tile.

"And you blame me for that?"

"You lied about my mother. Testified against her and put her in prison. Everything I am, I became after that. You and your brother created me." He opened a cupboard and reached under the sink. When his hand reappeared, he was holding a bat. "I'm no monster, Boyd. You can have your son. But first, take this bat into the garage. There's a mule out there. End its suffering. After that, you can go."

*

Ran hung from the rafters in the garage. Shot in the left leg, he bled onto the floor in a long, weeping stream, and as I walked through the door, he shook his head. The effort cost him, and his head quickly slumped. Blood ran steadily from his upper thigh, but the bullet had not hit an artery, or he would have already been dead. Then I saw Carter, gagged and tied to a chair in the corner. I ran to him, worked the gag away from his mouth, and pulled him close. His lips were cracked and red, but he stared at me with a dull gaze and looked unhurt. A bottle of scotch and an empty can of coke sat nearby. Moreno had evidently used the combo as a tranquilizer.

"Daddy?"

"You're okay, buddy. You're okay." Bulky knots held my son in place. Getting through the rope would require a blade. His face was flushed. I kissed him and promised we would soon go home.

"Daddy's got to talk to Uncle Ran. You'll be okay."

I moved close to my brother.

Ran saw the bat, and his lips trembled.

He tried to shake his head. "Wait," he mouthed.

"Moreno thinks we lied about Janis. He thinks we hurt Marty."

A slight head movement. "Wait."

"Did you call Fisk? Did you call the FBI?"

"Not you."

"What?"

"Marty. You."

"I never hurt Marty."

Ran shook his head. "Not you. Me."

"Ran, what did you do?"

"You were…leaving."

"What?"

"No Marty. No scholarship."

"Ran, what are you saying?"

"I hit too hard."

I stepped close.

"You hit Marty that night? It was you?"

"You were leaving me…with Dad. Needed my brother."

I lifted the bat.

Ran shook his head. "Please…wait."

"Moreno wants you dead. He's going to kill us all. He'll kill Carter."

"Wait."

After that night, whenever the police had interviewed my brother and me, my story had remained consistent because I had been certain about what I had seen. Marty hit Janis, and she retaliated with the bat. But I had only seen half of the truth. Ran swore he had watched the rest from the bottom of the stairs, and his version of events fit so neatly with my own, I never questioned it. But his version had been a lie.

"We sent an innocent woman to prison. We turned that kid into a monster."

"Please...wait."

The bat grew heavy in my hands.

I lifted it higher

"I can't. This has to end."

*

When I stepped from the garage, headlights illuminated the driveway, and footsteps ran toward the back gate. Then a loud crack echoed near the front of the house, as if the door had caved in. I lifted the bat and ran to the house. Before I got inside, two gunshots rang out.

In the kitchen, Danny Devlin stood over Carlos Moreno, and blood oozed from Moreno's shoulder in a slow-growing pool. Moreno watched me enter the room, took in the bat, and nodded.

"I told you, Boyd. We're not that different. Kill the mule and your son goes free."

"Ran isn't dead, Moreno."

Two men pushed through the back door then, moving into the kitchen, hauling my brother between them. A third man followed, carrying Carter. Ran winced as his leg dragged uselessly, but he mustered enough strength to spit at Moreno as they took him into the entryway.

"I'll leave you to finish it."

Danny Devlin placed a cell phone on the kitchen counter, next to Moreno's automatic, and left the room, probably headed for Moreno's car to find Selig's hard drives.

Standing over Moreno, I gripped the bat and moved it an inch closer to his head.

"Do it, Boyd. Your life is over. Your job is gone. Your reputation. Do you think your wife and kids will look at you the same once they know the truth? Finish it. Become what you made me."

I dropped the bat to the floor.

"Not like that, Charlie."

Then I opened the cell phone and called Fisk.

Chapter Thirty-Three

Assistant District Attorney Les Suarez sat across his dining room table from me, adjusted the digital voice recorder, and waited as I looked at the photograph. Standing in front of a run-down desert church, the Apple Valley Community Players squinted hard against the sun, bunching their faces into masks. There were twenty people in the group portrait. Even so, two of the faces were instantly familiar.

"That's Walt Schiff," I said, pointing to a man standing on the right. "And that's Janis Goodman next to him."

Suarez leaned back in his chair and nodded.

"That's where they met," he said. "Janis Goodman became involved with Schiff's theater group shortly before her release from prison. At some point, she told Schiff her story." Suarez put another photograph on the table. "This is Jennifer Pierce, another member of the group. She's the one who tracked down Janis's son. You knew him as Charlie Moreno. His real name is Carlos Moreno y Sanchez. He was a cop in Mexicali."

"A cop?"

"Dirty. Linked to the cartels, but not in a major way. Three years ago, he shot an illegal immigrant from Guatemala. The judge dismissed the case as justifiable after receiving a briefcase full of money. That kind of payoff is standard procedure for the cartels. According to Schiff, tracking Moreno down was Janis's idea. She was sick and dying and wanted her son. Jennifer Pierce is on the run, and Moreno isn't talking, so we don't really know how they found him."

"The cartel had no part in it?"

"He's a minor player for them. Good for looking the other way. Not a *sicario*. If they were sending someone north to do a hit, it would not have been him. This seems to have been personal, Boyd. At least for Moreno."

"Schiff and the woman? What was their motive?"

"When she was released from prison, Janis Goodman pulled most of the equity from her house and bought stock from MicroLine's competitors, I guess as a way of hurting you. She gifted some to Walt and Jennifer; the rest she left to Moreno. They obviously expected to drive the share price up by damaging MicroLine, but like I said, we don't know everything yet."

"Moreno won't talk?"

"He says you're to blame. The dead guys in the desert, MicroLine. He lays it all on you."

"He wants to ruin my life."

"Obviously."

"Dead men don't suffer."

"What's that?"

"Something he said. So where does that leave me?"

"If Roger Saldana had died, you'd be in a world of hurt. But with him a supporting witness and saying you saved his life, the San Bernardino DA has no interest in filing charges. That's assuming you'll cooperate against Moreno. As for Keller and the bikers, the feds have been out there twice. The place is abandoned, and that number you gave us leads to a dead line."

"I'll cooperate."

Les Suarez nodded. "How's Carter?"

"He's okay. He's getting counseling. We started him at a new school. This empathy problem, they think it provided a kind of blanket, insulating him from what he saw."

"That's good." Les pushed the digital recorder close and pressed the record button. "Now, tell me what happened to Martin Goodman."

While I talked, Les said nothing—no comments, no clarifications—holding questions until the end. For nearly an hour, the past flowed out of me in a constant stream, as if once breached, the dam built brick by brick over the years could no longer contain the dark water.

After a few beats, Les reached out and turned off the recorder.

"Your brother was a kid," he said.

"Yes."

"Thirteen years old."

"That's right."

"An innocent woman suffered in prison for twenty years."

"I know."

"An innocent man nearly died."

"Yes."

"And twenty-two years later, it nearly cost you everything."

"I'm ready to pay for that."

"From what I've heard today, you did nothing wrong." Suarez peeled the back off the recorder and removed the memory card, pinching it between two fingers. "Your brother faces charges for what he did to Walt Schiff. He's agreed to plead guilty to false arrest and assault with a deadly weapon as long as you're left alone. With his priors, he'll do time. A few years, possibly more. Maybe that's his act of contrition for what he did to Marty Goodman."

"And that's enough?"

"He was a kid, Jack." Suarez pressed the memory card until it snapped in half. "Janis Goodman is dead. Nothing can bring her back, and your brother was a juvenile, so he wasn't legally responsible. No DA is interested in retrying history, not unless someone goes to jail for it. Whatever debt you and your brother owe Marty Goodman, you'll have to pay it in the present, not the past."

I pointed at the crushed memory card.

"You know that erases nothing," I said.

"I know." Les Suarez nodded. "Nothing's ever deleted."

*

Sitting in Marty's room at Evergreen, I watched a hawk cruise the ridgeline, no longer on the hunt, simply riding warm updrafts that swept above the pines as if trying to enjoy the last sun before winter. I followed the bird for a while, then got up and emptied Marty's urine bladder into the toilet. My arm throbbed from the bullet wound, and the sling slowed me down, but once I hooked up a new bladder, I went to the foot of the bed and lifted the sheet.

Marty's nails were long, yellow, and cracked. "You need another trim," I noted.

Marty said nothing in response.

After retrieving the nail cutter from a drawer near the bed, I stood over his left foot and began to trim. He didn't flinch. I did the right foot, then got a handful of lotion from the bathroom and rubbed his feet for a while. I thought I heard him moan.

A few minutes after that, voices rose in the hall.

Then my family appeared.

Sara and Carter.

Then Abby.

Carter spent several minutes recounting his day at The Phoenix Academy. Along with class time, he was getting daily sessions with a counselor and had begun to talk about some of the terrible things he had witnessed. We knew the effects might not show up for years, but we would deal with them when they came, as a family.

When everyone had calmed down and crammed into the little room, I went back to the bed and touched the sheets. This time I heard the old man groan, or maybe it was a sigh.

"Marty," I said at last, "you've got some visitors. I'd like you to meet my kids."

ABOUT THE AUTHOR

Michael Harbison is a writer and photographer living with his wife and daughter in California. Over the past fifteen years, he has written numerous magazine articles on subjects ranging from adventure travel to digital forensics. *Road of Bones* is his second novel.

www.harbisonbooks.net

www.martinsisterspublishing.com

www.ingramcontent.com/pod-product-compliance
Lightning Source LLC
Chambersburg PA
CBHW070755280626
47162CB00016B/532